NEVER SPLIT THE PARTY

NEVER SPLIT THE PARTY

MIDDANG3ARD™ BOOK ONE

RAMY VANCE
MICHAEL ANDERLE

DEDICATION

*This book is dedicated to Ham Alnijjar, the guy
who taught me that entire worlds can exist
in the role of a twenty-sided die.*

—Ramy Vance

*To Family, Friends and
Those Who Love
to Read.
May We All Enjoy Grace
to Live the Life We Are
Called.*

— Michael

LMBPN Publishing
PMB 196, 2540 South Maryland Pkwy
Las Vegas, NV 89109

Version 1.02, August 2019
ISBN 978-1-64202-397-8 (ebook)
ISBN 978-1-64202-398-5 (paperback)

THE NEVER SPLIT THE PARTY TEAM

Thanks to our beta readers
Sarah Weir, Nicole Emens, Mary Morris, Kelly O'Donnell,
Larry Omans, and John Ashmore

Thanks to the JIT Readers

Dave Hicks
Diane L. Smith
Jeff Eaton
Deb Mader
Crystal Wren
Dorothy Lloyd
Misty Roa

If I've missed anyone, please let me know!

Editor
The Skyhunter Editing Team

1

Today the Expansion would be announced, and Myrddin Emrys felt an emotion he hadn't experienced in nearly three thousand years.

Nervous.

It was nearly ten o'clock at night, and the guests were beginning to trickle into the auditorium. Dignitaries and delegates from across the world looked around with disappointment.

This was where Myrddin Emrys, the richest man in the world, had summoned all the world leaders? They had expected something grand. Something awe-inspiring.

Instead, world leaders—all of the world's leaders, to be precise—were welcomed to a plain-looking theater with stark white walls.

Sure, the desks were labeled with the names of the countries and sovereignties, but the placards were a simple white, with the dignitaries' names hastily written in black marker.

Still, they entered.

Such was the respect most of them carried for Myrddin.

Or maybe it was respect for the game he had created: the virtual world of Middang3ard, where over seventy percent of the world's population—the world's *voting* population—spend the majority of their day.

As the last few entered, the auditorium quickly fell into a silence as close to death as possible for over two hundred breathing bodies. They waited in anticipation for Myrddin to enter.

Most of them, that is.

"Where the fuck is he?" growled the newly-elected US President.

One of his security guards hurriedly bent over and whispered something in his ear. From the look on the President's face, he was being scolded. Whatever the guard said, it worked, because the President sulked back into his chair, pouting as he waited.

Myrddin Emrys shook his head as he watched them from backstage through the disturbed surface of the water in his scrying pool, which was set in a giant black cast iron cauldron.

The cauldron not only showed him what was happening, it also revealed what was being felt by the leaders. The ancient sorcerer was hit by a wave of emotions that were a mixture of confusion, anticipation, and fear.

Today, Myrddin thought, *I'll finally get to see if all my centuries of planning and preparing have paid off.*

He doubted it. He doubted anything could prepare them for what would come next.

He had hoped there would be more time, but in the last six months, the Dark One had become far more aggressive, conquering one world and destroying another. Whatever the Dark One's plans were, they were accelerating, which meant Myrddin had no more time to prepare.

He needed to act now.

Earth needed to act now.

Waving a hand over the scrying pool's surface, he watched as the faces of the dignitaries blurred together into a massing of black figures marching, converging into one shape—a black amalgamation that stood to the height of a tower.

Orcs, trolls, ogres, and all manner of the Dark One's forces were amassing. Soon they would overrun Middang3ard.

The *real* Middang3ard.

And when Middang3ard fell, Earth would soon follow.

The old wizard had protected his home and fellow humans for as long as he could. He had also prepared them for a war of magic and mythical creatures through games, stories, and legends that most humans believed to be make-believe.

He had prepared them as best he could through his game, something that VR uniquely allowed.

Through the game, millions of humans had learned how to swing a sword, cast a spell, and navigate the complex inner workings of the real Middang3ard.

But was it enough? No, of course not. A game was just a game. The real thing was...well, real.

A fact, humans would learn quickly enough.

But if Earth was to survive the Dark One, he needed soldiers to come to Middang3ard to fight the Dark One's forces.

He needed adventurers. Heroes.

Human heroes.

Perhaps then, and only then, could they stop the Dark One from invading their home. That, too, he doubted, but better to fight and try than submit and die.

However, to get any of that, he first needed to convince these world leaders that the threat was real. To make them understand that they needed to commit resources—serious resources—if there were to be any hope of defeating the Dark One.

That would take time, and tonight was just one step. But while these human leaders were taking their time committing their forces, Myrddin would start to recruit his own army.

He sighed as he mentally prepared himself for what was to come next. He needed to persuade the world leaders, and that required proof.

"Fine," Myrddin snarled as he slammed his hand into the water's surface, destroying the image of the Dark One's army. "They will have their proof, for tonight I will take all of them to Middang3ard to breath its air, touch its soil, and taste the blood of all those who have fallen to protect its hallow grounds. Tonight, I will release the Expansion."

R obert "Suzuki" Fletcher stared into the flames of his campfire, his avatar's kite shield resting against his knee, as he ran a whetstone over the edge of his sword. The stone gave off a soft, almost crystalline hum as he went about his work.

Suzuki knew he was sharpening a virtual blade. That his hand, encased in its virtual reality glove, was empty back in his apartment as he ran it over nothing. But it felt so real, the stone resistant against the hardness of the blade. Of course, it was just his VR suit's exoskeleton hardening to give the illusion of resistance...not that he really cared.

In the game, sharpening his sword would increase his percentage chance of success, and right now he needed any edge he could get.

Pun intended.

He also needed to think, and the methodical repetition helped clear his mind.

After all, he was in the Expansion of Middang3ard, and the gamemasters hadn't made it easy. He and his fellow party members—the Mundanes—had been here for days, trying to puzzle out how to enter the Expansion's temple.

And they weren't alone.

Throughout the forest, dozens of small campfires burned as if the other players were trying to light the earth on fire to fight against the blackness of the firmament hanging above. Players crowded around the fire as they nursed their wounds and spoke in soft murmurs.

Even though there were hundreds of adventurers, most of them allies, Suzuki had never felt more unsafe in Middang3ard than he did at that moment.

Suzuki stopped running the stone along the blade, silencing the hum, and turned his ear toward the tree line, trying to listen for danger.

But the forest sounds of Middang3ard were an indecipherable blur next to the hushed whispers from the other camps.

Being huddled together in such a group made everything too loud.

Safety in numbers, he mused. But then again, if they were away from the group, they wouldn't be such a large target, and they could, well, listen for danger.

Suzuki really wasn't sure which would be best, alone or in a group, and, figuring that it was half a dozen on the one hand and six on the other, he went back to his thoughts and his blade as he tried to figure out how to solve the secret to opening the door to the Expansion.

Beth, Stew, and Sandy were sitting by the fire, no longer bantering. They'd all been there for hours and were getting bored, as Stew made clear when he stood up and yawned. "I can't keep doing this. I mean, I got a life."

Beth smirked. "What life? This is our life." Of all the Mundanes, she was the most dedicated to the game. "I mean, you deliver pizza, I'm a telemarketer, and Sandy here...what do you do again?"

"I'm part of a marketing enterprise dedicated to fulfilling your make-up and accessory needs."

"In other words, you're part of some pyramid scheme?"

Sandy nodded. "That I am."

Beth pointed the dagger she had been using to whittle a virtual twig at Stew. "So, what life do you need to get back to, exactly?"

Stew cracked his neck. "Whatever. My point stands. We should be doing something."

Sandy threw some twigs into the fire. "Sitting is something."

Stew "Leeroy Jenkins" Harris rolled his eyes. He was a good head taller than anyone else in the party, his massive body perfect for the role of barbarian. He stood and started to pace. The loose animal skin that covered him swayed to his movement so realistically that one might believe they were actually in a forest and not at home, strapped into VR suits.

Beth "GameOver" Lovett glared at Stew, putting back her dagger before pulling out her sword and pointing it in Leeroy's direction.

Her armor was not as heavily plated as Suzuki's, but still thick enough to offer a good amount of protection. "Don't you fucking dare start, douche nozzle." She pushed back her short-clipped hair, exposing the handful of small scars that covered her left cheek. "Do you remember what happened on the last raid when you started to get all antsy?"

Stew shrugged. "If I remember correctly, it was me pulling goblins off of your ass."

"Because you triggered every trap in the damn building."

Sandy "DeeStruck" Poples nodded as she stretched her

long slender body in exaggerated boredom. "None of us are playing this so we can sit around. Plus, Stew has all those gorgeous muscles that he has to put to use."

As she spoke, she absentmindedly cast a spark spell that sent tiny glints of electricity floating up in the air. Loose robes draped the sorceress's body, and she appeared to be a priestess from ancient times who worshipped pagan gods using dark arts long lost to humanity.

Stew struck an Olympian's pose. "Thank you very much, DeeStruck." Even though Sandy's handle—DeeStruck— was a bit camp, he pronounced it reverently, because he knew exactly how she'd gotten the name.

He also knew that anyone who made fun of her in-game handle would quickly die for the mistake.

Stew flexed his avatar's pecks, making them dance to some silent drum. It was impressive because it meant Stew actually had those pecks. The VR game only exaggerated your traits, it didn't make them up.

Unlike so many of the other, far less successful VR games on the market, Middang3ard did not let you play other races or customize your looks. You were what you were in real life.

Only a bit more so.

"These biceps crave destruction." Stew did a couple more body-building poses before plopping himself down by the fire, saying, "Can we at least go check out the door again?"

He slapped Suzuki on the back, jarring the warrior-mage from his thoughts and back to reality.

Well, what passed as reality these days.

"You know what?" Suzuki asked with a nod. "For once, Stew is right. We *do* need to do something. Gear up. Let's check the door and see what we missed."

"Oh, hallelujah." Beth groaned. "I'm pretty sure that Stew being right is one of the signs of the apocalypse."

The Mundanes walked into the forest, Sandy at the front, with a small fireball that she cradled in her hand to help illuminate the darkness.

With almost every step they took, Suzuki checked over his shoulder, trying to relieve the sense of dread that sat like an unwanted dinner guest in the pit of his stomach. His instincts told him something was there, but his heads-up display, his HUD, didn't report anything.

Then he heard it. Crackling leaves. Something *was* in the forest.

Something large.

Something that was trying to flank them.

Suzuki checked his HUD again, but even though he heard the danger, it still didn't alert him that anything was there. Which meant it was masking itself.

But what could do that? A dark elf or evil mage masking its intent? Or maybe some kind of new monster they'd never encountered before? Something conjured just to kill players in the Expansion?

Suzuki moved up closer to Beth. His hand lightly brushed hers, and he felt his skin burn under his armor. Even in VR, it made his head race to touch her.

Beth looked at him and smiled. "Something on your mind?"

Suzuki continued to scan the area. "We're being followed. It sounds big."

Beth touched her own HUD as she scanned the

surrounding forest, "I'm not registering anything, but my perception skills aren't as high as yours."

Suzuki shook his head. "My HUD's reading nothing too."

"So how do you know something's there?"

"I know," Suzuki said.

Beth nodded. She trusted the Mundanes' leader. She trusted Suzuki. "What do you need me to do?"

"Prep a distress signal. I'm pretty sure we'll make it to the dungeon door before anything happens. But when the shit hits the fan, I want to know we got backup."

"Lure it to the open and call for reinforcements. Good plan. I guess that's why we pay you the big bucks."

Suzuki chuckled. "Last time I checked my bank account, it was empty."

"Ahh, we must have the wrong account, then."

"Must have," Suzuki said with a smile before his face went deadly serious. "Now get ready."

3

I t only took them a few minutes to cross the forest into the clearing where a massive stone door appeared at the foot of a mountain. Elvish runes decorated the door, glowing brightly as if they had been traced into the stone with gold dust.

Another party made up of a massive barbarian and two rangers was already at the dungeon's door. They watched as the Mundanes broke the tree line, and as soon as they did, one of the rangers waved them over, displaying both hands to signify no ill intent.

Suzuki welcomed the gesture.

Especially given what was lurking in the forest.

Suzuki gestured for the others to go on ahead, and as soon as they were a few steps away, he turned and listened. The cracking of leaves and wood had stopped, which meant that whatever was stalking them was getting ready to attack.

Fine, then, Suzuki mused, let's get ready. He jogged to catch up with the others, and as soon as he caught up, he whispered to Beth, "Go ahead and fire the distress signal."

"Got it." Beth winked at Suzuki. She reached into her

pack and pulled out a small red bag. "Yo, douchenozzle," she called to Sandy.

"What's the deal?"

"Can I get a light?" Beth lifted the red pouch for Sandy to see.

Sandy snapped her fingers and a little flame jumped from her fingertips. The red pouch in Beth's hand caught fire. Beth crouched, then leapt and sent the flaming pouch soaring into the sky. It erupted in a cascade of fireworks.

"What the hell are you doing?" one of the rangers shouted.

A shriek broke through the silence of the forest. The two rangers jumped, crowding around their barbarian as the Mundanes turned to face the forest.

"Should take a couple minutes for everyone to show up," Suzuki shouted. "We can handle this until then, can't we, Mundanes?"

Stew ran up next to Suzuki, cracking his knuckles as he prepared to charge. "Let's get good," he growled.

"No." Suzuki put a hand on Stew. "No Leeroying it up now. We wait until whatever it is breaks through the forest line and attack it out in the open."

"Got it, my fearless leader," Stew said, as he unsheathed his sword and cried, "LEEROY JENKINS!" With that, he bolted toward the forest.

"No, Stew! I said, 'No Leeroying' this!" But it was too late. The barbarian was already behind the tree line.

"You can't keep a good Jenkins down." Sandy laughed as dark shadows swam over her. She was going into full DeeStruck mode. "This shit is on."

The childlike look of fun drained from her face. She swiped her hand slowly over her cheeks and an ancient death mask materialized on her face. Her terrifyingly large black eyes had blood pouring from them, and her mouth was nothing more than a carved snarl.

Her robes flapped open as she rose off of the ground, magic crackling around her. Everyone was about to be reminded where she had gotten her handle. "Let us bathe in the frothing blood of our enemies," she shouted.

The rangers and the other barbarian came up behind them. "Does he usually do that?" one of the rangers asked.

"Leeroy's gotta Leeroy, I guess." Beth shrugged.

"And yeah, the joke is not lost on any of us," Suzuki added.

There was a monstrous shriek, followed by a bloodcurdling scream of pain, the latter much more human and much more frightened, before Leeroy's body came sailing through the air. He hit the ground and skidded until he was laying at Suzuki's feet.

"How'd it work out?" Suzuki asked as he scanned the forest for whatever was strong enough to toss Stew like a stuffed doll. His HUD still didn't read anything. It was definitely using something to mask itself.

Leeroy groaned as he sat up. "Reconnaissance finished, oh Fearless Leader. We got ourselves a haphnax. A big one."

Suzuki's sword materialized in his hand as he raised his shield before him. "Haphnax? Shit. Of all the creatures they'd throw at us, it had to be a goddamned haphnax. Let's get ready, Mundanes," he called as he cast the Rally spell on his teammates.

Immediately everyone's HUD pinged with the effects of the spell. Now they would be better at coordinating their attacks, and better coordination meant a higher percentage of success.

Looking to the side, Suzuki noted the other party standing together, mixed looks of terror and fear painting their faces. With a heavy sigh, he looked at his Mana pool. It was still pretty full, but he knew this battle was just the beginning. He needed to conserve his magic.

But there'd be no magic to conserve if he died. Casting Rally on the other party, he said, "Come closer. We stand a better chance if we band together."

The sound of cracking trees filled the air as the haphnax stepped into the clearing. It was vaguely insect-like, with a tail the length of its body that ended with a sharp claw swooping over it. It had no eyes, only a large, oval mouth filled with rows of snapping, razor-sharp teeth.

The haphnax reared up on its hind legs and let out another shriek.

"All right," Suzuki shouted. "HUDs, shields, and weapons up, everyone. Remember Mundanes, stay calm. This isn't our first terror bug."

Suzuki's HUD targeted the haphnax, finally registering it as a threat. "Thanks for the heads up," he muttered to himself.

His health was displayed to the right, alongside his mana. At the bottom was a list of his available quick skills. In the top left corner was a series of equations and percentages that currently read Likelihood of success: 12%.

Very low. As in, this-could-be-the-death-of-them-all low.

That was the thing about the *Middang3ard* game. Everything was measured in percentage terms of success and failure. A complex algorithm measured the players' skills, ability to work as a team, weapons, and the enemy's power, processing it through complex equations that calculated their chances.

Come up with one plan, and the chances were only so high. Modify that plan, coordinate better...and suddenly your chances went up.

Or down.

There were no stats or levels or even experience points, XP for characters to improve on. They simply had to get better in the way one got better at anything in real life—through practice.

It was like this game wasn't a game at all, but rather a safe place to learn new things...and often Suzuki felt this was more of a school than a game.

No one knew exactly how it worked, although thousands of mathematicians, scientists, data analysts, and nerds had spent and continued to spend countless hours to try to figure it out.

No one could, and in the end, everyone chalked it up to Myrddin Emrys being one of those avant-garde geniuses capable of coming up with the impossible equation that literally took everything into account.

That or he was an alien.

Whichever it was, Suzuki knew to trust his HUD, and at twelve percent , their chances of survival were way too low. He almost liked it better when his HUD didn't say anything. At least then he could pretend he wasn't in any real danger.

"Why the hell is that so low?" Suzuki mused. The Mundanes were four highly-experienced players with tons of great gear. Plus he'd cast Rally, so their HUDs would help them coordinate their attacks.

And it was only one creature.

The Mundanes had faced worse before. They should be in the mid-50s. Easy.

Plus they had this other party with them, and new players were starting to show up, having answered Beth's call for help.

Beth stepped closer to Suzuki, jerking her thumb at the barbarian and the rangers cowering behind the Mundanes.

"Those three pussies behind us are filling this whole place with newb fear," Beth lamented.

"So what?"

"So what? That haphnax is just eating it up. That's what. And look." She pointed at the tree line. "More players are showing up all the time, and when they see that thing, they freak out too, feeding it more of their fear. Pathetic."

The haphnax shrieked again as it tore the ground up with its claws, swiping its tail at three players who were stupid enough to think they could sneak up behind it. Instantly the three players were wiped out, their bodies disappearing into pixelated heaven.

Suzuki did a quick calculation, checking the monster's abilities. It could feed off of fear, and right now, it was having one hell of a meal. Beth was right.

"Typical psych-out," Suzuki said in agreement. "Dee-Struck, get up in the air and get me a perimeter so we can lock this asshole in. Leeroy, tank him. And do it right this time. And GameOver," Suzuki turned to Beth as he used her in-game name. That was something he only did when things were going to get messy. "Do what you do best."

Sandy's eyes rolled back in her head, exposing eerie white orbs as she floated up into the air. "Not fair. I wanted to rip its heart out."

Beth unsheathed her sword and took the front ranks with Stew. "You'll get a chance, babe, don't worry."

Suzuki looked over his shoulder as more and more players showed up, surrounding the creature. When he looked back at the haphnax, his HUD now read a thirty percent chance of success.

Good, the odds were looking up.

"Give him the juice, Mundanes," Suzuki shouted.

Beth and Stew raised their swords, slamming them

against their chests and casting Enrage and Battle Shout. The haphnax screeched, growing noticeably more aggressive. Dozens of other players were in the clearing now, trying to get their bearings.

The haphnax screeched again as it leapt into the air, soaring over Stew and Beth and landing in front of Suzuki, swiping him with its tail.

Suzuki lifted up his shield and deflected the attack, but the haphnax was enraged. It flipped around and struck one of the rangers with its claw, instantly decapitating him.

Stepping back, Suzuki slashed at the haphnax and joined with the rest of the Mundanes. The haphnax started flailing around as the rest of the parties converged on the creature, but there was too much fear in the group.

Even with the haphnax surrounded, confused, and enraged, it was still soaking up the fear of the other players. With another shriek, the creature spun in a circle, taking a player out with its deadly tail every few seconds.

"Any bright ideas?" Beth stared at the flailing mosh pit of freaked-out players and gnashing teeth.

Suzuki's HUD now read ten percent. *What the fuck?*

"Just one," Suzuki shouted. "DeeStruck—"

"More support," Sandy moaned.

"Sort of. Y'all ready for glory?"

"For glory, for honor, for XP," they shouted.

That had been the Mundanes' mantra since their early days of playing before Middang3ard. "You know, guys," Stew said, "the game got rid of XP for percentages. Maybe we should change our catchphrase to something like—"

"Shut it, Stew. Focus." Suzuki pointed at the other players. "DeeStruck, paralyze everyone you can see from above. Everyone but us. After they black out, they'll stop feeding it fear. Then I need Beth and Stew to get in close and pin it down. Once that's done, you can rain sweet death down on our little friend."

Sandy's fist pumped and then blasted into the sky. She screamed loudly as clouds massed above her. Lightning rained down, striking every player and the haphnax, as the night filled with screams and the smell of singed hair.

Once the lightning strikes stopped, Beth and Stew sprang forward. They sprinted past the stragglers who had avoided the blast and leapt over the pile of bodies that had fallen next to the haphnax.

The insect-like creature sought to run now that the fear was gone, but it was too late. Stew and Beth were already on him.

Stew brought his great sword down and impaled the haphnax while Beth used two short swords to pin its tail to the ground.

Then Stew pulled out two daggers and beat his chest with them, drawing blood as his eyes bulged with the casting of Battle Shout. "Now you taste fear," he growled.

The haphnax tried to recoil, but before it could move, the two Mundanes jumped on its back, pinning it further. This time, they used spears that their HUDs called forth from their inventory.

Once Suzuki saw that the haphnax was pinned, he raised his sword, and his whole body glowed white as he shouted, "I cast Holy Protection!" The white glow exploded from his body and flew through the air until it attached to all the players in the area.

Suzuki's HUD now read eighty percent.

"Bring the pain, DeeStruck," Suzuki shouted. "Get clear, Mundanes."

Beth and Stew didn't need to be told twice. They knew what was coming. DeeStruck was about to destruct.

The two Mundanes leapt over the paralyzed players, seeking to put as much distance between them and the monster as they could.

Suzuki's HUD read one hundred percent.

"My enemies know only fear of my name," DeeStruck shouted from above. "They dream of my hand when the nightmare of death takes them. I am *Death*."

Fire burst out over DeeStruck's body and she plummeted to the earth like a meteorite. Fire erupted and washed over the haphnax as it screeched and writhed in pain.

DeeStruck burrowed her way into the haphnax, her body disappearing inside the insect-like creature.

She was out of sight until Suzuki made out a hand that jutted out of the haphnax's back. It held a still-beating heart in it.

DeeStruck shimmied out of the thing's back, standing on what was left of it. She was drenched in greenish-blue blood that hung from her like thick mucus. "I fucking love this game," she shouted with unabashed glee.

4

Suzuki and the rest of the Mundanes gathered around the pile of twitching players. This was going to be a problem. They'd be pissed that DeeStruck had put them down, only a few of them understanding that the move had saved their lives.

Still, there was a way to manage some of their anger. Suzuki held his sword up again and healed the crowd, spending more precious mana.

It was a good move. The other players would be less pissed off now and, given that danger still lurked, Suzuki felt comforted by having strength in numbers—and if he was honest with himself, more cannon fodder.

The other parties had suffered massive causalities, but a few of the players were left. He checked his HUD on his and his teammates' status, but because the game mirrored real life, there were no Hit Points. Not exactly.

There were exhaustion and pain, which the VR suits simulated by making it more difficult to move. And as for the pain, that was accomplished by the suit literally poking the players wherever they were wounded.

Suzuki cast some more healing spells, which, in practical terms, lowered the resistance the suit offered and removed some of the painful spots.

All those spells had nearly depleted his mana pool. If another haphnax appeared, Suzuki doubted he'd have enough magic to deal with it, let alone heal his party from the wounds they'd inevitably sustain.

Beth clapped Suzuki on the back, and he jumped from the shock. She was smiling at him in that way she seemed to reserve only for him.

Or at least he hoped it was only for him.

He tried not to spend too much time thinking about how Beth smiled at other people. He felt it might be a complicated circle of thoughts.

Thoughts best left unthought.

Still, he felt there was something special about the way she looked at him after a battle.

Beth smirked. "That was a ballsy move, douchenozzle. Great job."

One of the players—a cleric, judging by his robes—who had been paralyzed walked over to Suzuki and stuck out his hand. "I'll say that was a ballsy move. I'd also add it was a dick move, just to round everything out."

"You're still alive, ain't ya?" Stew snapped. "Even if you did get humiliated, you still get to play another day. Not like some of your newb-ass friends."

"What the hell did you say about my friends?"

Suzuki stepped between Stew and the other player. Emotions were starting to run hot, and they could all still be in grave danger.

"Hey, hey." Suzuki stood between them. "Sorry I didn't give you guys a heads up, but I had to figure something out fast. And we're all here now to figure out this dungeon, so what's the big deal? We're here to help each other out."

"Yeah, I guess. Whatever. Thanks."

The cleric walked away, and Suzuki knelt down to start a fire as Sandy and Stew went off to talk. It was their post-battle ritual...mage and barbarian talking through everything that happened.

Beth knelt next to Suzuki and put her hand on his shoulder. "That was a solid plan, Suzuki. You did good. Better than I thought we were going to do, with so many kids here fucking things up."

"Thanks." Suzuki nodded reluctantly.

Beth always gave him a post-fight pep talk. A few years ago, he had thought it was because she believed he needed cheering up. He wasn't much of a fighter compared to players like Stew or Sandy, but Beth always made him feel like he was an important part of the team. Sometimes she made it seem like he was the *most* important part, a tactician a grade above any she had ever played with before.

"So what are you thinking about the door?" Beth asked.

Suzuki shook his head. "Hm. You noticed how the haphnax scaled everyone's fear?"

"Suzuki, what are you talking about? The only reason it was doing so much damage was that those kids didn't know what they were doing."

"No, it didn't scale damage. It scaled fear, and then it projected out on us. That's new. I think that's why it kept shrieking. It was trying to scare us and then feed off that fear."

"Yeah, so?".

Suzuki looked around the clearing. Across the way was an all-barbarian party heating themselves by the fire. "So, it was purposely trying to accumulate as much fear as it could to power itself up. This wasn't a one-on-one thing, either. It was designed to feed off multi-combatants from multiple parties, and if Sandy hadn't gotten that under control, I think it might have kept doing it until it was unstoppable. And that," he snapped his fingers twice before walking off, "gives me an idea."

"Hey," Beth called. "So, what? Conversation over?" Beth knew Suzuki well enough not to disturb him when his mind was turning, so she just watched as he went over to the barbarian and ranger who had been standing there when they first arrived.

They looked up and Suzuki could tell they didn't really trust him, not after what he did. But they didn't draw their weapons either.

"Hey," he called. "I'm Suzuki."

The barbarian stepped forward. He was covered in war paint and tattoos, and a giant scar ran the length of his chest.

"Saw what your party did to that haphnax. Dick move," the barbarian grunted. "But it saved us. I'm still standing because of you, so you're all right with me. Name's Conan_119876."

Suzuki silently groaned. Another player with the wholly original name of Conan. And judging from the long string of numbers after his name, it seemed Mr. Originality here was just one of almost a hundred and twenty thousand others who thought Conan was a good in-game name. "Yeah, your guys held your shit together pretty well."

"Well enough, until...you know." He made a sleeping gesture. "What do you want?"

"I been thinking 'bout this door. You guys tried to open it already, right?"

The barbarian nodded to the door. "Been banging on it for two days. You?"

"Long enough. So there's this inscription on the door. 'The power is more than one.' And you saw how that haphnax aggregated its fear and used it against us. I think the game's pulling some weird shit. I mean, this is the Expansion's secret dungeon. It's not going to work like the rest of the game, just like that haphnax didn't work like the rest of the game."

The barbarian took a few practice swings with his ax before pointing at Suzuki. "So what do you think we need to do?"

Suzuki walked closer to the door, pointing at its center. "Attack it together. Just like the haphnax used our collective fear, we need to work together. Collectively. I think that's what distinguishes the Expansion from the rest of the game. Shit only works if different parties work at it together."

"Uh-huh," the barbarian said, pursing his lips. He clearly doubted Suzuki's logic.

"OK, how 'bout a wager then, Conan_119876?"

"It's just Conan. Don't worry about the numbers with the name. You'd be surprised at how many Conans are running around on this server."

"Yep, I'm *real* surprised," Suzuki said, trying to avoid smirking. "OK, here's the deal. If we get it open, I get first dibs on sword loot. If we don't get it open—"

"You convince your girlfriend to raid with me next week."

"My girlfriend?"

Conan jerked his head in Beth's direction. She was wiping the blood from her sword with some ornate fabric. She whipped the fabric, and the blood snapped from its end and hit Stew in the face. Suzuki couldn't remember a time he'd ever seen her look so beautiful.

"She's not my girlfriend." Suzuki blushed.

"Then it shouldn't be too big of a problem, right?"

"Fine. Deal."

Conan and Suzuki made their way to the dungeon door. There was a thin disturbance in the air around it—a force-field of some sort.

Suzuki and his party had been attacking the door for the better part of the last few nights, fighting off the occasional spawns of mobs trying to sneak up on them.

So had every other party camping in the forest. No one had broken the secret.

Usually, Suzuki wouldn't have stuck with the door so long. There was a lot to do in Middang3ard, and dungeons were only part of what he enjoyed. The game was so much more than just running through mob after mob of enemies.

The amount of variation in the magic system alone was enough to spend a lifetime on. Some of the best parts of the tabletop version of the game had been expertly ported into the VR version.

That said, Suzuki was invested in this dungeon. A close friend of his, RealDeal_0300, had cleared the dungeon a few weeks earlier and disappeared from the game altogether.

But since they were offline friends, RealDeal had been in touch. Not with any real information, because he'd had to sign some NDA and risked being banned from the game for life if he said anything. The only thing RealDeal had hinted at was that whatever was in the dungeon would break Suzuki's world.

Then there were the rumors that *Middang3ard* was more than just a game. That it was a real place, too.

And that this door in the Expansion set opened the gateway.

But Suzuki dismissed that as hype designed by master marketers, pushing the Expansion to millions of users. Still, it would be cool if Middang3ard actually existed.

And RealDeal's disappearance did give credence to the rumors.

"On the count of three," Suzuki said, lifting his sword over his head. "One, two, *THREE!*"

Conan and Suzuki brought down their swords on the door's shield. There was a bright flash of light, and an electrical current pulsed out from the shield and through the forest. Players from every party looked at the dungeon door as the shield fell.

The door swung open.

Suzuki raised his fist in triumph. "Yes!" Glancing at Conan, he added, "If you find any barbarian shit in there, you can keep it. Thanks for the help."

The Mundanes, along with the rest of Conan's party, had rushed over as soon as they saw the door open. They all stared into the darkness of the dungeon, where thousands of red eyes peered back at them.

"Holy shit," Beth murmured, staring at them.

Stew cracked his knuckles again. "There's a lot of things to kill in there."

"Hold it together, Douche Nozzle, and don't spill your load too fast."

Stew smirked. "I don't ever spill my load too fast. I explode my passion when I feel it's appropriate."

"Is that true, Sandy?"

The mage ignored Beth's question, her gaze fixed solely on the cavern before her. "I can only hear the future death cries of my enemies. Everything else is noise."

Suzuki gestured for the others to huddle around him. "All right, Mundanes. For honor, for glory—"

"For XP," they shouted in unison.

Stew shook his head. "There's no XP in the game. Maybe we should—"

Before he could finish, the Mundanes were running into the dungeon, followed by Conan's party—what was left of it, at least. The darkness was tangible, almost as if it had a life of its own, and even though the red eyes had seemed so close, they hadn't come across anything yet.

It was almost as if it were empty, and the farther they ventured, the more anti-climactic it became.

Stew yawned loudly as he playfully pushed Beth.

"Will you stop dicking around?" Beth growled. "Stay focused."

"Why? It's empty," Stew replied.

Suzuki stopped walking as they entered a large cavern where a small goblin child stood alone about fifty yards ahead of them. "Not empty," Suzuki said, pointing at the child, who stared at them with huge, baleful red eyes.

Stew pointed at the creature. "What the fuck is that?"

"HUDs up," Suzuki whispered. "I'm not getting any read on the enemy type. It's some kind of goblin, but I've never seen a goblin child before."

The goblin child was holding a small doll in its hand. When the players took a step closer, the goblin opened its mouth and started wailing.

"Oh, shit," Beth exclaimed. "It's a goddamn sentry."

The ground shook, and through the dungeon echoed the sounds of feet hitting the floor and steel clanking. Suzuki looked at the ceiling, and he could see that there were holes dug into the cavern's walls. At the center of the cavern, directly above the wailing goblin, was the largest hole. The goblin child wailed again, and that was when the first wave hit. Goblins flooded out of the holes in the walls, coming from all over the dungeon.

Suzuki drew his sword as DeeStruck launched herself into the air, tossing fireballs in every direction. Leeroy drew his daggers and cast Enrage on himself. His body bulked up, and his eyes went red. GameOver drew her sword and shield and threw herself into the fray. Suzuki and Conan went barreling after her, their swords connecting with goblin flesh as fire rained from the sky.

"May death ring through the ears of all who dare challenge my power," DeeStruck shouted.

Conan slid his sword into the stomach of a goblin. "She really gets into roleplaying, huh?"

"Hey, Stew?" Suzuki called. "How much does Sandy actually like to roleplay? She got you dressing up like a maid yet?"

"Eat a goblin dick," Stew shouted.

Suzuki blocked a goblin with his shield and Beth jumped over him, landing on top of a goblin and driving her sword through its chest.

There were still more goblins, and it was impossible to tell when they were going to stop spawning. Suzuki checked his HUD.

Five percent.

It was time for a plan, or they would be overwhelmed in the next couple of minutes.

"GameOver," Suzuki shouted. "On me."

"Gotcha!"

As Beth and Suzuki pulled away from the mass of goblins, Stew caught their eyes.

"Are you guys splitting?" Stew cried out. "You never split the party!"

A mob of goblins swarmed over Leeroy and he drew his greatsword to cleave through them as Sandy swooped down, generating an electrical storm as she hit the ground. Even with all that effort, the goblins quickly washed over them, drowning them in a sea of gray bodies.

Suzuki sheathed his sword and held up his shield. He checked his mana on his HUD; there was enough. He cast Find Hidden Traps and Pathways, and bright gold light flew from his shield to the walls of the cavern. Suzuki and Beth chased the light until they came to a far wall where there were no holes. The gold glow outlined a door.

Before Suzuki could gauge the situation, Beth pushed against the outlined stone and a door in the rock opened. Beth fell through the door, and Suzuki followed.

The room was empty except for a stone with a sword in its middle.

Suzuki shook his head, "This doesn't look right."

"Fuck it, it's the sword in the stone." Beth pointed at the damn thing. "Cliché, but classic as hell."

Beth crossed the room and grabbed the sword, and the VR simulation around them dissolved. Stew and Sandy manifested next to them.

The game completely disappeared, and the only things left were their four avatars, hovering in cyberspace.

"I can't believe you two left the party like a bunch of newbs," Stew growled.

"Fuck off, douche nozzle," Beth shot back. "Looks like it worked."

A long gong sounded, startling the normally fearless warrior so much that she grabbed for Suzuki.

When she realized what she had done, she quickly looked away before muttering, "Sorry."

"No, no, it's all good," Suzuki told her, tripping over his words.

"If you two are done being awkward as fuck," Stew said, "check your emails."

Suzuki looked at his HUD, and there was a new message blinking. He opened it.

The message read **You have completed the final dungeon. You are cordially invited to Middang3ard.**

"But this *is* Middang3ard." Stew's voice was filled with confusion.

Sandy looked the invitation over. "How the hell can we get invited to a videogame we're already playing?"

Another message popped up. It included a PDF of a plane ticket to New York City and a receipt. The receipt was signed by none other than Myrddin Emrys.

The game shimmered out of existence. Suzuki was laying on his bed, staring up at the blank screen of his VR visor. A message flashed, **Game Complete.**

He took off the visor and shouted, "Fuck, yeah! We're going to Middang3ard!"

5

Despite Suzuki's initial doubts, the tickets were real. He was picked up by a limo around the crack of dawn and driven to a private airfield, where he was greeted by a young man holding up a plaque with the name "Suzuki" on it.

He shrugged, agreeing with their decision to use his nickname instead of Robert. After all, he'd been playing as Suzuki for so long, everyone called him that.

Even his mom...before.

Suzuki shook his head, driving away his thoughts of names and the past. Now was a time to be consumed by the future, and as he stepped onto the plane, that was all he thought about. What would the future hold?

Middang3ard, he hoped.

The young man gestured for Suzuki to board the plane, and, as soon as he was seated, the plane took off, ascended into the clouds, and sped toward Manhattan. There were no pre-flight safety videos or flight attendant to make sure his seat belt was properly fastened.

So much for playing it safe, Suzuki thought as he stared out of the window.

Suzuki was exhausted because the excitement of this moment had denied him any real sleep over the last couple of days. Now he wished he had slept.

Knowing that this plane ride was his last chance, he closed his eyes for a brief moment before opening them again.

Sleep was impossible. His body was a live wire, with everything he had read about Middang3ard conspiracies crackling through his head.

It was all conspiracy theories about the true nature of the game.

Weird shit, with people theorizing that the VR game was a simulation of a place that might actually exist. But that was old news mostly, spouted by the same people who believed the moon landing had been faked and the Earth was flat.

But then there had been the announcement by Myrddin, which fueled the rumors to the point where the more moderate players started chiming in.

And now there was this? Suzuki was flying to New York City to meet the game-makers and the other Mundanes.

———

The five-hour trip hardly felt like half an hour, and Suzuki's heart pounded with excitement and fear as the private jet circled the city skyline, getting ready to land. He watched the skyscrapers as they loomed like the titans of another world. Having grown up in a small, nondescript town, Suzuki thought about how the pictures he'd seen didn't do this skyline justice.

Not even close.

The plane wasn't heading toward the skyscrapers, though. They were flying a little farther out of the city, closer to upstate New York.

After a little more time, Suzuki could see that they were quickly approaching a solitary skyscraper poking through a canopy of trees. The plane landed on a small landing pad near the towering glass building.

Suzuki grabbed his luggage, slung it over his shoulder, and followed the young man in the black suit off the plane. They approached the building, where two people were standing by the entrance. Even though Suzuki had never seen them in real life, he recognized them instantly.

Stew was nearly as large as his avatar Leeroy, but unlike the smooth, almost baby-like cheeks on his avatar, Stew's real cheeks were covered with splotches of acne.

Sandy resembled her avatar even more closely. Petite, cute, with flowing black hair, she was almost her avatar's spitting image. All you needed was her hands glowing with destructive magic, and you wouldn't be able to tell the difference.

Stew saw Suzuki approaching and waved him over, giving him the biggest bear hug as soon as he was in reach. Once he was put down, Sandy embraced him with a hug as vigorous as Stew's.

Sandy broke the hug, "It's so good to finally meet you in the flesh."

Stew slapped him on the back. "Yeah, it's good to know you look like as much of a punk-ass in real life, too."

Suzuki nodded. "Yeah, yeah, good to see you asshats too."

"I think he looks a little more stately in real life," a voice called from behind.

Beth.

Suzuki recognized her voice. He'd recognize it anywhere and under any circumstances. *Beth.* He was finally going to meet her in person. Turning around, his heart pounded as if it were trying to escape his chest.

Even though she hardly broke five feet, she seemed to tower over all the Mundanes. She was wearing shorts and a tank top, and her biceps were even more impressive outside the game. Her hair was cut even shorter than her avatar's, too.

"A lot less pasty." Beth chuckled. "Like you might actually know what the sun looks like."

Suzuki stepped forward, hand outstretched. He tripped over his shoes as he approached her, almost falling. Somehow, thankfully, he caught his balance at the last second. Embarrassed, he stuck his hands in his pocket, glanced at his feet, and then back at Beth. "Yeah, I still go outside and shit. Gotta get some exercise from time to time. It's important. One of the most important—"

Beth crossed the space and hugged Suzuki. She held on to him, and Suzuki hugged her back. They stood there together for a while.

"Bet I know what kind of exercise Suzuki *really* wants," Stew whispered to Sandy.

"Shut up." Sandy elbowed him in the stomach. "They're cute together in a gross, uncomfortable way."

The Mundanes grouped around the entrance of the building and stared up at the thousands of windows reflecting the sunlight.

Beth opened the door and stepped through. "Guess even real life comes with castles. Even if they're made out of steel and glass." The rest of the Mundanes followed. The building opened to a large foyer filled with an assortment of different people.

The other players of Middang3ard.

Most everyone was still split up into their gaming parties, little clusters of individuals ranging from scraggly zit-riddled teenagers to middle-aged women and frat bros who had seen the terrors of steroid abuse.

The Mundanes waded through the group of parties and looked around at the vast scope of the glass building. Suzuki found that his eyes kept drifting to Beth's, hoping to make eye contact, but she appeared to be captivated by the majesty of the building's construction.

"Ahem."

Myrddin Emrys stood at the top of a crystal escalator. He straightened his tie and stepped forward, his feet not even touching the escalator's steps. There were gasps throughout the crowd as he floated down what looked like a set of invisible stairs. His eyes were deeply set in his face, and his brow was furrowed and dark.

"That's a pretty sick hologram," Stew mused.

Suzuki shook his head as Myrddin floated into the center of the room.

"That's not a hologram. That's the real deal. Look, there's no light refracting from him anywhere. Even the best holograms can't do that. He's really floating." Suzuki's eyes widened with unbridled excitement.

Stew shrugged, still not shaking off his skepticism. "Or they're just a fuck-ton more advanced than anyone else."

Myrddin raised his hands as his feet touched the ground and gave a weak smile. "I am glad to finally see the winners of my...ahhh...experiment."

Suzuki saw Myrddin speaking, but he heard nothing. There Myrddin was. In the flesh. The creator of a massive part of Suzuki's life. Suzuki was in awe, as if he had just met God. In some ways, Myrddin *was* a god.

Nostalgia hit him like a freight train for all of the hours spent with his nose in character and strategy guides. Suzuki pulled out his keys and looked at his keychain. One of the limited-edition twelve-sided dies that had come with the original tabletop version of *Middang3ard* hung next to his keys, right next to the 3D-printed replica of the ring he and Beth had looted in their first raid.

If it weren't for Myrddin, Suzuki wouldn't have anything. Not his interests. Not his hobbies. Not his friends. He would have never met Beth.

He felt it coming up—something worse than vomit. Words.

His mouth started moving, and a gush of words came pouring out.

"Myrddin, sir... Mr. Myrddin, ahh, I mean Dr. Emrys. Thank you, sir. Thank you. I mean, yes, I-I owe you every-thing," Suzuki blurted.

The crowd of players' heads rotated toward him at a snail's pace, and soon every eye was focused on Suzuki. This was worse than any goblin horde he had ever faced.

"I mean the loot," Suzuki stammered. "I mean I owe you for the loot drops."

Myrddin looked Suzuki over before muttering, "Mun-dane" and stepping away, evidently wanting to put some distance between them.

Suzuki couldn't tell if the word was because Myrddin recognized him from the game or if he really meant that Suzuki's reaction to him was average and boring. Either way, Suzuki was reeling with excitement. Myrddin had spoken to him.

Directly to him!

Stew put his hand on Suzuki's shoulder and squeezed tight as he leaned in and whispered, "Dude, I know you have a hard-on for Beth, but you are embarrassing us right now. There is no amount of hand wipes to clean up the bukkake you just shot all over Myrddin."

"Shut up. I'm just being grateful."

Myrddin, now in the center of the room, gestured for them to follow as he floated back up the escalator. "Please, come with me."

The players walked the same path, but they didn't float. They took the escalator instead, their feet firmly planted on the metal stairs.

"Hologram or not, that's some effect," Sandy remarked as she lined up behind her party members.

At the top of the escalator were a series of floating surfaces. They looked as if there were entire floors of buildings condensed somehow so that they were two dimensional.

All around the room were holograms of different characters from the *Middang3ard* game, characters Suzuki had never seen before: elves riding horses through fields while firing arrows, an uncomfortably beautiful orc straddling her lover next to a fire, a dwarf fleeing from riders dressed in black, brandishing torches.

Suzuki couldn't wrap his head around how he could look at an image as simple as an elf standing and watch it transform into near-pristine video quality of the same elf reaching toward him, slowly gyrating her hips, her daggers glinting enticingly.

Sandy walked past Stew, who was transfixed by the images of a raiding party of orcs eviscerating a village of halflings. "Sploosh." Sandy's face was scrunched up in a mock orgasm. "I think I'm so, so, *sooo* splooooooshing."

"Oh, shut up," Stew groused. "You can't possibly think this is hot?"

Sandy's face grew serious. "Only the entrails of my enemies arouse me. Splayed out, warming my hands. Nothing else moves my loins." She had spoken in an ominous tone.

Stew looked down at Sandy with horror before the petite, fashionable girl burst out into giggles. "I'm just messing with you, Stew. Or maybe not? It's all part of the mystery that is me."

"I knew that," he said, trying to pull off a laugh. Instead, all that came out was an awkward giggle. Turning to Suzuki, Stew mouthed, "She's a freak."

"You love it," Suzuki mouthed back before looking up to see that Myrddin was slowly gliding through a few of the images. His suit shimmered in and out of existence and there appeared to be stained, time-worn crimson robes underneath.

Myrddin raised his hands. "By now, you have all heard of the Dark One."

Suzuki felt his feet lift, and looking down, he saw that he was hovering a couple of inches above the ground. Looking around, he saw that it was happening to everyone. They were all floating up into the cascades of images overhead. When Suzuki looked at Beth, her smile was the widest that he had ever seen.

"Most of the world does not believe me. Even many of your leaders, who have been to Middang3ard, don't believe me," Myrddin continued. "They think that this is some sort of prank by a rich eccentric, but they will come around. Everyone will. Eventually. And when they do, the Earth will send an army like no universe has seen before to combat the Dark One. Until then, you are all my chosen champions.

You understand the danger our worlds are in. The Gnomish world has fallen, the Dwarven world is near-ruined, and should Middang3ard fall, Earth will be next. Make no mistake, should the Dark One conquer us, all humans will either be slaves or dead. The time for action is now. It has never been more important."

Suzuki looked down at the ground, which was at least twenty feet away. His heart was racing, and he almost couldn't contain the giddy feeling welling up in him.

He was floating.

Really floating in the air, with at least two hundred other people. It was magic.

Honest-to-God magic.

"Yeah, but that shit is just game hype, right?" someone called.

How could anyone think that? Suzuki thought. They were literally floating in the air.

"No," Myrddin snapped. "This is not hype, adventurer. We need recruits. We need heroes. The world governments have their thumbs up their asses, so we need you. Professor Grimpston, please enlighten the children of this world." He gestured to his left, which had just been empty space, and a short figure with pointy ears wearing a tweed jacket, a tilted red cap, and rimless glasses appeared.

That wasn't right. He *manifested*.

"Whoa!" Sandy spoke with unhidden awe and respect. "Is that Professor Grimpston? From in-game?"

A few players yelped at the surprise, and others cheered and laughed. Everyone was pleased to see one of the legendary NPCs of the Middang3ard. There wasn't a player in existence who didn't know the gnomish mage. He was the game construct who welcomed all to Middang3ard, walking new players through the game's tutorial and set-up.

Professor Grimpston swatted at one of the prancing unicorn images that floated in front of his face before shouting, "Oh, my! You must warn me when you teleport me during one of your 'The world is ending and we need heroes' speeches."

"Please, Professor. Explain the direness of the situation."

"Okay, okay, we get it," someone shouted. "You have a makeup and special effects department. Big deal. If you're expecting me to shell out any more cash for an update, all you had to do was email me. This is a little over the top."

"How far the children of dust have fallen." Grimpston sighed. "Not even magic seems to interest them anymore."

"It's the video games I designed," Myrddin lamented. "They dull the imagination in some. How about we impress them? Dazzle them with magic that cannot be ignored?"

"Must we?"

"When a crowd demands a spectacle..."

Grimpston's beady eyes lit up. "Fine. A spectacle is what they need? Then a spectacle is what they shall have."

Grimpston attempted to straighten himself while he was floating, but the distorted gravity only made him spin a bit. He huffed and grabbed his hat before it fell off his head.

"Impressive," a player murmured as muffled chuckles echoed in the room.

Grimpston took off his hat and held it close to his chest. "Hold onto something if you can." Then he stroked his long white beard three times before waving his hand. As soon as he did, the world turned upside-down.

As in, literally.

Suzuki felt something hook into his stomach—a sharp pain that quickly vanished, followed by a tug, as if someone had reached into his chest, grabbed his lungs with both hands, and yanked him forward. Suzuki's body started vibrating, his teeth chattering so violently that he thought they might shake out of his mouth.

The images of fantasy creatures that had been floating in the room melted into giant pools of color and began swirling together.

Suzuki searched for the gnome's face in the crowd, and when he found it, he could see the color dripping from Grimpston's face as if he were a fresh oil painting being held outside a speeding car's window. Suzuki touched his face and looked at his fingers, which were covered with a wet-paint-like substance that was eerily the same color as his skin. Suzuki wondered if he was melting.

The world jerked forward, and even though Suzuki wasn't standing, he felt the ground drop out from under him. The structure of the building tore itself apart, splitting every which way and out into space as the players rose, yet stayed stationary.

New York was falling apart around them. Buildings shot up from the ground, bridges unraveled themselves, and girders flew around in a vortex of steel, screeching as grass uprooted itself and the world as they knew it fell apart. They were all suddenly in the deep of space and stars zoomed past them.

"Warp speed," someone said, and Suzuki agreed. This was exactly like the visual effect on *Star Trek*. The only difference was that on the tv show, you experienced it from the safety of your living room couch. Here, you were experiencing it for real. Without a spaceship—or a couch, for that matter.

Suzuki clutched his chest, terrified that he was going to suffocate, but before he could lose his breath, he was on firm ground. He fell forward and stifled the urge to vomit.

That was when he noticed he was looking at grass. Grass greener than anything he had seen his entire life.

It took him a moment for him to find his feet before he realized that they were all standing in a plain that stretched as far as they could see.

Myrddin was floating down from the sky, and in a moment, his feet daintily touched the ground.

Grimpston was picking himself up off the ground like the rest of the players, knocking grass out of his beard as he cleared his throat. "Impressed," the gnome more declared than asked.

"I knew it," Beth cried with abandoned joy. "I fucking *knew* it."

"Yeah, you did." Suzuki was glad he hadn't talked more to Beth about the Middang3ard conspiracies. He doubted he could have helped thinking she was a little crazy or avoided her thinking that he was a tool. At least now he knew they both knew the truth of it all.

Grimpston and Myrddin stepped away from the players so they could be seen better. Most of the players wouldn't have noticed. They were enamored with the world around them. The trees were larger, the air crisper, and the sun was beaming down with a heat that many had never experienced before.

It took the combined effort of Myrddin and Grimpston to catch their attention again.

Myrddin clapped his hands twice, the palm-strikes sounding like thunder, while Grimpston spoke in a voice that seemed to both echo in- and outside the spectators' heads. "As you can see, this is not a game. This is reality. Another plane of reality, but reality nonetheless."

Grimpston waved his hand, and a globe that looked very much like Earth appeared. "This looks like your home planet, right? But it is not. That is Middang3ard." He gestured as if pulling at an invisible string and zoomed out until they saw Middang3ard at the center, being orbited by nine similar-looking planets.

The gnomish mage touched the planet that seemed to be farthest away and it glowed bright blue. "That is Earth, and these planets are the eight other known realms of each of the races: Elf, Gnome, Goliath, Ratfolk, and Catfolk worlds. And before you ask, Ratfolk and Catfolk are the strongest of allies." Each planet lit up the same bright blue as he spoke its name. "Middang3ard is the planet in the center. The tenth planet, if you will. And as for these three, they are the Gnomish, Dwarven, and Dracon. All three worlds have already fallen to the Dark One." The last three worlds named were colored in blood red.

"The Dark One will not stop until all nine worlds have been conquered. This is an ancient war that has been raging for over two thousand years, and it was only in the last eight years that the Dark One managed to conquer all three. How? We do not know. What we do know is that the Dark One is moving fast, and this is why we opened the expansion set and brought you all here."

Myrddin zoomed out until a giant black moon was visible, orbiting the nine planets. "I designed the VR game to prepare you. Train you. But limits on technology can only allow me to do so much. I had hoped that this moment would come later, when the game had evolved to be more real. However, we must make do with what we have, and the rest of your preparation and training will be conducted here on Middang3ard." Myrddin scanned the crowd, and even though he was speaking to dozens of people, everyone there felt he was looking directly at them. "Those of you who pass the coming tests, that is," he added.

Then, sighing deeply, Grimpston chimed in with, "We have prepared you as best we could. Here on Middang3ard, we will make our stand. You and your party members are our latest batch of recruits. We have been searching for the best warriors your world has to offer for years, and you are this season's candidates. The Dark One is coming for all our worlds."

Grimpston sighed again and hung his head. There were tears in his eyes, and his beard caught them as they fell down his cheek.

"Some of our worlds have already fallen, and he is still coming. You are the hope of Middang3ard and the remaining realms that circle it. One of those realms, let me remind you, is your own."

Stew leaned over to whisper to Suzuki, "I don't know about this. This is freaking me out, and I'm *sure* I didn't sign up for this part when I downloaded the update."

Suzuki glanced around at the new world, which looked close enough to Earth, but just a few minutes ago, they had been in New York, surrounded by buildings and skyscrapers. This? Just plains and woods in the middle of nowhere, with a gnome and an old man wearing robes? This was something new. Whatever was happening seemed important.

And it was very real.

Beth stepped forward and the Mundanes gathered around her. She put her hand out in the middle. "For glory," she said.

Sandy put her hand on top of Beth's. "For honor."

Suzuki put his hand on top of Sandy's. They were really going for it. "For XP," he said.

They all looked at Stew, who was standing with his arms

crossed. He was clearly still freaked out by everything that was happening. Still, he wasn't about to split the party.

With a heavy sigh, he put his hand on top of Suzuki's. "I know we keep saying for XP, but the game doesn't give us XP," Stew grumbled.

"Come on, you big lug," Sandy grinned.

"Fine," Stew muttered before growling, "For glory, for honor, for XP!"

The Mundanes were united, and they were in Middang3ard.

6

M yrddin and Grimpston led the group of a dozen or so parties through the plains. Grass grew wild, and many of the new recruits were too awestruck to speak. In the distance was a forest, and in front of it stood some sort of construction.

A barracks, perhaps?

As they trudged forward, Myrddin and Grimpston spoke among themselves, mostly ignoring the recruits. It wasn't an easy trek; the plains turned to hills and the grass was wilder the farther they went. Still, the Mundanes stuck together.

They always stuck together.

None of them spoke to any of the other parties, and none of the others attempted to speak to them. A sharp breeze blew through the plains, and it carried fragrances that Suzuki had never smelled before. He wondered if there were different plants here than at home.

There must be, but then again, where was "here" exactly?

Neither Grimpston nor Myrddin had been very specific as to where they were, other than stating it was Middang3ard. True Middang3ard. Suzuki had seen his world melt before his eyes and the cosmos spread out before him. This couldn't just be another place on Earth. He wondered if it were an entirely other plane of existence. Perhaps a place folded on top of a place? It must be. Suzuki had never seen anything like this in either the game or the real world.

Beth walked close to Suzuki. She bit her lower lip and stared at her feet as her hands mechanically parted the grass in front of her.

"Was this what you were expecting?" Suzuki resisted the urge to reach for her hand, fearing rejection. Maybe he'd try later.

Then again, maybe not. Given the way he usually operated, he'd probably find an excuse not to do anything, now or later.

Beth shrugged, and when she spoke, Suzuki noted tiny indents in her lip from biting so hard. "You feel that? Even the air feels different."

"Yeah. Feels lighter. Easier to breathe."

"Might just be because I'm not inhaling so much smog."

Suzuki laughed and took a deep breath. "True. Might just be that we're breathing fresh air for the first time."

"Hey, Suzuki. Where are you from?"

Suzuki almost stopped walking as he stumbled over his words. They'd been playing together for nearly two years, and he still had no idea where Beth was from. Same with Sandy and Stew. They'd spent hours and hours together every day, and he had never thought to ask where they lived.

Or maybe they had mentioned it at some point, and the information got lost in the daily raids. It was an odd feeling to be so connected with other people and yet know nothing about who they really were. The sheer oddness of seeing Sandy wearing makeup still hadn't worn off.

"A smallish town in Orange County called Brea. You've probably never heard of it. No one has. How about you?"

"Like you, a small town about forty minutes outside of New York City." She chuckled at some joke that probably only New Yorkers would get. "But because New York City is the biggest, closest place, everyone in town just says they're from there. I wonder where they're from." She nodded in Sandy's and Stew's direction. "Are they enjoying the smog-free air as much as I am?"

Stew and Sandy were walking close together. Their hands brushed as they spoke in soft whispers, Stew occasionally looking around or picking at his face. Sandy did not look at Stew much, but her fingertips continued to touch his.

Beth pointed at their hands. "You know, I thought all that in-game flirting they were doing was just a joke. It's kinda cute to see that it wasn't all roleplaying."

"Yeah. Guess we're all real people in a real world."

"Real people in a real world?" Did I just say that? Real smooth, Suzuki. Smooth like sandpaper, he thought, wishing he were alone so he could bang his fist against his forehead.

But if Beth thought he was stupid, she gave no sign of it. "You guys were more real to me back then than most people I know in real life. And seeing you in the flesh only makes it more so."

Suzuki wasn't sure if it was this place or the air or the excitement of being on Middang3ard. Whatever it was, he suddenly felt an urge to tell Beth how he felt, like it was now or never. "Hey, Beth," Suzuki stammered as he slowed down and contemplated his next words.

He was going to ask her out.

Then he thought about it. Do people even do that anymore? Ask someone out? How would you even go about doing that? Ask her to go steady? Too archaic. Maybe ask her to be his girlfriend? Too grade school.

Shit, he thought as he looked up, meeting her eyes. She had stopped and was staring at him.

"Yeah?" Beth asked.

Suzuki froze. His words wouldn't come out of his mouth. The words he'd rehearsed time and again failed him.

But now seemed as good a time as any to ask. The veil had been pulled back and they were both here, walking through a field, off on an adventure neither of them fully understood, nor had ever imagined possible.

And if Suzuki had learned anything from the books, now was the time to say something. Still, his jaw was locked shut, refusing to budge.

Beth chuckled. "You know, I still have that ring you gave me." She pulled up a keychain with an old-school Tamagotchi. On it hung a *Lord of the Rings* replica ring that Suzuki had won in a gaming competition. When he had shown it to Beth, she had remarked on how pretty it was, so Suzuki, being the sap he was, had sent it to her.

"Are you fucking serious?" Suzuki blushed. He had sent her that ring years ago, and she still had it. "I thought you weren't into nostalgic shit like that."

Beth slipped the ring off of her keychain. It was small, barely wide enough for any of her fingers. Still, she managed to slip it onto her pinky finger and held it up for all to see.

"Hey, douche nozzles," Beth called to Sandy and Stew. "Did you guys ever see the ring Suzuki got me?"

Stew looked back and rolled his eyes. "Looks cheap."

Sandy pushed Stew, nearly knocking him over. "It's the thought, you idiot."

Suzuki blushed again and focused on moving the grass out of his way.

"I thought it was a nice gesture," Beth whispered as she leaned closer to Suzuki. "Even if it's something an old man would do."

"Maybe, but then again, you kept it, and I'm pretty sure that's something only an old broad would do."

Beth chuckled, starting to walk again. "You're probably right. Still, I liked it. I kept it on me for, you know, good luck and shit like that."

"Yeah, sure. Good luck," he muttered. His chance to say something slipped away with every step they took.

The groups followed Myrddin and Grimpston over a large hill and began their descent into the valley, which stretched for miles. They could see multiple structures—barracks of a sort with tracks for sprinting or jogging.

People were moving about the larger structures. Some of them looked to be human-sized, while others were shorter. Dwarves and gnomes were doing heavy labor. A large, glowing blue orb with spikes that fractured and reformed was in the middle of it.

It reminded Suzuki of a bootcamp.

Once they reached the barracks, Grimpston found a large stump to stand on. Myrddin had disappeared, leaving him alone with the recruits.

Grimpston stroked his beard and cleared his throat. "Welcome to the Pain Field," he shouted, his voice magically echoing through the valley. "Years ago, we used to hold a sort of fitness routine for a few months to make sure our cadets were capable of withstanding combat. However, thanks to the ingenious creation of Mr. Emrys, we are quite certain of *your* combat abilities. Think of this more as a physical. We know what you are capable of, but now we need to know if your bodies can withstand the strain of Middang3ard—the true pain of success."

"Did he just say *pain*?" Stew looked worried. He was such a big guy, but he didn't seem to be into pain of any kind. "Nothing in Middang3ard hurt before. I mean, not really. The suit would poke you, but you could always change the pain settings if it got too much and—"

"Shit wasn't real before," Beth shot out. "Besides, how'd you get those muscles without a little bit of pain?"

"It's not the same."

Grimpston went to open the doors of the barracks just as they swung open on their own. A trio of dwarves came out carrying pots and pans, grumbling as they walked. The dwarves' beards were impressive, nearly touching the ground, which wasn't really saying all that much since they barely stood over four feet.

Still, their bodies were magnificent. One of the women pushed past Suzuki, stopping for a second before sniffing loudly and spitting at Suzuki's feet.

"Fucking humans," she snarled as she shuffled past.

Grimpston clapped his hands. "Please excuse them. Nerves are tight around here right now, especially among the dwarves. They lost much in this war, and it doesn't help that today a platoon of their soldiers disappeared in the Flats of Jer-Suay. But that is why you are here: to help. Now come with me. It's time to get you fitted."

Grimpston led the cadets behind the barracks. There were racks of weapons, including longswords, bows, shields.

Along with the weapons, there was a human mage dressed in what appeared to be a military-issue robe. It fit him perfectly, yet still flowed. A red stripe ran down the front of his robe.

The mage motioned for the cadets to come closer. "Time to get you outfitted," he cackled as Grimpston pulled one of the cadets forward, a teenager no older than seventeen. Looking the teenager over, he announced, "This one's not even old enough to drink." His voice came out old and brittle, like a clichéd wizard in some 1980s movie.

"Shut up," Grimpston snapped. "Most of the newest batch is this young. Or impressively old." The professor pointed at two elderly men who looked like they were having the time of their very, very long lives.

The mage shrugged and walked around the teenager. He nodded as he took measurements with a thin measuring tape. Then he raised his hands, drew them together, and spread them apart.

Runes floated in the air between his hands. They looked like small icicles or snowflakes with a glowing nexus, then they suddenly burst with a loud *pop*. Bits of the runes swirled around the cadet and attached to his body.

They started to glow and spread. The cadet's clothes turned bright blue, then began melding together. They morphed into a sleek suit of armor consisting of thin, basic plate mail on top, with fine black chainmail underneath, all with the consistency and elasticity almost of nylon.

The helmet was a tight fit, and there were electric nodes on the side. The visor was a dull blue.

Five more mages walked out of the barracks and motioned for the cadets to come forward.

They broke into queues, lining up behind anyone with whom they felt remotely comfortable. The Mundanes stuck together as they approached one of the mages, an old man with a battle-worn face marked with scars.

The sheer unbelievability of the situation was making itself evident to Suzuki. Everything was getting more and more surreal. Gnomes. Dwarves. Battle armor?

It was Suzuki's turn to stand before the mage, who looked him over once and nodded. He cast the runes, and Suzuki felt his clothes dissolving and then hardening. His vision went black for a second as a helmet materialized over his head, and then his vision returned. There was a brief crack of energy, and Suzuki's HUD came online.

He sighed. Here was something he was at least comfortable with. He'd spent enough time in the game world of Middang3ard to feel as if he were slipping on a second skin.

His HP was displayed in the top right-hand corner, rate of success on the left, and at the bottom were slots for inventory and skills. But there were also variances from the original HUD he had come to love and trust.

On the left-hand side was a list of attributes: Strength, Intelligence, Dexterity, Endurance, and Etheric Potential. These had all been taken care of in the game's leveling system.

All of these attributes were out of twenty, and in the game, his strength was 16, well above average. Now his strength read 10—in other words, average for a human.

Just like him.

These attributes weren't some idealistic level. The HUD was literally reading the recruits and giving them real scores based on their true abilities.

The only number that read higher in real life than in the game was intelligence. In life, Suzuki was a solid 18. In the game, his warrior-mage was only a 16.

Smarter than I look, Suzuki mused.

Finally, at the bottom of the HUD was something that

Suzuki had never seen before: the lower left-hand corner showed a question mark icon.

Suzuki tried to select the icon for more information. When none was forthcoming, he queried the mage. "What's the question mark for? And how come I can't get more info?"

The mage ignored his question, and Grimpston motioned for Suzuki to get out of the way and join up with the other cadets who had been outfitted. "Come on, boy. Hurry it up."

Most of the cadets with uniforms were already grabbing at the weapons they preferred. Suzuki noticed that there were minor variations for different kinds of cadets and he assumed they were based on the different classes the cadets had played during the in-game version of Middang3ard.

Warrior characters tended to have bulkier armor, with the addition of chest and shoulder plates. Most of the dagger-wielders and archers had lighter leather armor, with a selection of pouches and straps.

The mages were the only characters who stood out. They had militarized robes similar to the mages who were equipping everyone. The robes fit tighter than anything in Middang3ard, though, somewhat giving the impression of a Catholic priest.

As Suzuki looked over the different weapons on the rack, the rest of the Mundanes joined him. Stew was fiddling with his chest piece. "It's too big," he grumbled after finally giving up and grabbing an ax.

"I'm assuming that's because it's meant to protect you," Suzuki pointed out.

Beth took a couple practice swings with her sword to gauge its weight. "Yeah, I don't care how big you think your muscles are, they're not going to stop a sword. Besides, things are so much lighter here for some reason."

Stew flexed. "Not sure about my muscles not deflecting blows. I'm pretty hard."

"Hard head," Beth said. "The rest of you is stab-able for sure."

"We won't know that for sure until we try it out."

Sandy tugged at the hem of her robes. "Don't joke like that. They all seem so serious about everything."

Beth sheathed her sword. "It's because it's fucking serious. The email, the CNN announcement—all of it was real. You guys get that, right?"

They all nodded, their initial enthusiasm dampened.

"Myrddin said that the gnome world already fell," Beth reminded them, her voice excited and hurried. "As in, the gnome world doesn't exist anymore. As in, the Dark One fucking genocided an entire race, a whole fucking planet."

There was intensity in the way she spoke, and although Suzuki couldn't see Beth's face behind her helmet, he could hear what was cracking her voice.

Fear. And that fear was going to spread to everyone.

"Yeah, that's true." Suzuki stepped up beside Beth. "But that stops here. With us. We rose to the top of the ranks before. If we had been playing on the gnomish world, we would've kept that from happening. And we're going to keep it from happening here. Got it?"

Suzuki pressed the node on the side of his helmet. The HUD flashed, and he could breathe fresh air again.

Beth and the rest of the Mundanes did the same. Sandy touched her ear as well, even though there was no helmet. She nodded in solidarity.

"So let's get ready to show the Dark One what the

Mundanes fucking bring, all right?" Suzuki shouted. "For Honor!"

"For glory," they shouted.

"For XP!"

After the cheer, Stew looked at the group and scratched his head. "You know guys, there isn't actually any XP in the game. Hasn't been since the early tabletop RPG versions. And now that this is real and not VR, there really, *really* isn't any XP. Maybe we should change our cheer."

"To what?" Suzuki asked.

"I don't know. Something like—"

There was a loud gong, breaking Stew's train of thought, and the chattering between the cadets stopped.

Grimpston was standing on top of his tree stump again. His face was long, and his eyes were wet. The dwarves surrounding the tree stump looked haggard as well. It was as if they couldn't see the beautiful valley they were standing in, the sun beaming down from above.

They were all someplace else.

"Let us begin our first round of training," Grimpston said. "You will split into your default parties, and each party will meet with a mage. The mage will place you in a magical simulation of a combat scenario. Your goal is to survive. Remember, this is not a game. You will feel the consequences of your actions, and a dead cadet is no use to our world or yours. Now get going."

7

The Mundanes marched over to the closest mage, a young human with bright, clear eyes. He nodded to acknowledge them before raising his hands and tracing a sigil in the air.

A bright green light flashed, and the now-familiar tugging sensation of transportation engulfed them as the green world melted around them. It was replaced with something vaguely familiar.

They were in an alley filled with trash. It was dark, and the walls of the buildings surrounding them were covered in what looked like blood. Steam rose from the sewer in front of them.

"All right," Suzuki whispered, "HUDs up."

Suzuki touched his ear, and the helmet materialized over his head. His HUD popped up before his eyes.

It was slightly different from what he had seen earlier. His health was still displayed in the top right corner, alongside with his mana, which read twenty percent, far lower than it would have read in the game.

Class restrictions? Suzuki wasn't sure why he was so

hobbled, not that it mattered here. A hundred, twenty, or zero percent, they were going to win the day.

The lower right-hand corner was inventory, spells (of which there were none), and equipped weapons: a longsword, a shield, and a pistol.

Suzuki felt his waist, and there was indeed a pistol. He made a mental note to check it out later. The upper left-hand corner was an approximated map, on which the Mundanes appeared as tiny blue dots huddled together. Up ahead, there was a jumble of red dots.

"Sandy, do you have any mana?"

"Yeah, a hundred percent."

"Hmm. Guess our HUD loadouts are specific to each player. Er...cadet, I mean."

"I'll fucking say," Stew growled as he pulled a short sword from his back. "At least this says barbarian. I can't believe they gave me a dinky longsword. Might as well just have handed me a limp dick. No offense, Beth."

"Not all of us need to overcompensate, douchenozzle."

Suzuki put up a hand. "Seriously, guys, cut the shit. We can joke after we prove we're supposed to be here."

As soon as those words left his lips, he realized that was exactly what he wanted to do: prove he belonged.

There was the small voice in the back of his head, the one he was almost too embarrassed to even acknowledge was his. *He'd been training his whole life for this.* Every tabletop game. Every book. It felt as if they had been placed in front of him for a reason. Now was the chance to prove it to himself.

To prove it to the Mundanes.

To prove it to the world.

To prove it to Beth.

"People need us," Suzuki continued. "No one's needed the Mundanes before, not really. Now they do."

A voice piped through their HUDs' communications. "Welcome to your first mission. The objective will be simple, but success will not. Remember, up until now, the only experience you've had was in your VR suits. That was a poor substitute for the real thing. And make no mistake... this is the real thing. Here, pain is very real. Here, death is very real. Prepare yourselves."

"You heard the man," Suzuki said as his HUD flashed with the objective **DEFEAT ENEMIES**.

That sounded easy enough.

The Mundanes stepped out of the alley and into an open street intersection. It was empty, except for a little old lady pushing a mop and bucket. She smiled sweetly at the Mundanes and slowly made her way across the street as if she didn't have a care in the world.

Behind her was an old derelict building with a glint of blue light emanating from one of its windows.

Stew pointed at the old woman, then back at the building. "Who the fuck is she? The janitor? Where are we, Detroit?"

"Get down," Beth shouted as she lunged and knocked Stew over just as a glowing blue arrow whizzed past them both, landing in the ground. It flashed brightly, as if it had a pulse.

"Book it," Suzuki shouted, and the Mundanes scrambled.

The arrow exploded, sending the Mundanes and chunks of concrete flying. Suzuki skidded across the concrete and leapt to his feet.

"Sandy," he shouted, "I want you airborne now! I need to see what we're up against."

Suzuki couldn't believe this. He was in a real, honest-to-God fight. This wasn't a game, not anymore. This was real and all the game elements—shit like stats and avatar skins, classes, and anything else that you could log out of—didn't matter anymore. All that mattered was winning the fight.

Somehow, Suzuki felt confident. He didn't know why. This was his first real fight, but he felt strong. Capable. Ready.

"Got it." Sandy rose, covering herself in a magical aura. The smile on her face was nearly as wide as a truck. "This feels so fucking awesome," she cried as she floated into the sky.

From up in the building, dozens of arrows rained down on the street corner. The old woman continued slowly crossing the street, ignoring the cacophony of explosions and bright lights. Beth, Suzuki, and Stew took cover behind a semi.

"What have we got?" Suzuki spoke in his HUD comm, which was eerily similar to the VR simulator's.

"Goblin archers in the windows," Sandy's voice piped. "Magic arrows, obviously."

"It's also obvious that they're in the windows! Gimme something I can work with."

"Well, excuse me. I'm kind of busy trying not to get nixed right now."

Suzuki looked out from behind the semi. Sandy wasn't exaggerating. She was dodging multiple projectiles, and he could tell it took every ounce of her concentration to do so.

The voice had been right; this was nothing like VR. In VR, they had equipment and time. In VR, they could pause the damn game. Here it was real-time, and Suzuki felt like a newb jacking in for the first time. "Stew and I will draw their attention," he yelled. "Beth, you just hold tight. Come on, Stew, and please don't Leeroy this up!"

Stew unsheathed his sword. "Gotcha."

"Beth, when we've got their attention, I want you and Sandy to regroup."

Suzuki looked at his HUD—sixty percent chance of success. Not good enough. "Stew, cast Enrage on yourself."

The barbarian nodded as Suzuki exited cover and pulled out his shield to offer cover. He listened as Stew clanked his sword three times against his breastplate, casting the barbarian spell on himself.

Suzuki checked his HUD. It now read eighty percent. That was more like it.

Within seconds, arrows crashed into his shield. One of them lodged, and Suzuki felt his shield heating up.

The arrows exploded, and the blast flung Suzuki against the wall. Blood trickled down the side of his face and his side spasmed with pain, reminding him that this was real and not some VR simulation.

A surge of adrenaline ran through him.

"Beth, scratch what I said," Suzuki shouted as he did a quick calculation. "Hit the foundation, all four corners. Got it? You too, Sandy."

"On it," Beth yelled as she sprinted toward the building. She deflected arrow after arrow with her small shield and pulled out a red pouch. She tossed it at the corner of the building, sidestepping the onslaught of arrows coming down.

"Hit it, Sandy," Beth shouted.

Sandy flew out from behind the building and raised her hands. Four lightning bolts struck the corners of the building.

There was a massive explosion, and glass shattered and

flew everywhere as the building shook. Then it came crashing down, floor by floor, and goblins screeched from inside the building as it caught fire.

Suzuki brushed his shield off. "That was easy enough," he announced as Sandy and Beth rejoined the group.

Across the street, there was loud rumbling, and from the shattered concrete and rubble, goblins emerged. Some of them were on fire. Flames licked their flesh, but they didn't seem to care. There were at least a dozen goblins left.

Some of them drew their swords, while others nocked their bows.

Suzuki lifted his shield high above his head. "All right, Mundanes. Let's show them why we deserve to be in Middang3ard."

The Mundanes rushed into the fray, and the air filled with the clashing of steel and wood. Suzuki blocked a thrown goblin ax as Stew leaped over the goblins to flank them. The barbarian swung his broadsword and cleaved through a couple of goblin heads.

At Suzuki's side, Beth was dueling with a goblin. She wasn't even bothering to wear her helmet. She smiled and winked at Suzuki as she sank her sword deep into its chest.

"Fuck, yeah," Stew yelled. The barbarian was right. This definitely was a "fuck, yeah" situation. Suzuki was fighting for real, and he wasn't scared.

Nor was he getting tired.

It was like being in this place gave him the strength and courage he could never have dreamt of having back home.

He cut through another goblin as Beth rolled to the side and sliced the legs off an advancing goblin. The goblin horde was already noticeably thinned. Suzuki raised his shield and cast Protection over the Mundanes, dropping his mana pool to four percent. "Fry the rest," Suzuki shouted.

Sandy flew down into the midst of the remaining goblins and slammed her hands on the ground, forming a circle of fire around her. It spread with the rapidness of a tidal wave and washed over everyone.

The Mundanes were thrown back but remained unharmed. The goblins burned, and the street was filled with the smell of roasting flesh.

The stench was all-consuming. *Yet another difference from VR*, Suzuki mused as he surveyed the damage.

Across the street, the old lady stood on the street corner and waved.

Sandy grinned. "That trick never gets old."

The simulation shimmered out of existence, and the Mundanes were back in the valley. Some of the other parties were back too, but others were missing. Suzuki didn't know if they were still in their simulations or if they just hadn't made it. Either way, the Mundanes were done --- mission accomplished.

At least he hoped it was mission accomplished.

The Mundanes stood around waiting as the other recruits started showing up party-by-party. They looked the worse for wear, with some of them seemingly seriously hurt, but despite that still moving as if wounds and pain worked differently in Middang3ard. A cut here felt a lot less...Suzuki searched for the word before settling on "severe." Their bodies healed faster here.

Still, a wound was a wound, and those in pain were immediately attended to. As for everyone else, they were invited to rest in the barracks, where they could wait in relative comfort for the last of the recruits to finish their missions.

Inside, Beth cleaned off her sword with a rag while Stew paced back and forth. Sandy had wandered off to talk with one of the mages running the simulations. Suzuki wasn't interested in resting yet. He wanted to understand something, *anything* a little more.

He stepped outside the barracks and went around the back. He had expected to see a bit more of the base and terrain. What he hadn't expected was to see Grimpston sitting alone on a stump, looking grim.

Suzuki took a deep breath, knowing that this might be his only chance to speak to the gnome alone. Walking over, he took a seat by Grimpston. "Excuse me, Sir," Suzuki said quietly.

Grimpston jumped at the sound of Suzuki's voice before realizing Suzuki was sitting next to him.

"Oh, oh," Grimpston murmured. "You caught me in the middle of a thought. I see your party made it through, correct?"

"Yes, sir, we did."

"I wouldn't expect anything less from the Mundanes."

"You know us?"

"Of course I do. Robert, correct? Everyone calls you Suzuki. Even your parents, if I recall correctly."

"Yes, Sir. But how did you—"

"We've been keeping tabs on players the whole game. As we said before, we've been seeding this idea for a long time. It goes further back than I think any of you could imagine. Every book, every game. We've been placing the idea. Raising up an army. I'm excited to see what you were capable of once you got out there and into the *real* shit."

"Thank you, Sir." Suzuki hesitated, still wanting to ask his question.

"Out with it," Grimpston said. "Your propensity for over contemplation will be the death of you."

Suzuki was taken back. Did everyone know he over thought things? And did everyone have to tell him? "OK. I wanted to know why my access to magic was so severely throttled, but Sandy's wasn't. I barely had enough mana to cast one spell."

"Sandy's a mage."

"And I'm a warrior-mage. "Mage" being the key part of that. Mages have spells."

"The truth? You're not going to like it." The gnome stopped talking.

"Please." Suzuki gestured for the gnome to continue speaking.

"Not every warrior-mage's magic is restricted. Just yours."

"Why?"

"Because you're the leader of the Mundanes, a player we've watched for some time now. In battle, magic can be a tool or a crutch. We wanted to see how you'd perform without the crutch when all you really had at your disposal was your sword and your wits."

"How did I do?"

Grimpston clapped his hands together before slowly separating them. In between his spreading hands appeared a scroll with writing on it that Suzuki didn't recognize. Grimpston read it carefully, nodding as he did. "Not bad. Not bad at all, my boy."

"That's good to know." Suzuki breathed a sigh of relief.

Sensing that he shouldn't disturb the mage further, Suzuki stood.

"Hold on," Grimpston said. "That's not the real question

ye have for me, is it?" The old gnome tapped Suzuki's nose
with his finger. "Ask it. I will answer."

"But I did ask my question. And you did answer it."

"No, ye didn't. Not the one that burns in yer heart."
Grimpston was hamming up his in-game persona, hitting
the Scottish drawl harder than usual. "The one you swore
that you'd ask me if you ever got the chance. Now's the
time."

Suzuki gave Grimpston a confused look, and the gnome
sighed in frustration. "You know, the question you asked a
dozen times on all the forms."

It took a moment for Suzuki to make the connection, but
when he did, his face brightened as he realized that he was
about to get the chance to ask something that had been
bothering him since the game's inception. "About the game's
name." He snapped his fingers three times. "I want to know
about the name."

"That's the one. Now ask it."

"How did you know about that?"

Grimpston gave Suzuki an impatient look. "Like I said,
we've been watching you...all of you, for some time now.
Now ask."

"Okay, okay," Suzuki muttered. "Why is the game called
Middang3ard and not *Middle3arth*? I mean, *Middle3arth*
would be a much easier name to remember, wouldn't it?"

Professor Grimpston burst into laughter. "Because
Tolkien's people copyrighted it." His laughter grew into a
full cackle. "We didn't want to drain the war budget with a
lawsuit."

The gnome laughter was so intense that it was infec-
tious. Suzuki found himself crying while laughing. Even
cadets who were too far away to have heard Grimpston were
laughing.

But as suddenly as it started, it stopped, the gnome's face returning to its typical serious nature. "Now that that's out of the way, you'd better get back to your squad. You can't let them deal with all of this without their leader."

"I'm not their leader. We're just a party."

Grimpston shook his head and smiled. For such a crusty looking gnome, he could have moments of pure joy shine through his spindly beard.

"Suzuki." Grimpston voice was soft, caring almost. "I told you that we've been watching you all for some time. And you are their leader. You might not think you're ready for something like this, but you've been leading the Mundanes for a long time. Might as well keep going. Go take care of your party."

Suzuki stood and nodded. He felt larger, as if he'd just grown or leveled up. "A leader." He never would have used those words to describe himself. As he walked back to the Mundanes, he noticed that they all looked up at him as if they were waiting. He knew that he wasn't going to disappoint them. Deep in his core, he knew what he was here for.

There was going to be honor.

There would be glory.

It would be one hell of an experience.

8

The rest of the day had continued to be grueling: A litany of physical activities ranging from long-distance runs to being beaten with a stick. Grimpston assured the cadets that the next day was going to be even worse. He suggested the cadets retire to the barracks to get a good night's sleep before they found out who was going to be continuing on to the next stage of the admissions.

After hearing the groans of the cadets, Grimpston let them know that the tavern would be open all night. And there was no such thing as a drinking age in Middang3ard.

Before dismissing them, he called forth a few cadets to speak to them in private, Stew among them. "Don't say anything stupid," Sandy said as the barbarian trotted off.

"Always do," Stew called back.

"We'll meet you in the pub," Suzuki yelled out, wondering why Grimpston wanted to speak to Stew and not the rest of them. But as soon as they were in the old wooden tavern that smelled of hay and mead, he put Stew out of his mind.

He'd find out soon enough, and right now he was trying to brush off the various humiliations of the day.

Suzuki was sore.

Sorer than he'd been in his entire life. Still, he felt like he could keep going. It was an odd feeling. He hadn't been much of an athlete back on earth. Not that he was out of shape, but he wasn't the sort of guy to go on walks for the hell of it. Out here in Middang3ard was something different though.

He felt like he could have run drills all night.

It was probably the excitement.

The tavern was lit by candlelight, with candles on the walls and decorating the rows of tables which the cadets were rapidly taking up. But other than the obscene number of candles, this place was like any other old pub you'd find on Earth. Rustic, pungent with the smell of mead and already full of drunks.

Most everyone was drinking. Cadets with officers. Or whatever they called themselves. No one had been straightforward about the ranks yet. Suzuki could see that there were distinctions based on how the officers spoke to each other, but it was all over Suzuki's head. Still, it seemed that they were all having a good time without getting caught up in rank.

The dwarves were the only ones who seemed like they might have preferred to be somewhere else. They kept to themselves and slowly sipped on their mead as a group of human barbarians struck up a beer song. Something about the empty fields of hope stained with blood.

They had barely finished their first drink when Stew showed up, mead in hand.

"What happened?"

Stew brushed away the question, downing his drink.

"Alcohol now, talk later," he said in a Tarzan-esque voice, but Suzuki could tell something was wrong. Especially because the giant man had barely finished his first drink before standing up and announcing, "I'm getting another round. Anyone else want one?"

Beth and Suzuki raised their hands. They clanked their wooden tankards together and finished the last golden drops of mead.

"God damn," Beth slammed her hand on the table. "It feels good to be right."

"Yeah, yeah, yeah," Suzuki said. "We got it. You know everything."

"Not like that. I mean this. All of this," she spread her arms, motioning to everything around her, "it's like a movie. I could never have imagined anything like this."

Suzuki and Sandy nodded in agreement. Sandy wasn't looking at any of the Mundanes, though. She was staring off at the mage officer's table.

"You got a crush on one of the suits?" Beth snapped her fingers at Sandy.

"No," Sandy muttered. "Not like that. It's just...you know, we can be powerful here. Like really powerful. We could probably really fuck shit up."

"Leeroy's gonna go ham out there," Suzuki remarked. "We're going to have to make sure he doesn't get himself killed."

"You're not going to have to worry about that." Stew put the drinks down on the table, but he didn't sit down. The rest of the Mundanes looked up at him and saw the usual smug smirk sitting on his face was nowhere to be seen. It was like a shadow was resting on his face.

His eyes were damp, and he looked like he might cry. It was an odd image to see a giant of a man decked out in armor, barely able to keep the tears from rolling down his face.

"Hey, babe." Sandy stood up and went to him. "What's wrong?"

"I'm going home." Stew took a long draught from his tankard.

"Are you fucking serious?" Beth exclaimed.

Suzuki couldn't believe what he was hearing. "They can't send you home. You blew through that last exercise."

Stew shook his head as he took another drink. The tears were coming now. But his face was still straight, and he let them fall on the table.

"That's not what Grimpston told me," Stew said. "He said I was getting carried. Sandy was covering my ass. The whole time. Cleaning up anything that I wasn't finishing off. And keeping me from getting killed by shit I didn't see."

Stew looked at Sandy, but she wouldn't meet his eyes. She just stared at the table, wide-eyed and in disbelief.

"Is that true?" Suzuki asked.

"We always do that," Sandy's eyes were sad, and Suzuki knew she was racked with guilt at the thought that she was responsible for Stew getting kicked out. "It's just teamwork. I always cover his back. I didn't know it was going to count against him."

Sandy's lip was trembling. Her hands were shaking, and she was hardly able to lift her cup.

"Hey, hey." Stew drew her in close. "Don't worry about it, Sandy. You were just watching my ass like you always do. Can't swing that sword the way you like if I have to tip-toe around everything, right?"

Sandy looked up at him and forced a crooked smile. "When are you leaving?"

"Now." Stew gestured at the door where several other

cadets were already gathering. Suzuki guessed they were the ones who also didn't make the cut.

"I just had to come and say my goodbyes." Stew stood there awkwardly.

Suzuki could understand the feeling, and he knew Stew didn't know what to say. He didn't know either. So they all just sat there in silence. Stew wouldn't make eye contact with anyone at the table as he looked down at his tankard of mead and sighed. This wasn't the way that things were supposed to go.

"You guys remember that raid we did in March?" Suzuki asked.

"Yeah," Sandy said. "The one that I got that death mask from."

"Exactly. That one. I remember trying to prep that battle for at least an hour ahead of time. And I'd been thinking about it all day. And I gave that big speech about how we had to stick to the script if we were going to get anything done and right in the middle of the speech, Stew fucking Leeroys it. Everyone's shouting at him, and I tell him to stop Leeroying it up, and he just gets quiet. And then he says that he's never fucking seen the Leeroy Jenkins video."

"I just thought you guys thought I looked like a Leeroy," Stew chuckled before letting out a roar of a laugh. It was contagious. After a couple seconds, everyone was laughing except for Sandy. She was still looking down at her fingernails, picking at her nail polish.

Suzuki stood and raised his tankard. Beth followed. After a couple of seconds, Sandy stood up as well.

"To Stew," Suzuki raised his cup high. "When we need our asses saved, we'll think of you. Cheers."

"Cheers!"

They clanked their tankards together. A couple of folks

from the other parties were watching. A few nodded their heads in agreement. *They must have had people leaving too*, Suzuki thought. Not everyone's going to make it.

"Never split the party," Sandy lamented.

Stew shrugged and smiled weakly. "It might be time for a new party. I gotta get going." He lingered for a moment like a shadow of his former self. Then he finished his drink and left the tavern without another word.

Sandy was crying softly and Beth reached out, taking her hand. "It's not your fault. You were doing what any one of us would have done. Except maybe Stew."

Sandy laughed and took another sip. "Yeah. He would have at least put on a good show."

Suzuki woke up to the sound of a loud gong. He rolled over in bed and tangled himself in the thin sheets. When he reached for his standard duvet...the one with the cast of the Avengers printed on it...it was gone. Instead, there was a coarse green military-issued blanket.

Suzuki sat up in bed and looked around the room. Dozens of cadets were sleeping in stacked bunk beds. He had been dreaming of home.

But this was not a dream. He wiped the sleep from his eyes and tried to make himself wake up faster. He ran through the events of the last day.

Stew had been let go. The Mundanes were already broken.

He would have to give today's trials everything he had to keep the party from splintering even further. There was no answer for how he was going to do that, though.

Sandy had demonstrated amazing teamwork the day

before and Stew got nixed for it. More worries flooded Suzuki's mind as he got up and dressed. Across the room, Beth was sitting in bed, rubbing her face. A little bit of drool ran down her face as she met Suzuki's eyes. She quickly grabbed her sheets and rubbed her face clean.

"Stop perving," Beth rolled out of the bed and climbed down the trunk.

Suzuki's face went red and he looked down at his feet, then realized that looking at his feet would only confirm her accusations and tried to look up at Beth. He settled on shoving his hands in his pocket and pulling out some lint he pretended to be interested in.

Beth came over to Suzuki and shoved him playfully. "Come on. I'm just joking. I'm assuming you don't wake up to the glory of feminine beauty often."

"Where's Sandy?" Suzuki asked.

"Probably already outside," Beth put on her HUD, pressed the ear node, and her armor shimmered into existence.

Suzuki did the same. "Let's go."

They exited the barracks as another obnoxiously loud gong rang and the rest of the cadets started to make their way out of bed. Beth had been right. Sandy was outside, talking to one of the mage officers.

Sandy waved at Beth and Suzuki as the mage politely nodded his head and walked away. "I was just getting a scoop on what we're up against today."

"And the verdict?" Suzuki asked.

"Magical and physical resistance. Some random at the pub said that we're going to be poked and prodded until we feel sick." Sandy pointed at the line of cadets making their way toward the mages stationed over in the valley near where they had all been originally transported.

"Sounds fantastic," Beth groaned.

The remaining Mundanes followed the crowd. Without any ceremony whatsoever, the mages snapped their fingers and Suzuki felt the fishhook in his stomach and reality slid around him. When everything stopped moving, he was in something like a large gymnasium.

The massive building was split into different stations where there were mages and dwarves waiting. It reminded Suzuki of high school, when they'd give everyone a physical or some shit like that in the school's gymnasium. But unlike High School, stations both lined the ground and floated in the air. Each station was marked with a number that floated above the mages and glowed bright red with traces of sparks flying off of them.

An arrow guided their way until they came up to a red box painted on the ground with another flaming arrow that pointed up next to it.

"What the fuck are we supposed to do now?" Beth pointed up to a floating station with a burning number 1 next to it.

Suzuki shrugged. "Sandy, you got a spell that can get us up there?"

Sandy touched her HUD and shook her head. "I can't seem to access my magic here."

"Shit," Suzuki said, approaching the painted box. "What do they think we're going to do? Grow wings or some shit like that? I mean we're just—" His left foot stepped into the box, and instantly he shot up in the air.

Well, "shot up" implied some grace to what happened. It was more like he tumbled up, like someone helplessly falling in the wrong direction.

"Uh-uh." A dwarven attendee lifted his hand, stopping Suzuki before him. "Usually you just hop in the box and up you come. Not do whatever acrobatic feat that was. Like them."

The dwarven mage pointed behind Suzuki, and he watched as Beth and Sandy, having learned from his mistake, gracefully floated up next to him.

Beth was grinning ear to ear. "That was awesome, Suzuki. You looked like you were doing windmills."

"Reminded me of my nephew's tumble tots. But he was more graceful than you," Sandy chuckled. "He's three."

"Oh ha-ha, guys," Suzuki said, pointing at the dwarf. "Maybe we should concentrate on the task at hand." He gestured for the three of them to make their way inside the station.

"Uh, uh, uh," the dwarven wagged an admonishing finger at them. "These are individual evaluations. Please split your party and go to separate areas." He pointed to the other floating stations.

"Guess they're really into splitting up parties," Sandy mused.

"You can take this one, Suzuki," Beth pointed to the station in front of them. "Don't want you to do any more acrobatics today." She gave him an exaggerated thumbs-up before she broke into the most awkward breaststroke he'd ever seen.

"You're not doing much better than me," Suzuki called after her.

Beth continued to do her awkward strokes. "I am as graceful as a swan."

"More like a frog who just suffered a stroke," Sandy giggled as she tried the front crawl to get to her station.

"Good luck, guys," Suzuki called, and with a heavy sigh, he went inside the floating station where a grumpy-looking elf mage stared at him over the rim of his reading glasses.

The mage held a clipboard that he let go, but instead of falling like any normal object should, it just floated there as if the mage had put it away.

"First things first," the mage said, gracefully floating next to him. The elf stood, or rather floated, a full foot shorter than Suzuki and despite his obvious age, he was exceedingly beautiful "We're going to test your magical resistance."

"How exactly are you going to do that?" Suzuki was trying to keep the apprehension out of his voice. He was sweating so much that he thought it might be pouring from his armor.

"Please take a guarded stance." The mage crossed his arm over his chest, demonstrating a defensive pose.

"Guard myself with what?" Suzuki imitated the mage as best he could.

"Well, it's magic, so I guess with whatever helps you feel better."

Suzuki didn't know what to do, so he raised his fists as if he were a boxer. "Is this good enough?"

"Sure, why not."

The mage pulled a long thin wand from a holster on the side of his robes. He raised the wand to the air and brought it down with a quick slice. Suzuki's HUD read at the last second: Incoming Undefined Magic ATT.

Doesn't look too bad, Suzuki thought right before the attack hit. It was a blunt force that sent him spiraling backward. He skidded across the floor from the impact. It felt as if the wind had just gotten knocked out of him. He coughed and sat up. The mage motioned for him to step forward.

"Do you have any internal bleeding?" The mage didn't look too concerned. As if it didn't matter to him if Suzuki was bleeding to death or not.

"How the hell am I supposed to know if I'm bleeding internally?"

"Usually you cough up blood. Like, a lot of blood."

"No, I think my organs are safe."

"Good. Looks like you have fairly good resistance to magic. Now let's try elemental."

"Wait, wait!" Suzuki lifted his hands to plead with the mage, but it was too late.

The mage raised his wand again and fireballs appeared above its tip. Suzuki screamed and turned to run away just as the fireballs came down on him and engulfed him in a fiery explosion. When the flames died out, Suzuki was laying on his back—well, floating on his back—coughing loudly.

"Looks like you managed to avoid catching fire without even defending," the mage said. "You *do* have fairly good resistance to magic."

"Thanks, I think."

Suzuki was unsure what exactly he was thanking him for. He had just had a friggin' fireball thrown at him!

"Most cadets are either immolated or have broken bones by now."

"That's good to hear. What's next?" Suzuki had meant it sarcastically. He really didn't want to know what was next. And when the mage answered him, all Suzuki wanted to do was go home.

"Resistance to bludgeoning and piercing weapons."

"You're going to stab me?"

"Not quite. You are wearing armor, and you do have a shield. Also, it won't be me. It'll be him."

The mage whipped his wand again, and they were suddenly standing on the ground. A large troll materialized in front of Suzuki. The troll looked to be young, maybe a teen. Whatever its age, it was still huge. The troll easily stood a few feet above Suzuki and held a large club, and its dull eyes scanned the area, looking for prey.

"I suggest not *letting* the troll hit you," the mage said.

Suzuki whipped out his shield and sword. The troll and Suzuki made eye contact as they started to circle each other.

"Do you guys just keep trolls here to beat the shit out of cadets?" Suzuki shouted as the troll advanced.

"No," the mage said as he looked at his clipboard with a bored look on his face. "It's part of a new infantry program we've been working on. Trolls aren't like orcs. They don't care what they smash. You just gotta point them in the right direction."

The troll raised its club and brought it down on Suzuki, who only barely managed to get his shield up in time. The attack nearly drove Suzuki into the ground, but the shield took the brunt of the attack. Suzuki's knees buckled slightly, but he stood his ground.

This was unreal. He was standing up to an actual troll attack. And doing it fairly easily. The troll took a step back and then attacked again. This time Suzuki stepped to the side, raised his shield, and deflected the attack at just the right moment, causing the troll to lose its balance and nearly fall over.

Suzuki smiled from behind his helmet as it dawned on him that he could actually win this fight.

The troll roared loudly and pulled one of the swords from his side. He slashed at Suzuki, who raised his shield, this time pushing back when the sword connected, forcing the troll to step back as well. He drew his sword as the troll shouted loud enough to vibrate Suzuki's armor from the inside. The troll advanced.

"All right, that's enough." The mage waved his wand. The troll disappeared. "Come here. Let me check you out."

Suzuki came up to the mage and handed the mage his shield. The mage looked over it and nodded his head. There were tons of scratches, and the shield was slightly dented.

"How you feeling?"

"A little shaky." Suzuki patted himself down, checking for any signs of blood or broken bones. Anything. He felt surprisingly good, given a real-life troll just tried to kill him. He didn't seem to be hurt. "But otherwise pretty good."

"Wouldn't have been able to tell. Not a lot of cadets deal with staring down a troll like that. You got a pretty good all-around resistance. Come on, let's move over to the other station."

This time they didn't float up, just walked toward the station. Suzuki looked up at the floating stations. "Guess it's a good way to maximize on space," he mused.

Sandy was already at that station, lying flat on her back and groaning loudly as she held her stomach. When the mage and Suzuki got to her station, she stood up and gave Suzuki a thumbs up.

"You're gonna love this one," she grumbled as she limped off before he could ask what the fuck was going to happen to him.

"Oh yay," Suzuki groaned as he stood under the giant flaming 2 while the mage circled him.

"Looks like you have a fairly high magical resistance," the mage said. "Fairly high, indeed."

The mage raised his hand and the section of flooring they stood on shot up, nearly as high as the ceiling. There was enough room for Suzuki to walk a couple of feet, but he quickly found himself looking over the ledge of the magically articulated floor.

"First is Featherfall."

The mage waved his hands and cast his spell, which produced an ominous amount of chicken feathers floating in front of Suzuki's face. Then the mage gently pushed Suzuki off of the ledge.

Suzuki shrieked and tried to grasp the ledge, but he had been pushed too far. He closed his eyes and anticipated the inevitable splat of his guts and bones against the gymnasium floor. Yet it did not come. He opened his eyes and looked around. The floor was still what seemed like miles away, the mage's eyes still level with his.

Suzuki was suspended in the air, actually not quite suspended. He was falling, granted, at a snail's pace.

The mage raised his hands, and Suzuki felt a sharp pain in his feet. "All right, let's see what your body can handle."

Suzuki looked down where his feet should have been. But instead of seeing army-issued boots, he had a mass of hairy tentacles whipping about as if they had a mind of his own.

"What the ever-loving fuck?" Suzuki shouted.

There was a popping sound like a balloon full of water coming in contact with a needle. The tentacles were gone, replaced by duck's feet.

Suzuki opened his mouth to protest, but his voice was gone. Instead, a high-pitched quack came out.

"Hm," the mage mused, as he jotted something down in his notebook. "Looks like your body absorbs other properties of the cast species. Interesting."

"This is not funny," Suzuki tried to say, but only a series of quacks came out. He folded his arms to show his disappointment.

The mage was slightly grinning and turned away to hide it. He waved his hands again, and Suzuki felt a pinch on his shoulders as bones shifted and the skin on his back split apart. Suzuki yelped from the discomfort as he reached back to touch his shoulder.

What he felt was scaly and long. He instinctively flexed his shoulders and felt the massive weight of wings flagging. Looking over his shoulder, he saw that he had sprouted massive red reptilian wings that stretched out from side to side, giving him a wingspan of nearly six feet.

The red scales shimmered like rubies, and Suzuki found that he could will them to flap the same way he could his hands to move. They felt as natural as if he had been born with them.

The mage waved his hand again, and the roof of the gymnasium pulled back until there was open sky. "Go ahead and give 'em a try." The mage gestured to the clouds above. Suzuki didn't need to be told twice, beating his wings as he soared out of the gymnasium and into the open sky. The sun beamed down on him, and he rocketed toward the clouds. He was laughing as he shot into a large cloud, feeling its cold condensation chilling his skin before he burst out into the sunlight.

"This is amazing," Suzuki shouted, as he did a front flip in the air and spread his wings out.

"Good. One more test from me and we're done."

"Cool." Suzuki flapped his dragon wings with genuine amusement. "What are you going—" Then he heard another magical pop and the weight from his back was gone.

His dragon wings were gone, replaced by what Suzuki could only assume were tiny pigeon wings. He flapped them as hard as he could but to no effect. He was already plummeting back to the ground, and no matter how frantically he beat his little wings, the ground was still coming up at a frightening speed.

Suzuki's legs popped and he was covered in tentacles again, but this time, each tentacle ended in a pigeon's foot. His feet flailed around as he reached out for the ledge that was quickly passing. On the ledge, the mage raised his hands again, releasing a bunch of floating feathers into the air, seemingly taunting Suzuki.

Closing his eyes, Suzuki waited to become a red splat on the floor.

But the splat didn't come.

Opening one eye, Suzuki realized he was floating again. Faster than before but still not fast enough to cause any lasting damage. His multiple pigeon feet touched the ground, and he fell over as he tried to make sense of his new standing arrangement.

"Will you just give me back my feet," Suzuki shouted at the mage on the ledge.

"Excuse me," a voice said, startling him.

Suzuki jumped and tripped over his mass of feet and found himself eye level with a female dwarf wearing a white lab coat which matched her beard. She was standing in front of him, holding a clipboard and a wand.

Evidently, she was his next evaluator. The dwarf waved the wand, and Suzuki felt his bones swell. His whole body expanded faster than he could have drawn breath.

He went from his modest 5"9' to a whopping thirteen feet. His bones ached tremendously. It was like puberty's growing pains all at once. The dwarf took a few notes on her clipboard and then prodded Suzuki with her wand. He instantly shrunk back down to his regular size.

"Transmogrification is complete," his new evaluator said. "You are a resilient human. You pass."

Suzuki picked himself up and dusted himself off, feeling his arms and his back and then his legs, moving them around, as he made sure everything worked the way it should. Everything seemed to be back to normal, and he sighed in relief.

"Anything else that you want to do to my body?" Suzuki groaned with anxiety at the fifty shades of horror these guys could inflict on him. "Going to turn me into a fish or something now? Give me gills, then waterboard me?"

The dwarf looked up at Suzuki and without a hint of humor, shook her head. "All we have left is a brief questionnaire."

"Does it change me into anything?"

"Only into an official cadet or a reject. Shall we begin?"

Suzuki nodded.

"Good. Blood type?"

"B positive."

"Age?"

"22."

"Sex."

"Isn't that one obvious?"

"Your species is hideous by dwarf standards. No offense. And you are completely hairless. I honestly can't tell if you are a man, woman, or child. So I'll ask again: sex?"

"Male."

"English ancestry?"

"Excuse me?"

"Do you have any English ancestry?"

"Well, my grandfather was English, but he immigrated to the States something like fifty years ago."

The dwarf pulled a stamp from her pocket. She slammed it on the clipboard. The stamp read "Rejected" in bright red font.

"Wait, what," Suzuki shouted.

"Blood of Englishman. Giants will smell you from miles away."

"It was my grandfather! I'm not English!"

"Any more than twenty-five percent is too much. Please exit the gym. We'll be sending you home shortly."

Suzuki didn't know what to say. He wanted to fight, to argue, to find some way that he could stay, but he couldn't think of anything to say. And before he could simply launch into a rambling rant, the dwarf turned and walked away, leaving him with a sinking feeling of loss and remorse in his gut.

How could something this amazing just be snatched away from him? He hadn't had a chance to prove himself. Now he was letting everyone down. First Stew, now himself. The party hadn't even had a chance to make it to the wilds of Middang3ard, and everything was already falling apart.

Suzuki looked around the gymnasium. It was completely empty. He made his way outside, trying not to hang his head. Outside, there was a small group of, what Suzuki could only imagine, were other rejected cadets. It didn't seem like any of them could meet each other's eyes, and Suzuki sensed the cloud of failure that hung over them, not wanting to be anywhere near it.

"Hey, Suzuki," someone shouted.

Suzuki looked up and saw Sandy waving him over. He walked over to her. Her mascara was running, and she dabbed her eyes with a tissue that she then crumpled and put in her pocket.

"You too, huh?" Sandy said.

"Blood of an Englishman." Suzuki shook his head. He couldn't believe that his grandfather—a man he hardly knew—was the reason he'd never get to go to Middang3ard. "Apparently giants can smell it. What about you?"

Sandy blushed bright red and shrugged her shoulders. "They didn't tell me."

"This is fucking great, right? Chance of a lifetime and we didn't even make it out the gate."

A few feet from where Sandy and Suzuki stood, there was a loud crack of electricity. Suzuki looked at the source of the sound and watched in amazement as the field nearby folded over on itself, then unfolded again creating what looked like a massive, magical crease.

Then the crease split up, and a multicolored hole opened into a tunnel.

Beth and a few others walked out of the tunnel, each of them wearing what Suzuki assumed to be cadet uniforms.

And they weren't alone, each one of them paired with some kind of creature that Suzuki had only ever seen in Monster Manuals or when jacked into the VR game.

And they were all smiling.

As soon as Beth saw them, she waved at Suzuki and Sandy, crossing the field to join them. As she got closer, Suzuki saw what looked like a giant bee the size of a house cat sitting on her shoulder.

The insectoid had razor-sharp mandibles that seemed far too intimidating for its face and a stinger that hung low, more like that of a wasp than a honeybee.

Up-close now, Suzuki could see his reflection in its thousands of eyes. He looked pathetic even by his standards.

"What the hell is that?" Sandy asked.

"My familiar." Beth pointed to the creature on her shoulder. "You need it to do magic or get into Middang3ard proper. I guess this place is kind of an in-between plane."

"So, you made it?" Suzuki asked.

"You guys didn't?"

Suzuki nodded. The sense of guilt was overbearing. If it were just guilt, that was something he could have dealt with. But the shame he also felt was something far more difficult to bear.

Beth shook her head in disbelief. "This is fucking bullshit. First Stew, now you guys. I'm out. I'm out. I'm going to turn this down and head back with you guys," she growled as rage slowly took over.

"No, you can't," Suzuki said. "This is what you want. Middang3ard, fighting the good fight."

"Not without you."

Not without you? Had he heard her right?

Then she added, "Not without the Mundanes. We're meant to be together."

Suzuki nodded. "Maybe, but you can't quit."

"I can. Watch me," Beth started to turn on her heels when the large bee-like creature started nibbling on her ear. "What? Stop that...what?"

"What's going on?" Sandy asked. It was weird watching the insectoid do that.

What was even weirder was when Beth growled, "You're fucking kidding me. There's got to be a way—"

Beth nodded, her eyes narrowing like she was listening intently.

"You're fucking kidding me. Uh-huh. Uh-huh. What? That can't be legal!"

"What are you doing?" Suzuki asked, taking a step closer to her.

Beth lifted a hand, indicating that she needed a minute, nodded, and said, "Uh-huh," a few more times before her shoulders slumped.

Then she turned back to Suzuki and Sandy. "Fuck me,

guys."

"What just happened?" Sandy asked.

"My familiar." She gestured to the insect. It was looking at them now, no longer chewing on her ear. "I can't quit. I signed a contract."

"You did?"

"Except I didn't. I just agreed to go to Middang3ard three times. Apparently, in this place, that's like signing a contract and its serious shit. I break it, and I get cursed."

"Cursed?" Suzuki asked. "What the fuck does that mean?"

"Ros'ten isn't sure, but he said it usually involves losing teeth, boils, and leprosy."

"Fuck me," Suzuki muttered.

"Fuck me, indeed," Beth agreed. "I'm in now. No going back." She looked over her shoulder at the other successful cadets. She shifted her weight from foot to foot and cleared her throat.

A siren sounded, accompanied by a voice that said, "All recruits to the transportation deck."

"I can't fucking believe this!" Beth exclaimed.

"Go," Suzuki said. "Go. We'll find a way to Middang3ard, and when we do..."

"Yeah," Beth agreed. "We'll get the party back together."

"You bet," Suzuki replied. "We'll show these guys that the Mundanes are meant to be together."

"Promise?" Beth stuck out her hand. Suzuki and Sandy put their hands on hers.

"Promise."

Another siren. "Fuck. I got to go."

Sandy stuck out her hand, and Beth shook it. "It was good to meet you."

"We'll meet again. And soon." Beth took Sandy's hand

and pulled her in for a hug. "Glad to finally see your makeup in person. The pics don't do you justice."

Sandy nodded again, wiped her face with her hands, sighed, and walked off, leaving Beth and Suzuki alone.

Beth started, "You know, it's not understandable. The Mundanes might be a pack of douche nozzles, but we aren't anything without you."

Suzuki didn't say anything, just stared into her impossibly beautiful blue eyes.

"See you on the other side?"

"Yeah." Suzuki nodded. "See you on the other side."

Beth touched the side of his face, and they stood together for what felt like an eternity.

A blissful, perfect eternity.

Suzuki wanted to reach out and hold her. To tell her he'd always be thinking of her. To ask her to be safe.

But no words came out. Instead, he just looked at his feet. Then he felt Beth's other hand on his chin, gently lifting it so his eyes would meet hers.

Her green eyes flashed brightly and she leaned close to him, her lips only a few inches away from his.

"Watch it, human," the dwarf examiner grumbled as she pushed past Beth and Suzuki. She stopped and cast a disgusted glance at Beth. "Aren't you supposed to be shipping out?"

"Yeah." Beth straightened up, adjusting invisible creases in her uniform. "I should get going."

"Yeah. I guess you should."

Beth hugged Suzuki before hurriedly turning to leave. Suzuki stood there, helpless as he watched her go.

The dwarf who had interrupted what had promised to be their moment grumbled at Suzuki, "You should count yourself lucky. I can smell your blood from here."

9

Suzuki wasn't happy about it, but life went back to normal. Quickly, as well. One day he was training to be a part of Earth's last hope, then two months later, he was on his bed, plugged back into the VR. His blinds were drawn so that very little light could get into the room. He preferred it this way. When there was less light, there was less of the world to block out.

In the dark, he could lose himself to the VR and his imagination. Suzuki needed all the help he could get. He had stood toe to toe with a troll, been transformed into shapes he could never have imagined, met dwarves, and seen magic—real magic—first-hand.

The VR wasn't a substitute. It was just something to do to kill time while he tried to figure out a way back to Middang3ard to get the party back together. He knew it was one hell of a mission, but he was going to get that done, come hell or high water.

After a few weeks of dead ends, however, he was wondering if either hell or high water was ever going to make its way to his rural home.

When he got home, there had been rumors that *Middang-g3ard* would be pulled. Turned out to be bullshit. There were more people than ever online now. After the first wave of failed cadets returned to Earth, their story spread across the internet and news sources, and suddenly everyone wanted to be an adventurer on Middang3ard.

Also, with the steady flow of rejects blogging about what they had seen, people wanted in.

Into the real Middang3ard, that was, and they saw the VR game as their gateway. The result was that the game was full of newbs.

The world was waking up to the fact that Myrddin was telling the truth, so the secret wasn't so secret anymore. Sure, he and the other rejects had been forced to sign gruesome NDAs with both legal and magical consequences to keep what they had seen secret.

But that only meant that anything they leaked had to be kept vague.

And it was the vagueness of the rejects' reports that seemed to be driving curiosity to a frenzy. Suzuki wondered if that had been part of Myrddin's plan all along.

Sure, there were still some stragglers who refused to believe, but for the most part, the world had started to sing a different tune.

And now there were even rumors that the first batch of recent cadets was going to be coming home on leave in a little bit.

Suzuki tried to find out if Beth would be among those coming home, but information was hard to come by. Turns out communicating between realms wasn't as easy as it sounded. Suzuki had been waiting to hear from Beth for weeks. Three months, to be exact. He had the dates crossed out on a calendar hanging next to his bed.

So it was *Middang3ard* VR for now, while he tried to figure out a way to get back in...to get the party back together.

He was playing with Sandy and Stew as usual. They hadn't found a fourth to fill the party out, and Suzuki didn't think they ever were going to.

No one would ever be as good as Beth.

Beth.

Suzuki wished he had told Beth earlier; let her know how important she was to the party. Now all he had were regrets and unspoken words.

"Dude, could you please get your shit together?" Stew's avatar put its face right into Suzuki's view, breaking him from his thoughts.

"Ahh, sorry," Suzuki said, taking note of where they were.

Their avatars stood in the middle of an underground cavern. It was dark, the only light coming from their torches. Usually Sandy would be lighting the cave with a spell, but she had changed classes and refused to use magic. When Suzuki asked her why, she had told him it just wasn't the same.

VR couldn't compare to the real thing.

Suzuki was silently thankful he had never gotten a chance to use magic, and that he could still enjoy the basic mage and cleric spells since he'd never enjoyed the real thing. He would have hated for that to have been taken from him as well.

"Let's get this over with." Stew pushed farther into the cavern. It sounded as if it were a chore to him. Suzuki couldn't remember the last time he had seen Stew throw himself into the fray. He was a by-the-book player now.

Hell, he wasn't even that. Stew played like he was filing paperwork or finishing a paint-by-numbers artwork.

To most gamers, the dungeon would have been interesting. There were goblin mobs that would spawn sporadically, based on how many players were wielding certain kinds of weapons.

The traps in-game were all built around what kind of magic spells you were equipped with. The game had gone into overdrive since the initial recruiting of cadets.

No doubt to make the selection process harder, Suzuki thought.

The problem was that it wasn't getting any harder for the Mundanes. They were flying through each expansion without breaking a sweat, even with a three-person party.

Stew stomped a goblin into the ground and blood flew into his face. He didn't bother wiping it off.

Sandy impaled the goblin through the skull, spreading brain matter everywhere.

Suzuki took care of a few goblins with two effortless swings. "Stew, any news from your guy?" He didn't need to say more. They knew exactly what he was talking about. When the three of them weren't playing, they were trying to find a way back inside. And Suzuki, ever the strategist, was coordinating their research and efforts.

And part of that effort was Stew's guy-who-knew-a-guy lead.

Stew shook his head. "No."

"No, there's no lead, or 'no,' you didn't reach out to him yet?"

"I didn't reach out to him yet."

Suzuki slammed a goblin against a wall harder than he needed to. "Goddamn it, Stew, we agreed you'd get it done this week."

"Hey, I tried, but no dice, O great leader. And what about you? Any leads from your end?"

Suzuki pursed his lips. "You guys heard of the MERCs?"

"Everyone's heard of MERC," Sandy's character shot two arrows in rapid succession, felling a goblin. "Nobody's heard about how to get in, though."

"I heard that's where the real shit is going down. Not any of that army "jump through this hoop, weigh this much" type of bullshit...and I think I might know a guy." Suzuki's character took three more swings, killing two goblins who were foolish enough to get close to him.

For the first time in months, Suzuki saw Sandy's face light up. She threw a knife into a goblin who was sneaking up on Stew as she ran over to him.

"Are you serious?" Sandy's voice was filled with irritation. Then again, Sandy's voice was always filled with irritation these days. "How could you not have told us about this? How do we get in?"

"It's nothing solid yet."

"Still, it's something."

Suzuki nodded. "Maybe, but people are always saying that they know how to get into MERC. I mean, I've lost track of how many players claim they have a way to bypass the whole military bullshit and go straight for the glory and the loot."

"And Beth," Sandy added. It wasn't a jab at Suzuki. She was just as into getting the party back together as he was.

What Suzuki didn't add was that he wasn't sure the MERCs even existed. Still it was a lead and he was going to explore all possibilities.

It felt too much like some sad story that the losers were telling themselves. A consolation prize to help them sleep at night. What good would a mercenary group be when Earth was already having a hard enough time finding cadets who could go toe-to-toe with the Dark One?

Still, it was a lead, and he was determined to get back in. And get the party back together.

"So how do you get in?" Stew asked. "You know a guy."

Suzuki's avatar ran a nervous hand through his digital hair, obviously imitating what he was doing in his VR suit. "Y-yeah, I know a guy. A couple of guys actually."

"So who's your in?"

"Yeah," Sandy chimed in. "Who is it?"

"Just some guys I've been messaging on the forums."

"What are their names?" Stew asked.

"Like you know every player of Middang3ard? Come on. Let's finish up this dungeon." Suzuki was getting defensive. Truth was, he seriously doubted his leads.

"Look, it's a long shot, but these guys on Reddit said—"

"Dude, Reddit? Seriously," Stew growled. "You know that's just a bunch of bullshitters. They don't shit."

"It's a lead."

"It's a dead end."

"No, I think that—"

Stew turned to walk away from them, but Suzuki grabbed him by the shoulder and spun him around. Stew's avatar lost his footing and stumbled.

"Hey, what the hell is your problem?" The barbarian raised his voice in anger, drawing his sword. "Do you really feel like PVPing this shit right now? Because I will fucking wipe the floor with your character."

Suzuki pulled out his sword and raised his shield. He was hot with anger. Things had been getting like this a lot recently, and he didn't know how to stop it. Every couple of skirmishes, Stew would say something stupid, and Suzuki would get angry and want to do something about it.

"Hey, come on." Sandy stepped between the two of them. "Why don't we put our dicks away for just a moment?"

Suzuki and Stew glared at each other. Neither of them moved.

"Seriously, guys," Sandy shouted. "Stop it!"

Suzuki sighed and sheathed his sword and, putting out his hand, said, "Sorry, I shouldn't have done that. I'm just frustrated. We've been trying for weeks and nothing."

Stew nodded, taking Suzuki's hand. "Me, too. I've been looking around. But all I've found are lots of rumors, and nothing else."

Stew crouched down on a rock. He pulled up his inventory and built a fire.

"Nothing beats the real thing, I guess." He took a seat on the log Suzuki and Sandy were already sitting on.

Sandy leaned her head on Stew and slipped her arm around his waist, but Stew didn't seem to notice. He only stared at the flames as they flickered.

There was a ding on Suzuki's HUD. He looked at his notification. It read one new message. From Beth.

"Hey, guys," Suzuki started.

"Already got it, bro," Stew said. "Looks like Beth's still alive."

All of the Mundanes opened their group message from Beth.

Hey, douchenozzles the message read. **Finally got a chance to get a message out to you guys. You have no idea how hard it is to find time for that kind of shit. My parents didn't even know where I was for the first month. And even then, all I had time to do was tell them that I wasn't dead yet.**

I miss you guys tons. Can't say that enough. You guys

would love it out here though. It's fucking wild. What we saw before was nothing. Like nothing. You can't even begin to imagine. It's a whole other world. It's so weird cause it's kind of like home but also so different. I mean, there are so many orcs.

Like SO many orcs.

It's missions all day, every fucking day. It's exciting as hell but so tiring. Trust me, running raids all day in VR is nothing like actually having to run a raid. It's crazy how much I learned playing the game though. I owe it all to you guys. There's a couple of kids in my troop who only scratched the surface of Middang3ard when they were playing (don't ask me how they made it this far), and they've been having a real hard time.

We've been cleaning up orc camps. Mostly red and gray orcs. Some of the shit is gnarly. I don't want to get into all the shitty details, but it's war out here. The Dark One is up to some crazy shit. Still, haven't quite figured out what's going on but they keep a lot of that information away from grunts like me. But you don't need clearance to know something big is going on.

What Myrddin said was true. This shit is real, and we do need troops. Seems that Canada, the UK, and the Congo – of all places – have started training their military for Middang3ard. They've committed troops, but it's still not enough. We're going to need everyone... and I mean everyone to join. Total bullshit you guys got rejected. You're exactly the kind of people we need.

"Anyways, I don't have a lot of time. Just wanted to stop off and tell you guys I miss you and I'm doing well. I know you douche nozzles were disappointed that you couldn't come. I am, too. You would love it here.

"Sandy: The silk in the markets here is otherworldly. It

makes anything you'd pick up from Harrod's look like yarn.

"Stew: You'd fit in with these barbarians. Leeroying it up is a thing here. You'd think that these kids would be safer, but I dunno. Guess it's a personality thing.

"Oh! I was talking to some of the other troops about you guys, and they totally knew who the Mundanes were. We are kind of like a bootcamp legend for your in-game swag. There's even a bet to see who can figure out Suzuki's real first name.

"Anyway, hope you guys are keeping making a name for yourselves in-game. Remember to keep your eyes open. All of them."

Suzuki closed the message. Both Sandy and Stew got a shout out, but there was nothing for him.

"I gotta go, guys," Suzuki told them.

"Wait," Sandy said. "What's—"

Suzuki signed off and the VR screen went blank. He pulled off his headset and sat up in bed.

How could Beth just forget about him like that? Maybe she had met someone else. It's not like they had anything going on anyway. Nothing official at least but he'd always thought that there was something there.

Maybe it was just in his head. Maybe he was someone easily forgettable. Beth was amazing. She'd probably met someone who could keep up with her. Not some nerd sitting in his room trying to figure out if he was going to read through a D&D manual or jerk off.

Jerking off did sound like a good idea at the moment, so Suzuki started to pull off his sweatpants when he got a ding on his VR headset. He sighed and put the headset back on only to be greeted by Beth's face wearing a devilish grin. He rolled off the bed and pulled up his pants.

When he looked closer, he could see that it was a message, not anything that was real-time or live-streaming. *Thank God*, he thought, as he opened the video message.

Beth stared back at him. Her face was dirty, and it looked like she hadn't bathed in a few days. Her eyes were a little sunken, and her hair had grown longer. Suzuki thought she still was the most beautiful woman he'd ever seen.

Beth leaned forward and straightened out the camera.

"Hey, Suzuki. Just wanted to say hi. I miss you. A lot. It's been weird being away from the party. I always thought you guys would be here with me. I didn't want to freak out Sandy and Stew or anything, but this shit is real. Like real *real*. A couple of people from my squad...well...I mean, they didn't make it.

"We did a raid on this orc camp, and it wasn't planned well. It went bad. Which is why we need people like you here. There's a disturbing lack of strategists. It's mostly just meatheads. It's got me worried. The shit that I've seen out here...I mean, it's beautiful here, but what the Dark Lord is doing to these people, to this place! It could all be gone. Anyways, I'm not trying to stress you out or worry you. I'm safe."

Beth looked down at her watch. It was an old digital Casio that her mother had given her years ago.

"Let's see if I timed this right," she said. "In about ten seconds, you should hear a knock at your door."

Beth stared awkwardly at the screen. Suzuki counted: 7, 8, 9. He heard a knock on the door downstairs. He took off the headset, ran down the stairs, and opened his front door, where he saw a package sitting on his stoop.

Suzuki picked it up. It had some weight to it. Suzuki pulled up his private messenger on his phone. There was another message from Beth. It read: Get this dongle installed as soon as you can and use it when the time's right. It might just save your life.

Suzuki opened up the package. Inside was a small attachable dongle. He didn't even know what it was supposed to attach to. It was a slim cylinder, and it didn't have any ports that he'd ever seen before.

What the hell is this for?

He brought Beth's video message back up, but he didn't bother playing it. He just looked at Beth. He felt his stomach knot up. He was flooded with the same feeling he always got when he looked at a photo of her or checked through the loot they used to share. He should be watching her back. He knew that. Yet here he was, walking upstairs to go to sleep.

This was hardly an adventure.

10

K nock, knock. Knock.
Suzuki turned back to the door. He'd hardly made it a couple of steps away from the stairs, and there was already another knock on the door.

Another knock, this time louder than the last. Whoever was on the other side of the door sounded impatient. Suzuki reached over, gripped the doorknob, and flung the door wide open.

There was no one there.

Suzuki stepped outside into a typical day in his suburb. Every front yard had a pristinely-manicured lawn with patches of green grass stretching as far as he could see.

Most days it turned his stomach to see such uniformity. When he was growing up, his mother had told him that nausea was caused by allergies, but Suzuki knew the only thing he had been allergic to was the boredom and mediocrity.

And now that his mom was gone, having died from cancer three years ago, he'd inherited the house. Instead of selling it and moving to the city, he just stayed where he was, using the money she'd left him to game.

That's probably why he was so good at it and probably why it mattered so much to him. Since his mom died, in-game was the only place he didn't feel so alone.

Well, the only place he *used* to not feel alone. He felt it even more now since the adventure of true Middang3ard had been ripped from his hands.

Suzuki sighed, trying not to think about his mom or Beth or what he was missing out on, and went back inside. As he closed the door, there was another knock. Suzuki flung the door open, thinking to himself how much he was going to enjoy going off on whoever was pranking him.

Nothing.

He slammed the door. "What the ever-loving fuck?" he sighed under his breath.

Knock.

Suzuki didn't waste any time flinging the door open. "Okay, where the hell are you?" he shouted. Still nothing.

Nothing except when he looked down and saw something that made his jaw go slack in a mixture of disgust and awe.

A floating, fleshy orb was in the door's threshold. It was hovering about knee height and wasn't much bigger than a tennis ball. It had a mass of tentacles sitting on top of its head, each tentacle ending in a slimy eyeball. It had a mouth that turned up like a pug's and an overbite showing its numerous, small, dagger-like teeth. Its skin was gray and scaly. A large eye sat in the middle of the floating head's face. A thick eyelid rested over the eye so that the thing would have looked sleepy if it weren't for the halo of wide-open eyes surrounding its head.

"Ahem," the eye-covered creature said. "May I come in?"

The smell of dust and ancientness wafted from the floating head as all of its eyes appraised Suzuki.

Suzuki opened the door nearly as wide as his eyes. "Sure," he said. "Come on in."

The head floated into the house. Its tentacle eyes whipped around as they looked at every inch of the living room. They never stopped moving. Suzuki wondered just how much information must be pouring through that gray head all of the time. Finally, the creature turned to face Suzuki with its large middle eye. It didn't say anything, only stared at Suzuki with its dozen eyes.

Suzuki took a huge breath and scooted across the living room, trying not to look as if he were obviously trying to put some space between him and the ancient Beholder before him.

"Can I help you with something?" Suzuki asked.

"It is I who have come to help you," the creature said. "I am known as He with Many Eyes Who Watches throughout and beyond Time Unceasingly. Mortals refer to me as Manny."

Suzuki stuck his hand out for a handshake before thinking better of it. "Err...nice to meet you."

"You as well."

"Can I...uh...help you with anything?" Suzuki repeated, unsure exactly how to speak to a Beholder.

Manny's eyes bored into Suzuki. Someone staring at you was already bad enough, Suzuki thought. But this was unbearable. Most of Manny's eyes didn't even blink. Not even the massive one.

"You really live up to the 'Unceasing' part of your name, huh," Suzuki joked.

Manny opened its mouth and something like a growl and a thousand screams came barreling out. "Humor is not generally a strength of your race. I find you to be the exception."

"Do you want to take a seat or something?"

The living room filled with the sound of Manny's frightening parody of a laugh. "No," Manny said. "I have arrived on business. Business for you."

"What kind of business would I have with a Beholder? You are a real Beholder, right? Not some kind of mechanical trick to get me to order another update of *Middang3ard*?"

"Thankfully, Myrddin is finished with his tacky publicity stunts. I informed him such tactics are unbefitting for a wizard of his age and talent. Naturally, I was unheeded. As if I were not capable of seeing that which others are unaware of. One does not need twelve eyes to see that Myrddin was embarrassing himself. Greatly. But I am not here to speak to you of that which I have seen, I am here to speak to you of that which I have been told. I am a recruiter for the MERCs."

Suzuki took a seat as the news hit. He shook his head, running his fingers through his hair as he tried to wrap his mind around what he had just heard. Between all of the *Middang3ard* players going on about how they all knew someone who was in the MERCs and the rumors on the online message boards, Suzuki had stopped taking the existence of the MERCs seriously. Though, if he could accept a Beholder randomly showing up at his front door, he could imagine that the MERCS might be a real thing. But why were they at his front door?

Manny broke Suzuki's train of thought. "I can see that you are confused, human. Allow me to dispel your concerns."

All of Manny's tentacled eyes glowed. They looked like bouncing Christmas lights.

His middle eye rolled back so that only the white of his eye could be seen. Then he began spinning in a circle, faster and faster until he was only a blur. A bright light projected from his glowing eye until what looked like a massive scroll wavered into existence.

Manny stopped spinning and returned to his unnatural floating position as the scroll unfolded.

There were no words on the scroll, only a moving image of men and women in various kinds of armor. There were muscular, hardly-clothed barbarians covered in war paint; mages with flowing robes that reached to the ground and rippled and changed colors like the running waters of a river; archers and gunners; soldiers ---and warriors.

In the middle of the image was a paladin with bright, silver armor and a kite shield nearly the size of his body. A massive greatsword with a golden hilt set with jewels and precious stones rested in the warrior's hand.

The warrior reached for his helmet and touched its ear. The helmet rearticulated itself, bits and pieces moving back and forth like small building blocks being taken apart.

Suzuki's face was behind the helmet.

"At no time in history," Manny said, "has an army ever been enough. There are things that governments are not capable of. There are things that heavily regulated forces are not capable of. There are things that people simply do not want to do. That is when the different realms rely on the MERCs who are completely unsanctioned, untethered to race, realm, or government. When soldiers are afraid to get questionable blood on their uniforms, the MERCs relish in shedding that very same blood. And we are paid well for that bloodshed."

"Are you saying that you're working outside of the

government?" The thought of doing something illegal made Suzuki nervous.

"There isn't always a need for government. The government did nothing to stop the destruction of past realms, and the government will continue to step around what needs to be done. The realms are at war---make no doubt about that---and war is not beautiful. It is foul, disgusting, and unrelenting. Not everyone has the stomach to do what needs to be done in times like these. When your government hesitates, the Dark One destroys. He is a never-ending force of destruction and chaos. There is no room for hesitation."

Seven of Manny's eyes closed at once, as if to emphasize his last point.

"So it's illegal?"

More lights shone from Manny's eyes, and the image on the scroll changed. The soldiers were all gone, replaced by a battlefield with dozens of soldiers who lay dead in a green field, their weapons littering the field as if they were gravestones.

Manny floated beside the image. "Death is coming for your people. I have seen it. Your simple notions of right and wrong, legal or illegal, private or government will do nothing to save you. Are these dead men and women soldiers or mercenaries?"

Suzuki looked at the image of the dead. There were more than he could count. All that he could tell from the image was that they were humans, dwarves, elves, and gnomes.

So many different races, so many dead.

"When did this happen?" Suzuki asked.

"Answer the question," Manny bellowed.

Many of the dead soldiers wore armor. Some of them were impaled on long spikes and hung in the air as if they were some form of offering. The grass was stained with blood that wasn't only red, but other colors as well.

I guess not everyone bleeds red, Suzuki thought before saying, "I can't tell the difference."

"Exactly. Soldiers die. It does not matter if they are illegal or not. Their sacrifices all mean the same."

"So why not have regular soldiers?"

"We are the arm of force when situations are dire. Soldiers do not like low survival rates. We MERCs see that as a challenge. We're the unofficial cannon fodder."

"Wait, what?"

"The unofficial cannons," and under his breath, he added, "fodder."

The image on the scroll transformed again. This time, the warrior with Suzuki's face was surrounded by other MERCs. He knelt beside a large golden chest. Light shone out of the cracks of the chest.

The warrior opened the chest and stared down at its contents. Manny floated closer to Suzuki, filling the air with his ancient smell.

"The spoils of war are yours to keep. And these are *not* the spoils of your game. You will see realms and treasures that you could never imagine. Amulets which extend your life. Your real life. Not an HP gauge in a VR simulation. Armor which could show you the future. Gloves that can let you read the mind of your enemies. And all of it is for your taking. There is only one rule."

"And what's that?"

"Only fight the armies of the Dark One. There is no other law."

Suzuki thought back to the image of the dead soldiers and realized that Manny wasn't pulling any punches. The perspective that he was giving was vastly different than what Grimpston and Myrddin had hinted.

It wasn't that the others had lied or anything. But no one had mentioned death. Sure, things had hurt during training, but the thought of death had never really crossed his mind.

Listening to a gnome give grand speeches about missing or destroyed realms was not the same as seeing the destruction left by the Dark One. There had been so many bodies.

How many more were there going to be?

What would keep Suzuki from becoming one of them?

And Beth...she was in the same danger as those who lay dead and forgotten in that bloody field had been. Her assurances that she was safe meant something now. Truly none of this was a game.

Suzuki stood and paced back and forth, trying to calm himself enough so he could think clearly.

"Why did you come to me?" Suzuki asked. "I failed the basic exams. I couldn't even make it. Do you just pick up rejects to catch arrows?"

Manny smiled and laughed that screeching, inhuman sound. "You have so little faith in yourself. The MERCs are not rejects. We came for you because *they* missed a chance to have one of the best strategists that the *Middang3ard* game has ever seen."

"Flattery isn't going to help."

"You are looking for reasons not to come."

"What do you mean?"

"Do you fear death?"

Suzuki didn't answer. His teeth were clenched tight.

"Now tell me, Robert Suzuki Fletcher. Are you ready to face your destiny?"

"What if my destiny is to die?"

The image on the scroll changed again. Beth stared at

Suzuki. She was frowning, and she looked extremely annoyed.

"Beth?"

"Are you fucking serious?" Beth shouted. "Get your shit together, Suzuki!"

"Have you been listening the whole time?"

"Just to the part where you started acting like a little bitch. You and the rest of the Mundanes were so butt-hurt to get sent back home, and now you're afraid of coming back because something bad might happen? This is war, Suzuki. Real, scary, and fucking dangerous. And a shit ton of people are out here risking our lives so that people can be safe. You can sit at home and be scared shitless. Or you can come out here and do something great. We'll be on the same side. You'd get a freedom that I would *kill* to have. And who knows...we could even end up meeting. The MERCs go everywhere, and we work with them sometimes. We need you out here, Suzuki. Don't punk out."

Beth's image wavered in and out of focus until it vanished. Suzuki's own reflection stared back at him. He was wearing warrior-mage grade light armor. He raised his hand. His reflection did the same.

"There's only one rule?" Suzuki muttered.

Manny nodded, a bizarre and almost laughable image, the floating head rocking back and forth. "Only one rule," Manny repeated.

"Do you know where she is?"

"I have seen. And you will as well."

"I'm in."

"Good. Ready yourself."

Suzuki felt the now familiar hook of pain in his stomach and he lurched forward. A vortex opened beneath him and he felt the world flip upside down as he sank into the vortex, his body stretching, unraveling, and disintegrating. He didn't know where he was going, but it didn't matter.

Beth was somewhere out there, and that was all that mattered.

The ground was hard, and Suzuki hit it with a tremendous amount of force. He looked around, but couldn't make sense of what he saw. The world was still spinning, and he could hardly feel his legs. When he tried to stand, he fell to his knees. He immediately vomited.

Above Suzuki, the Beholder floated. "On your feet, MERC. Knees are meant for begging. And MERCs never beg."

11

W hen the fog in Suzuki's mind finally cleared, he pulled himself up and looked around at a disconcerting forest. The tree trunks were a bright, even red, the leaves various shades of pink and blue. Coupled with the almost neon green grass, the forest looked like something out of a cotton candy dream. The more that Suzuki looked around, the more unreal the place seemed. When he drew in a breath, it was sweet, almost like honey. Manny was floating beside him. He casually yawned as Suzuki took in the atmosphere of this new realm.

"Where are we?"

Manny's eye tentacles spread out as if he were using them to gesticulate. "It's an in-between realm. Not quite here nor there. Yet we are here. A pocket dimension within a pocket dimension. It is where our familiars are kept."

Suzuki followed Manny as he started to float away. "What familiars? I mean, I know what they were in the game. Creatures that kind of acted like sidekicks. But when Beth showed up with that messed-up giant bee, she made it sound like familiars have much more significance in

Middang3ard. Middang3ard the real place, as opposed to the VR game."

"Humans require a familiar to use magic," Manny answered. "The children of dust were able to use magic many years ago when our realms were freshly born. Humans were actually some of the most devout and skillful practitioners of magic. You and the elves. But the elves tended to use magic for themselves, predominately to extend their lives. Humans, on the other hand, seemed to have no overall purpose for magic. Each individual used it differently, based on individual needs or desires. This caused an explosion of magical creativity that humans became known for. Dwarves smithed, gnomes played, and elves studied. Humans, on the other hand, they experimented."

"What happened?"

Manny closed his many eyes. "Humans forgot how to use magic."

Suzuki eyed the Beholder, unsure. There was something about the shortness of Manny's answer that made Suzuki doubtful. The Beholder had already proved himself to be wordy. Why such a simple answer? Even more so, how could humans just forget how to use magic? Something didn't add up, but Suzuki could see by the look on Manny's gray face that he wasn't going to get an answer right now.

Maybe there would be a better time to try and dig the truth out of Manny.

The two travelers from separate realms walked farther and farther into the forest. Even though the trees had started to grow thickly together, the sun still shone harshly through the leaves.

As they walked through the forest, Suzuki could hear voices ahead. He wasn't certain how many people were there, but it sounded like more than a handful. The prospect of meeting more MERCs made Suzuki's heart race with excitement.

Seriously, Suzuki, he scolded himself, *not the best time for your social anxiety to kick in.*

There was a part of him that just assumed that this whole thing was one big scam. The magical equivalent of a Nigerian Prince scam or something similar. If there were people trying to take care of the different realms, there were bound to be individuals who were going to try and take advantage.

Suzuki wondered if the MERCs actually were doing just that. He knew enough about mercenaries from Earth's history. Mercenaries worked for coin, and anyone who worked for coin was loyal only to payment. That's probably why the MERCs had just one rule: fight the Dark One only. That left a lot of wiggle room for other kinds of illicit activities.

Manny and Suzuki passed a thin outcrop of trees and Suzuki could see that there were at least a hundred people in the small clearing ahead. Some of them were wearing armor, but most were wearing street clothes.

The ones in armor were something to behold. There was no uniformity among them. Instead, there was a wild diversity among the armored MERCs.

One soldier wore a gold-threaded chainmail armor that seemed to change length and visibility as he moved. The soldier himself dipped in and out of sight as he talked. His face was covered with small, intricate tattoos and a massive ax hung on his back.

One of the mages wore a finely-tailored three-piece suit. The collar of her suit was popped, and her sleeves were rolled up to show her gauntlets, delicate little things that were inscribed with elven runes. Her HUD was sleek and glowed with a dull white light. The armored MERCs were intermingling with the street-clothed MERC recruits.

They must be veterans, Suzuki thought. Manny wasn't joking about the spoils of war.

The older MERCs didn't seem to notice Manny and Suzuki as they walked past.

Good. Suzuki felt extremely underdressed. He was, after all, still wearing his pajamas. His mom had been right when she told him he should at least put on pants if he was going to play video games all day.

Manny led Suzuki to a small group of people, and as Suzuki got closer, he made out Sandy and Stew. Sandy's face beamed when she saw Suzuki and she rushed over to him, nearly knocking him over as she threw her arms around him.

"You made it too." She giggled as she let Suzuki go. "We were worried when we didn't see you here."

Stew sauntered up to Suzuki and put his arm around the man's shoulder. "Yeah, I thought it'd be a little fucked if I made it in, but not you," Stew joked. "Did eyeball give you the whole spiel? "

"He sure as hell did. Kind of a talker, that one."

"You'd think he had as many mouths as he does eyes," Sandy added.

Manny floated closer to the Mundanes, his eyes whirling about as he moved. "Just because I do not have ears does not mean that I cannot hear. I stand by what I have said about humans and humor, Suzuki. You and your friend Sandy are exceptional." Manny left out another one of his high-pitched, horrific laughs.

Stew leaned closer to Sandy. "Figures the only person

who'd get your sense of humor is a monster from another realm."

"My humor is multi-dimensional and beyond you," Sandy fired back. "I think that's what you're trying to say."

Manny cleared his throat, and the older MERCs left the groups they had been speaking with and surrounded him. Being flanked by fully-upgraded MERCs provided Manny with an even greater sense of authority, and the whole scene looked like a MERC propaganda photo-op.

Doubt kept creeping into Suzuki's head.

This was illegal.

They were unsanctioned.

What was the catch?

But whatever the catch was, he was in now. They all were.

"Now that we have gathered you all here," Manny shouted above the murmurs of newb cadets, "we can begin. You should have had the nature of your human inadequacies explained to you by now. Farther into this forest is a place called The Garden of Familiars. Many of the familiars of the realms gather here to drink from its lake. I do not know why. Do not ask me. We will be going to the garden, and you will all pick or be picked by a familiar. This is an important step of your initiation into the MERCs. Without a familiar, you will continue to be cut off from magic. You will not enter Middang3ard. So I will emphasize this one point: choose carefully. Your time in Middang3ard is extremely dependent on your familiar. Try to choose a companion who will compliment you, rather than tear you down. Are there any questions?"

A middle-aged man with a short beard and heavy brow freckles raised his hand.

"Yes, you," Manny boomed.

"What if we can't find a familiar?"

"You will. They want to get out of this place just as badly as you want to get into Middang3ard. Now follow me."

Manny floated away, followed by the veteran MERCs. The newbs followed as close behind as they dared, while Suzuki and the Mundanes took up the rear.

Suzuki wanted to watch the other MERCs trying to figure things out as best he could before wading into the thick of it all.

Stew nudged Suzuki in the side. "Are you doing that thing you do?"

"What thing that I do?"

"The one where you overthink everything so much you can't enjoy an amazing experience. You know, like you did with that easy raid on Shoyenguard. Or the whole Beth thing."

"What whole Beth thing?"

Stew turned to Sandy, who was absentmindedly staring at the leaves overhead. "Hey, babe, how long has Suzuki been obsessing over how he feels about Beth?"

Sandy scrunched up her face as she thought. "Two years and seven months."

"Two years and seven months," Stew repeated. "Almost as long as we've all been playing together."

"I have not been obsessing," Suzuki countered. "I just like to understand things. Some of us like to know what's going on. We can't all just live in a testosterone-filled haze. Shit, and who are you to talk? I don't even know if you and Sandy are dating half the time."

"Babe, are we still dating?"

Sandy cheerfully nodded her head as she skipped to catch up with Stew and Suzuki. "Yep," she chimed. "First-year anniversary next week."

Stew cracked his knuckles and smiled in a way that made him look like a wet salamander. "See my point."

"Do you really need me to point out the sheer stupidity of you giving me love advice? That's like asking Jar-Jar Binks about the finer points of galaxy politics. Or asking the Punisher to give a lecture on the proper use of police or military force in overseas diplomacy. Or—"

"All right, all right," Stew butted in as he waved away Suzuki's rant. "I get it. You have a Netflix account, too much time on your hands, and your virginity's still intact. All I'm saying is let's give this a chance. This could be something that blows our minds right out of the fucking realm."

"You've been practicing your MERC lingo," Sandy quipped.

"Gotta talk the talk before you walk the walk."

"Yeah, yeah," Suzuki said. "I get it's exciting and shit, but this isn't a game. None of this is. And none of us asked to be a part of this. I got a message from Beth earlier."

Suzuki looked over his shoulders to see if anyone was listening. Most of the other newbs were a good distance away. He couldn't see Manny anywhere.

"She said people were dying, not getting sent home. Dying. And just think about this whole thing. We were playing a video game with no indication that it was anything other than a game. We won. Then we got whisked off to another fucking dimension without even being asked. Myrddin laid all of this shit on us, and we just jumped into playing soldier as soon as possible. Then they started shipping people off without even asking a fucking question. Even the military doesn't do that. And there's all this shit that still makes it seem like a game sometimes. The HUDs and junk. No one's even asking what's going on. We're just taking it at face value. And we're taking it from someone who's already tricked us once."

"But this isn't Myrddin," Sandy argued. "These are the MERCs."

"Yeah, but do we really know the difference?"

The crowd of new and old recruits, led by Manny, came to the Garden of Familiars.

The garden was a more open section of the forest with a large lake in the center of the clearing, the water as clear as glass. It was surrounded by a grove of roses and other plants that Suzuki didn't have a name for.

There were so many kinds of multicolored foliage that the garden looked to be nothing other than a rainbow grounded onto the earth. Yet these paled in comparison to what was causing every new recruit's jaw to drop.

The garden was filled with an assortment of creatures, many of them crowded around the lake. Some of the creatures were obviously from Earth. Or at least similar to those on Earth. Deer, bears, falcons...a litany of different animals. They stood near each other as if they were conversing.

Then there were the creatures that Suzuki could not take his eyes off. Creatures that he had only seen in books, comics, video games, and monster manuals: fantastical creatures on par with anything that had ever been dreamed in Middang3ard. Most of them were vaguely familiar from different myths or media.

The Mundanes stopped in their tracks. A giant deer had walked directly in front of them. Yet there was something off about the deer. It was noticeably taller, its legs long and spindly. Light seemed to pass directly through the deer so that it had the look of embodying water. Its antlers stretched up and out to the sky, ending with a bloom of wildflowers. The deer also stopped. It stared at the Mundanes.

"Hmm." The deer sighed. "More humans."

The deer trotted away, leaving the Mundanes speechless. Suzuki eventually brought himself back to attention and went to join the crowd of other recruits.

Everyone was crowding around Manny. "There's not much which can be explained about this process. Please...go make a friend."

The recruits looked around, with few of them able to meet the eyes of the creatures who walked around this bizarre garden of Eden. Suzuki's heart was racing. Everywhere he looked, there was a fantastical beast he'd never seen before. Between his feet, five pink mice scurried, stopping for a moment to look up at Suzuki before chasing each other off.

Stew nudged Suzuki and motioned at a few nymphs bathing in the lake. "I heard from one of the older guys that you have to get *very* acquainted with your familiars."

"Jesus Christ." Suzuki sighed. "Sandy's right there, you dick."

Sandy shrugged as she looked around the garden. "He's just kidding. He's like a dog chasing a car, he wouldn't know what to do if he ever caught one. Besides, he knows I'd find someone with a lot of tentacles to crawl up into me."

Stew's eyes widened in reaction.

Sandy smiled and kissed Stew on his cheek. "Now who do you think is right for me?" And before Stew could answer, Sandy walked into the trees.

"You were joking, right," Stew shouted as Sandy walked off. "Babe! You were joking, right? I thought we already talked about the tentacle thing."

Suzuki slapped Stew on the back and laughed. "Not only is she better looking than you, but she's also funnier, too. I'll see you in a bit."

Suzuki left Stew to his insecurities as he searched for his own familiar. Somehow being here made the fears running around in Suzuki's head all but disappear.

This place was magic. Not magical.

Magic.

Nothing about it was close to anything he could have fathomed before. Suzuki wondered if these were the same familiars that the military used. It probably didn't matter either way.

He wandered around and let his eyes soak up everything. Fairies drifted around the flowers near the lake. Their wings caught every ray of light and acted like a prism, casting rainbows across the grass. The nymphs in the water were splashing each other until a raccoon the size of a bear leapt through the air, cannonballing into the lake, sending water flying everywhere. The familiars sunbathing next to the lake screeched and laughed.

Suzuki wanted to observe some more before he made a move, so he took up an open spot near a small patch of gardenias.

By now, many of the familiars had gravitated toward a recruit. Suzuki was glad that nothing had come near him yet, and he was able to take it all in. He wondered how it was that familiars helped reestablish humanity with the magical world. Perhaps it was some kind of symbiotic relationship or bond? Or maybe it was just an agreement, plain and simple. The familiars helped humans access magic and humans ... what did humans offer them? He wasn't sure.

Suzuki was tossing theories around in his head when he noticed a figure at the far edge of the garden-- an imp sitting alone on a giant stone facing the darkest part of the forest.

The imp's back was turned from the garden, as if it

wanted nothing to do with the matching of familiars and humans.

Suzuki knew exactly what the creature was doing. He recognized it because it was what he so often did -- sit alone, away from everyone else, contemplating. Suzuki didn't know how to explain it, but he was drawn to the creature, almost as if they were kindred spirits.

Or maybe it was more magic, guiding his thoughts and actions.

Whatever it was, Suzuki stood and started in the imp's direction.

Manny floated up beside Suzuki, his many eyes tracking the young man. "Finally decided on a familiar to pursue?"

"Maybe, I'm not sure. But I did want to ask that imp a few questions."

"Don't take any of his answers seriously. He may try to mislead you."

"I thought this garden was filled with user-friendly familiars only."

Manny made a motion as if he were trying to shrug. "Not all is as it seems. Besides that creature is an imp to begin with, an eldritch imp on top of that."

"You guys really hold onto your notions of racial good and evil, don't you?"

"Only when the hold fits. And even then, my definition of good and evil is not simply put in terms for those who can only see one thing at a time."

"Just because you have a ton of eyes, doesn't make you omniscient."

"If these were my only eyes, I'd agree."

Suzuki stopped walking and stared at the Beholder. He tried to meet Manny's many eyes, but there were too many to focus on. "What are you trying to tell me?" Suzuki probed.

"The imp is eldritch. It is not like other imps of its kind. It has existed for longer than I can see. And with that lengthy existence comes a somewhat peculiar concept of morality. Let me say it simply: I have rarely met an eldritch creature with even the smallest inkling of care for mortals."

"So what's he doing here? Isn't this a place to hold familiars to help mortals?"

"He is here because he is a traitor. He once worked for the forces of the Dark One. He defected over matters which mortals cannot seem to grasp. Once he was on our side, he bonded with a human for a brief period of time. It did not go well. Only the imp remains. Since then he's refused to cooperate with any other mortal. He refuses to give any explanation. And since he is an eldritch creature, there is only so much which I can see."

Suzuki watched the imp from afar as it spread its wings and curled its tail. If Manny had been trying to deter him from approaching the imp, he'd failed. His warnings only served to deepen Suzuki's curiosity. "Thanks for the pep talk, but I think I'm gonna find out what this guy's deal is, anyway."

Manny silently nodded his head, giving some kind of consent or encouragement. Suzuki crossed the length of the garden, approaching the imp. The flowery scent of the garden faded, and the closer Suzuki got to the imp, the stronger the smell of brimstone and sulfur. The imp was crouched low as if it were holding something between its hands. Its scales were interlaced beautifully over each other, and they shone in the sunlight. Two large horns curled over its head like those of a ram.

As Suzuki approached the imp, he raised his hands as

if he'd been stopped by the cops. It seemed like a good idea to at least show he wasn't armed. "Hey," Suzuki called.

The imp looked over its shoulders. Its eyes were black as death. "What do you want, human?" the imp hissed. His voice was deep and sultry. "I am contemplating."

"What are you thinking about?"

"Thinking" is not the same as contemplating. And what I am *thinking* about would hardly be of interest to you."

"Try me."

The imp turned around so that it could face Suzuki. It was larger than it looked from behind. Its wiry, frail body exuded an air of power that confused Suzuki. Just looking at the imp made Suzuki uncomfortable. Its black eyes bore deep into Suzuki, and he felt as if the imp could see anything within him that it wanted. Even if Suzuki didn't.

"Time," the imp said. "I am thinking of time and dreams. Those which we have seen and those which have yet to come and all of that which has always been."

"What makes you think that I don't understand time?"

"Time is not a concept you humans tend to grasp easily."

Suzuki walked closer. He took a seat on a rock near the imp's as the imp's scales ruffled like that of a giant bird. "You mean like quantum mechanics? Or are you talking in a more abstract sense? Like the very nature of time itself?"

"Child," the imp spat. "I existed before your kind pulled themselves from their bacteria-laden womb and shat themselves across your realm. Do you honestly think that a cursory knowledge of Stephen Hawking is going to impress me?"

"No, but I think an extensive knowledge might."

"Interesting. You are proud, yet also reek of insecurity. Still, nothing more than a simple human paradox."

"You never said what you were thinking of. Specifically. I mean, any human undergrad can *think* about time."

The imp clutched its branch while it leaned over to get a better look at Suzuki. "I was born in a place that no longer exists in time. I am spending my eternity locked away in this timeless prison, waiting for a half-witted human savior to take me away from a place where nothing dies, and everything stays green and full of life. I wonder how long I must wait to taste air, true air, air full of decaying molecules. And I wonder how long it will take my new host to die so that I may be released into the world anew."

Suzuki shrugged his shoulders and leaned back on his rock. "That's not really a question about time. That's mostly about your place in time."

"What is time without the individual to experience it?"

"Good point."

"I know."

"What's your name?"

"My name has been whispered across the barren caverns of space for nearly a millennium. It requires two tongues and a thorough understanding of the first words to even whisper it."

"How about Fred then?" Suzuki extended his hand. "I can pronounce Fred with one tongue and a mediocre grasp of English."

The imp laughed. Not that it sounded like anything more than gears in an unoiled machine cracking against one another. Then Fred eyed Suzuki carefully, as if he wasn't just looking at him, but through him. "Interesting. Death follows you but has yet to choose you. Why?"

"I don't know. Maybe—"

"It was a rhetorical question. Your kind is wholly unfit to even contemplate such things. Still, you amuse me, mortal.

Very well, then, I have been here long enough. Time to breath the air of death once more. Your name, human?"

"Robert, but my friends call me Suzuki."

"You are tolerable, Robert. Barely."

"Suzuki, please. Call me Suzuki. Everyone does."

"Very well, Suzuki," the imp said, turning back to the darkness of the forest.

"So now what?"

Fred sighed as if he were debating something in his head. Then with a growl, he jumped off of the branch, flapped his wings, and floated beside Suzuki. "I suppose that I follow you around on any asinine quest you see fit to exploit my powers for. And why not? Asinine quests or endless meandering in this garden are my choices. And to that end, I guess following you will be slightly more interesting than being here. At least it will be a change of scenery. So, as the mortals say: lead on."

Suzuki wasn't sure how to take any of these statements, but it seemed he had landed himself a familiar. He took a tentative step away from Fred, who flapped his wings and floated after Suzuki.

"So we're kind of like a buddy movie?"

"And what is a buddy movie, exactly?"

"You know, like *Lethal Weapon* or *Turner and Hooch*?"

Fred closed his eyes, and Suzuki felt something enter his mind. "Ahh, I see. You are speaking of human stories." The imp probed some more. "Not *Lethal Weapon*. More like *Turner and Hooch*—where you are the canine destined to die. Shall we?"

12

The duo made their way back to the main part of the garden. More recruits were paired up with familiars, enjoying the shade next to the lake. It looked like a lazy Sunday morning, with recruits and familiars chatting casually in a park.

It would have been quite a peaceful scene if some of those familiars weren't downright terrifying monsters.

Suzuki looked around, hoping to spot Stew or Sandy in the crowd, but he couldn't see them anywhere. They must be in the forest, still looking for their familiars.

Suzuki wandered the surrounding area of the lake for a bit until he spotted Sandy. She was sitting in a small plot of daisies, weaving a handful of flowers together into a flower crown. Next to her was what looked like a very large rabbit with a foot-long spiral horn coming out of its forehead. Suzuki recognized the creature from a tabletop game that he used to play before *Middang3ard*: an almiraj.

If he remembered correctly, they were pretty docile creatures with a habit of getting themselves into trouble. They were also sought out by poachers because of the innate magical abilities stored in the horn.

Suzuki wondered if Sandy knew that. He didn't remember her being an avid tabletop fan before *Middang3ard*, and she'd never seemed to care much about lore in-game. Still, if anyone could find a familiar to boost her magical capabilities, it would be Sandy.

Suzuki waved over in Sandy's direction. "Hey, Sandy," he shouted. "You got one yet?"

Sandy scooped up the almiraj and held it close to her chest as she nuzzled it with her face. "Oh, my God, Suzuki," Sandy exclaimed. "You have to see this adorable fucking fuzzball. His name is Niv."

Niv leapt out of Sandy's grasp as Suzuki and Fred approached. His nose was trembling like prey before a predator, but he still hopped up to Suzuki and Fred, stood on his hind legs, and slightly bowed his head so that his horn pointed in their direction.

"Nivens McUnicorn McTwisp at your service," Niv said.

Suzuki knelt down and bowed as well. "That's quite a name you got there, buddy," Suzuki said.

"My true name is 47 consonants and must be screeched if you are to get the cadence right. But I've found that humans respond better to cute names. And from what I've been told, I'm very cute. 'Painfully cute' as Sandy has put it."

Sandy leaned over and scratched Niv's rear, causing his hind leg to jump and tap the ground percussively. "You *are* painfully cute. Looking at you is literally killing me."

Fred landed on Suzuki's shoulder and dug his claws in deep. Suzuki jumped and winced from the pain, but caught himself before he gave any other indication of how uncomfortable he was. Niv looked up at Fred and smiled sweetly, as only a bunny can.

"Hey," Niv called. "A human actually chose you? I thought you'd be rotting in this garden until someone remembered they used to worship you."

"Thankfully, there are some actual adventurers in this bunch of whelps. Besides, I chose him, lowly beast."

"Mine's a bit of a grump." Suzuki saddled up next to Sandy. "Have you seen Stew anywhere? I haven't been able to find him in the crowd."

"A little while ago," Sandy answered. "He was talking to the nymphs…actually, I think he was trying to flirt with them, but they pulled him in the water and left. He slunk off after that."

"Trying to flirt with them? Doesn't that bother you at all?"

Sandy shrugged. "Nope. He's all mine, and I know it. What's the harm with a little flirting? Especially if it ends up with him looking like an idiot."

Suzuki and Sandy laughed while their familiars watched. "Come on. We should probably go find him."

The four of them left the grassy knoll by the lake and wandered through the rest of the garden. After a few minutes, they came across Stew, wandering around with another recruit. Stew looked almost frantic. There were no familiars around, only a large patch of bright yellow flowers roughly the size of Suzuki. The two Mundanes and their familiars jogged over to catch up with Stew.

"How's the monster hunt going?"

Stew shrugged as he looked at the flowers, not even bothering to meet their eyes. "Harder than it looks like it was for everyone else," he finally said. "Figured I could at least try to pick Sandy some flowers while I was out here."

Sandy shrieked and ran over to hug Stew. "You were gonna pick me flowers?"

"Of course. You love flowers. And these are pretty, right? I thought they were pretty."

Stew reached out to grab one of the flowers and Sandy's eyes went wide. "Wait," Sandy shouted, "those are—"

One of the flowers leaned over, and its petals split open. It snatched up the wandering, unaware recruit and started munching.

"Holy shit," Suzuki shouted as he leapt back.

Niv jumped to the front of the group and lowered his horn. "Don't worry mortals," Niv said. "I got this." And with that, Niv charged full-force into the carnivorous plant. The plant jerked open and spit the new recruit out. The recruit shrieked and tried to wipe off the sap covering his body as he wandered away, clearly dazed by the experience.

"Thistle Bite," Sandy finished.

Stew cautiously leaned forward for a better look. "Never seen such a big, hungry plant before."

The Thistle Bite leaned over and snapped at Stew, causing him to stumble backward and fall flat. Sandy stepped forward, her eyes flashing brightly. "Who would plant something like this in a garden with a bunch of new recruits?" she exclaimed, irritation dripping from every word. "It's so irresponsible."

Sandy waved her fingers, and the Thistle Bite burst into flames. She looked down at her hands, surprised. Then she started giggling and pointed at the rest of the Thistle Bite. Flames shot out of her fingers, and the whole patch of flowers caught flame.

Niv hopped up and took a seat on Sandy's foot. "I know how to pick 'em," he said. "Not even bonded and you're already using magic. You've got a talent."

"Thanks," Sandy cooed. Then she looked at Stew, who had already started to wander off. She leaned closer to

Suzuki. "He still hasn't found one. This is like tryouts all over again."

Niv cleared his throat. Sandy and Suzuki looked down at him. "I could help him in this department," Niv offered. "I have a friend who's a little too shy for these kinds of things. They might get along. And it would help keep some of his... err...carnal desires in check."

"Let's see him! And hopefully not too in check."

Niv twitched his nose three times and then dug his horn into the ground. Up ahead, Stew was walking, kicking stones in his path. The ground in front of him started shaking and Stew stopped. The ground continued to quake as if something were drilling itself out.

A head popped out. It was shaped like a donkey's head, and it wore a goofy smile as if it were aware of how ridiculous a donkey burrowing out of the ground was.

But it didn't stop there. The donkey's head forced itself out and was followed by sharp, stone claws which made way for the five-inch squat body of a stone gargoyle. It had been carved with an impressive set of pecs and biceps and short, stubbly wings.

The gargoyle must have been sculpted by someone who was obsessed with the human form, Suzuki thought. *That and donkeys.*

"Well, look at you, little dude," Stew exclaimed. "Where did you come from?"

The donkey gargoyle bashfully looked away. If stone could blush, the gargoyle was doing it right then. "From underground," the donkey gargoyle said.

"What are you doing here?"

"What are you doing here?"

"Looking for a familiar."

"I'm looking for a human."

"Uh...do you want to be my familiar?" Stew said in a tone that mirrored a toddler asking another toddler if they wanted to be friends.

"Would you be my human?"

"I'm down!"

The conversation was oddly simple, which by Suzuki's estimation meant it was perfect for Stew. The donkey gargoyle smiled and nodded its agreement. It wobbled over closer to Stew and threw his arms around Stew's leg.

Stew started to take a step back before he caught himself and awkwardly petted the gargoyle's head. "What's your name?"

The gargoyle looked up with its disconcertingly innocent eyes. "Good and Bad," he said. "Because sometimes I'm good. But other times...I am very, very bad."

"Uh...err...okay. Nice to meet you. But Good and Bad is a bit of a mouthful. How about I call you 'GB?'"

The donkey gargoyle nodded with unbridled excitement.

Stew turned and waved at the other Mundanes. "Guys! I got a familiar."

Sandy knelt to pet Niv's ears. "Thanks," she said.

"My pleasure," Niv replied.

Manny's voice boomed over the entire garden. "Recruits," he shouted. "I trust you have found your familiars by now. Please return to the lake so that we may begin the Ritual of Digesting."

The Mundanes looked at each other. "Digesting?"

Fred clutched Suzuki's shoulder again. This time Suzuki didn't flinch. Fred leaned forward so his hot breath was on Suzuki's ear. "This is the fun part."

One by one, the recruits surrounded the lake with their familiars. Manny floated in between them, checking each familiar and recruit with his many eyes. Most of the recruits squirmed under the scrutiny. The familiars did not seem to notice, other than Fred, who looked extremely uncomfortable.

That's a weird look for such a demonic creature, Suzuki thought. What would make something like Fred feel uncomfortable?

Manny floated in front of Suzuki and Fred while the imp's scales bristled. "So, you two are deciding to leave for Middang3ard together?" Manny floated up to be at eye level with Fred.

"Yes." Fred sneered. "The human and I believe we will make a good team."

Manny eyed Suzuki. "Is that so?"

"Yeah, I think so," Suzuki replied. "Can't you see the chemistry?"

Manny looked hard at them with all of his eyes. Suzuki tried his best to give a convincing smile as Fred grinned widely as well, his serrated teeth shining brightly.

"Very convincing." Manny sighed as he floated away to a higher vantage point. He cleared his throat, and all of his eyes narrowed. "If you are all comfortable with your hosts, I invite you to begin the Ritual of Digesting. Kneel before your familiars, and they will complete the ritual for you."

The recruits looked warily at each other, but most of them knelt quickly enough. The rest took a few more moments but nonetheless knelt. Suzuki touched his knee to the ground and looked into Fred's pitch-black eyes.

Fred smiled devilishly. "Finally, human," Fred growled. "I can be free of this hell."

"Wait, what are you doing?"

Fred leapt onto Suzuki's chest and he felt the imp's hot scales against his mouth as Fred tried to pry his mouth open. They both fell to the ground and wrestled with each other as the rest of the familiars began completing the Ritual of Digesting.

Next to Suzuki, GB was braying loudly, stamping his feet on the ground. Stew backed up slowly.

Sandy was being cornered in a similar way. Niv bowed his head at Sandy, his horn shining brightly. "I'm sorry, Ms. Sandy," he muttered softly. "It's not as bad as it looks."

"What the fuck are you all doing?" Sandy shouted.

"Completing the ritual."

Niv jumped onto Sandy and knocked her down. He shoved his horn in her stomach and she screamed as the small, magical animal burrowed in. She gasped and rolled on the ground as she tried to pull Niv out, but it didn't stop the creature. He burrowed and burrowed with his horn and his legs, and as Sandy screamed, the almiraj disappeared.

Sandy stopped screaming. She felt her stomach. There was no blood. No wound. Nothing. "Huh. I'm OK. I'm OK!" She turned to the others wearing a manically wild smile, "That was...huh...hey guys, it's not that bad!"

Fred pried Suzuki's mouth open, his eyes locked on the human's. There was something almost intimate in the way that Fred was looking at Suzuki. The fear that had been pulsing through Suzuki's veins a moment ago disappeared. Then Fred opened his mouth and boiling hot magma poured from his gaping maw. Suzuki tried to jerk away, but Fred was stronger. The heat of the magma felt as if it were boiling Suzuki's skin before it even touched. Suzuki tried to scream, but the magma poured into his mouth, and he felt his entire body catch flame.

But he didn't burn.

It was just a feeling that soon passed. Fred's body fell over lifeless. Suzuki felt his face, his mouth. Nothing bad had happened. If anything, he had a minty taste in his mouth. At Suzuki's feet lay Fred's body. It shriveled into a thin black husk and broke into a million pieces that drifted away in the breeze.

Around the lake, the rest of the recruits had finished the bonding process. None looked to be too shaken. Manny cleared his throat to catch the recruits' attention.

"As I said before," Manny lectured, "your familiars will allow you to enter into Middang3ard proper. If you have not figured out by now, your familiar is now residing within your body. The level of interaction you have with your familiar will vary from recruit to recruit. They are your responsibility. Let me iterate again, your familiar is your tether to Middang3ard. Always keep that in mind. Now that you are fully equipped, I ask you, are you ready to be a brother of the MERC?"

"Aye," the recruits shouted.

Suzuki murmured a weak, "Yes."

"I ask again," Manny shouted. "Are you ready to face the depths of hell, to stand against the Dark One for all we hold sacred and beautiful? Are you ready to be a brother of the MERC?"

Another resounding cry came from the recruits.

Makes sense that a Beholder would be OCD about war chants, Suzuki thought to himself. *Or it could be some kind of contract.*

"I ask again," Manny repeated. "Humans, are you ready to risk limb, life, and soul for the safety of your realm? Are you ready to be a brother of the MERC? Can I get an A-fuck-ing-men, humans?"

Suzuki cast a glance at Sandy and Stew. Sandy's face looked a little pale, but she was smiling widely. Her hands were balled into fists. Stew was grinning as well. His chest was puffed, and he looked as if he were imitating his ideal of a soldier. Above them all, a massive vortex had opened in the sky. Suzuki looked up, and he could see millions of stars swirling and stretching and taking the shape of lands that he could have only imagined.

"Fuck it," Suzuki cried out. "Amen!"

The familiar fishhook hit him again, only this time Suzuki flexed his stomach and there was no pain.

Then the world turned to nothing and they were gone.

13

W hen the world came back into existence, the garden was gone.

Suzuki was on his feet, his stomach gurgling but holding. They were somewhere else now, somewhere less bright and pristine than the Garden of Familiars. They were somewhere dirtier with air that was thick and musty.

It took Suzuki a minute for his eyes to focus before he realized that they'd been transported to a murky swampland. Massive cypress trees stretched out of the swamp water into the sky. A dim, red sun shone through the overstretched leaves. A network of wooden pathways had been built into the wetlands. Off in the distance was a village which the pathways connected to. There was a large log house in the middle of the village. A heavy plume of smoke poured from the log house's chimney.

Manny floated to the front of the company of MERCs. "Come on, recruits. It is time for you to be outfitted. Today is the first day of your glory. I must leave you here. Although you are but paupers, soon you will know glory. Soon you will bring honor to your race. And soon we will put an end to the Dark One's reign of terrors."

As Manny talked, he started to fade away. He was gone within a couple of moments, leaving behind a troop of bewildered new recruits.

New recruits for whom Reality was starting to settle in.

They had all been dropped into a world they knew nothing about, completely weaponless, with something crawling around their insides now.

Suzuki wondered where Fred was exactly. The imp couldn't actually be in his body, resting in his ribcage or anything like that. Fred must be taking up some kind of psychic space in his mind or something like that. Maybe he had bonded physically with Suzuki. However, there were more important questions that needed to be answered at the moment.

Some of the recruits were hesitantly shuffling toward the village in the distance.

They were all dragging their feet...every single one of them...unsure what to do next.

Suzuki was unsure too, but what he did know was that standing on the outskirts of a town build near a swamp in Middang3ard probably wasn't the best place to mull it over.

"Come on," Suzuki said as he pushed his way through the crowd and to the front. "We should check the village out. It's at least a place to start."

Stew and Sandy forced their way through the thick crowd of recruits until they were standing next to Suzuki at the front of the pack. And so they marched forward to whatever awaited them.

As they walked, Suzuki would regularly check over his shoulders to see how the rest of the recruits were taking everything in. No one looked comfortable. Suzuki smiled and waved for the recruits to follow him.

"We gotta put on a show," Suzuki whispered to the Mundanes. "Everyone is freaked the fuck out."

"I'm freaking the fuck out," Stew responded.

"Yeah, but we don't have to let everyone know," Sandy added. "I get it, Suzuki. People freaking out all over the place isn't good."

The Mundanes led the recruits down the creaking wooden pathways, up to the giant log house that was churning smoke. They stood in front of the doorway, Suzuki unsure of the proper course of action. He had no idea what was behind the door. If it was something terrible, there was no doubt he was going to be blamed for whatever happened.

Still, they had to do something, and it didn't make sense that Manny would drop them in the middle of enemy territory without any weapons. Even if this was some elaborate ploy by the Dark One to kill off players who had shown any slight promise during Myrddin's tryouts, this would have been one roundabout way to do it.

So Suzuki lifted his hand, made a fist, and knocked on the door. Behind the door, a harsh voice called, but it was muffled. Suzuki could hear furniture being shuffled around, scraping the floor. The door suddenly swung wide open, and a gruff-looking dwarf with a burn scar on his forehead appeared.

He eyed Suzuki and the Mundanes, before stepping out and looking at the rest of the recruits.

The dwarf's frown turned into a smile that stretched

from ear to ear. "Took ye long enough. Name's Gorgol. Come in, and let's get you little shits processed."

Gorgol swung the door open wider and the Mundanes stepped into the log house. The rest of the recruits trickled in after them.

The log house did not carry any rural charm inside. Its interior was that of a log house that extended much farther than it appeared to from outside. The walls were lined with tall filing cabinets which were packed tightly next to each other. Tables and desks covered the floor. There were benches for waiting at the far side of the building.

Inside, dwarves and humans sat behind desks, each of them with a mountain of paperwork piled before them.

The log house looked like a cross between a medieval mess hall and the DMV.

"Is it everything that you were hoping for?" Fred asked.

Suzuki jumped and looked around for the imp, but he was nowhere to be seen. It was then that Suzuki realized he hadn't heard a voice, at least not heard it in the proper sense, but rather felt it.

He'd felt it within him, almost like when he was thinking to himself, but different somehow.

"Fred?"

Fred cleared his throat, which made no sense because Fred obviously wasn't talking through traditional means. "In the spirit. Or something close enough to it. Also, you don't have to speak out loud. I can hear you well enough if you just think. You should get in the habit. I'd hate to see what would happen if a group of goblins heard you talking to yourself in the middle of a quest. I imagine they'd eat you alive. Something of that sort."

"Where are you?"

"Within you. Part of the bonding experience. It would be

a little conspicuous to have your familiar constantly on your person. This gives me a way to retreat without having to open a small pocket dimension. You are my pocket dimension human. Think of yourself as a glorified taxi."

"Except you don't get to decide where we're going, right?"

Fred growled low, under his breath, but said nothing else. While Suzuki searched the rest of the MERC recruits to see if they were also communicating with their familiars, Gorgol came up to Suzuki with a stack of paperwork and a quill pen. "Excuse me," Gorgol said.

Suzuki jumped at the sound of the dwarf's voice. "Oh, shit. I didn't see you there."

"You're a little on the jumpy side, aren't you, recruit?"

"You just caught me off guard."

"Better work on that, as you'll find a lot of things will catch you off-guard in Middang3ard. Now, if you don't mind, please fill these out and come back to me when you're done."

Dwarves were moving through the crowd of recruits and handing any empty hands paperwork. The recruits made their way to the benches that filled the log house's halls. The Mundanes stuck together and grabbed seats next to each other.

Stew was already groaning about the paperwork. He held his papers in an awkward position on his lap.

Sandy didn't seem to mind at all. Or if she did, she didn't show it. She just got to work, filling out the forms.

Suzuki opened the packet of forms and checked them out. The first page was almost as generic as a doctor's form. Age, sex, height, weight, and that sort of thing. There was also a section dedicated to ethnic and cultural heritage.

Suzuki noticed there was nothing that flagged him for English ancestry.

Suzuki leaned over to Sandy. "Hey, have you heard from Niv?"

Sandy nodded her head but didn't look over from her paperwork. "Yep," she answered. "It's pretty fucking weird. He's pretty funny, though."

Suzuki turned to Stew, who was tapping his foot neurotically and chewing on his pen. "How about you?"

Stew jumped up as if he had been prodded with a stick. "What?" was his hazy reply.

"Have you heard from GB?"

"Only when we first got here. I don't think the little guy likes to talk much. He's a great listener, though." Stew gripped his paperwork and wrung it in his hands. "I didn't think I was coming to Middang3ard to fill out paperwork."

"Guess bureaucracy is everywhere."

"My mom says the world runs on paperwork," Sandy added.

"Your mom works at the DMV. Of course, she would say that."

"I'm just saying that it doesn't look like she's wrong."

It took Suzuki nearly twenty minutes to fill out his paperwork. When he was finished, he wandered around the log house, looking for Gorgol. He hadn't paid too much attention to any of the dwarves that he had seen before, and now that he was looking for one in particular, he found it difficult to tell them apart. All of them were short, bearded, and had a glint in their eyes that made it seem they could attack you at any moment.

Now though, he was starting to pick out individual faces. Even different demeanors. None of the dwarves pushing paperwork reminded him of the rough and tumble MERCs he had seen at the Garden of Familiars. Not that these dwarves looked soft by any means. They just appeared to be concerned with other things.

When Suzuki finally found Gorgol's desk (he'd passed it twice before he realized that was the dwarf he was looking for), he delicately put the papers down in front of him.

Gorgol looked up and smiled. "Thank you." Gorgol's smile never wavered despite taking form after form after form. It was as if he could do this all day, every day, and never get bored. Once the papers were in his hand, he gestured to the benches behind him. "Please take a seat."

Suzuki did as he was asked. Gorgol waved his hand and a holoscreen popped into existence in front of them. He scrolled through the screen, waved it away for another one, and spent some time looking at the new screen.

Then he snapped his fingers and the screen disappeared. Gorgol grabbed another, thicker stack of paperwork and handed it to Suzuki. "Please take care of these," Gorgol said. "Bring them back when you are finished, please."

Suzuki took the stack of paperwork and sighed. "No problem." He turned to make his way back to the Mundanes, who were also saddled down with entirely new packets of paperwork. They all gave each other looks of disbelief, but accepted their fate and dug into this new batch.

It took an hour before Stew got bored. He put his pen on Sandy's knee and stood to stretch. His eyes did not look like he was stretching, though. His eyes looked as if they were going to pop out of his eye sockets.

Sandy reached out and took Stew's hand. She caressed his palm and, with her other hand, pointed to the stack of papers. Stew shook his head and looked ready to protest, but he said nothing and sat down. Sandy handed him his pen and he continued with the paperwork.

There was an uncurling in Suzuki's mind. That was the only way that he could describe the feeling. It was as if a snake wrapped around his brain had suddenly decided to relax. "Why did you walk up to take the lead, human?"

Suzuki opened his mouth to answer and then remembered what Fred had said about thinking instead of talking. "What are you talking about?" Suzuki asked, directing his thoughts at Fred.

"When you first arrived. The other recruits were confused, and you went to the front to lead them to this driveling place of tedium. Why did you do that? Do you fancy yourself a leader?"

"No, not really. It just seemed that no one was going to make a move. I figured it was pretty obvious that we were supposed to come here."

"So you do see yourself as a leader?"

"No."

"I've known many leaders in my lifetime. What is it that you lead for? I have yet to see a MERC who is concerned with anything other than loot."

"I came here to fight the Dark One."

"Yes, I wonder if you did."

"What exactly are you trying to say?" Irritation was sneaking into Suzuki's voice. He could hear Fred's condescending sneer with each question.

"I have known many MERCs. I've seen them come and go. It is a rarity to see one with such pure, angelic purposes as yourself."

"So what if I want to be a leader?"

Suzuki snapped his quill pen. He hadn't even realized he

had been holding it so tightly. He sighed as he stood and went looking for Gorgol.

Fred circled Suzuki's mind. It felt as if the imp were trying to invade his thoughts. "A soft spot should be guarded more thoroughly," Fred chided. "You do see yourself as a leader. Or at least you want to be a leader. What is it, may I ask, you wish to lead for? I have seen many *leaders* succumb to the various strains of their office. Power does ultimately corrupt, as I have heard."

Suzuki picked up a quill pen from the desk of a random dwarf. The dwarf looked up at Suzuki and sniffed loudly to voice his displeasure. Suzuki managed a weak smile before walking off. "Corruption seems like something you might have a good idea about," Suzuki said.

"Yes," Fred hissed. "It is something which I've established a good understanding of. A good enough understanding to offer a word of wisdom. I believe that the Dark One was an admirable, kind-hearted leader at some point."

"Did you know him?"

"It is difficult not to know him when you are as ancient as me. I knew of him much like I have known of and watched many leaders. And I can say safely that leadership is not for you, Suzuki. I do not believe it will suit you, even if it does feel intoxicating."

"Shut up," Suzuki spat. "You don't know me or what I want."

"True. I doubt you do either."

Suzuki sat back down his chair. He was shaking with anger. Sandy looked at him, her face soft with concern. "Suzuki, what's up?"

"Nothing. My familiar is just kind of an asshole."

"Dude," Stew broke in. "You chose an imp. What the fuck were you expecting?"

"I dunno. Maybe some slyness. Not an outright troll asshole."

"Beggars can't be choosers," Sandy said. "And we are definitely in the beggar spectrum. At least we're in Middang3ard."

Sandy was right, and Suzuki knew it. There was no way around that uncomfortable tidbit of information. The Mundanes had barely made it into the cut to save Middang3ard, though Suzuki wasn't completely certain that's what they were here for.

But Suzuki didn't air his concerns. It didn't make sense to worry any of the other recruits. It also seemed like it might have been impossible to worry anyone else.

Even though dwarves came, collected their paperwork, and handed out more, everyone in the log house appeared to be extremely excited. There were smiles and laughter in abundance. Suzuki felt as if he were the only person with doubts about the whole situation. Even Stew and Sandy didn't seem all too worried.

A passing dwarf handed the Mundanes a seventh package of forms. This last stack was dedicated to outlining the last ten years of video game experience he had. The stack before this one had been about the last fifteen years of his reading list. Suzuki and Sandy had to provide Stew with a handful of titles to flesh out his list. It had looked a little bare.

Once the dwarf meandered off, Suzuki shook his head as he started on what he hoped was his last checklist. "Why did you guys even want to come here?"

Sandy put down her pen. She reminded Suzuki of a child who was getting ready to lie herself out of a lie. "The same reason anyone else did. To fight the Dark One."

"Come on, Sandy, don't bullshit me. We're supposed to

be friends. A party. And what's the first thing that we said that a party needs to do to work?"

Sandy lowered her eyes and avoided Suzuki's gaze.

"What was it?" Suzuki repeated.

"Trust each other," Sandy whispered.

"And how can we trust each other if we can't be honest with each other?"

"We can't."

"So why did you want to come to Middang3ard?"

"Because I want to get good." Sandy folded her hands over her paperwork. She looked as if she were getting ready to defend a dissertation. Her eyes still refused to meet Suzuki's. Even Stew had finished fussing with his paperwork to listen to what was going on. His eyes were locked on Sandy's, but hers strayed from contact with anyone else's.

"What's that supposed to mean?" Stew put his hand on Sandy's. "You are good. Great even. The best."

"In a game. I want to get good for real," Sandy interrupted as her eyes sparkled with electricity. "Suzuki, you remember when we first started playing together? Before Stew joined the party? Back when I couldn't get any of the hotkeys right. I kept screwing up all my spells and roles. I couldn't get why you kept playing with me because I was always fucking up our missions and getting booted from raids and shit. I asked you what I could do to get better. And what did you do? You sent that stupid ass meme of a cat dangling on a string. You know, the one with the caption, 'Hang in there'. Do you remember that?"

"Sort of." In truth, Suzuki didn't.

"So I hung in there. I got good. I spent hours every day trying to get good. And then I was. But this...this is something so much bigger than that. I can get good for real. I want to get good here. I'm sick of sitting in a fucking cubicle, answering phones and coming home to play make-believe. I know it's a walking cliché, but I don't give a fuck. This— here. I can find out if I'm capable of something. Every taste of actual magic I've gotten...it's just...I can't give that up. Ever. That's why I'm in Middang3ard. I'm tired of pretending to be a badass. I want to find out if I can actually *be* a badass."

"You want power?"

"No." Sandy stretched out her hand and a flicker of flame and a fireball burst into existence, hovering in her palm. "I want to be godlike. I want to be the strongest mage any of the realms have ever seen. And I want to torch the Dark One with that power."

"Damn," Stew said as Sandy closed her hand and extinguished the fireball. "I thought that whole 'death and murder' thing was just a joke."

"No," Sandy whispered. "I'm tired of being weak. I don't want to be that anymore." And then her demeanor changed completely, as if she hadn't been displaying her power as she revealed her desire to take on the Dark One. "That's me," she chirped in a cutesy voice. "What about you, Stew?"

Stew fidgeted in his seat. He looked as if he would have been more comfortable running away. Suzuki had never seen him look so uncomfortable before. Stew was actually turning red. He gave a heavy sigh and pushed up his glasses. "It's nothing as heavy as Sandy. I just want to wreck shit. And there's nothing to wreck on Earth. Not like here. What about you?"

Suzuki felt Fred surfacing in the back of his mind. "Yes, human," Fred growled. "What about you?"

"Beth," Suzuki said without hesitating. "I want to see Beth."

The Mundanes sat in silence for a few moments before

they returned to their paperwork. Suzuki felt that this was the first time that he'd ever truly seen Sandy or Stew. No amount of gaming or talking had prepared him for this moment. They were his party.

His family.

Yet there were so many parts of them that he had no understanding of. He wondered how much of Beth he didn't know.

"You guys had much cooler reasons than me," Stew grumbled.

Sandy and Suzuki stared at Stew. Then they broke out laughing. Sandy laughed so hard that she had to grab Stew and lean against him. The other recruits stopped their writing and looked at the Mundanes as the trio laughed hard enough to bring tears.

"Guess that's why the MERCs have the one rule," Suzuki said. "Cause we're all here for fucking stupid reasons."

A slew of dwarves were now walking down the aisles of benches. They were collecting paperwork, finished or not. A surly dwarf with a stained beard and burned overalls grabbed all of the Mundanes' paperwork and scuttled off. There was a loud gong (Suzuki had figured this was Middang3ards equivalent to a siren), and a loud voice magically projected itself.

"MERC recruits, please assemble in the back of the office to receive your equipment," the voice commanded.

The recruits slowly rose and made their way to the back of the log house. A queue formed. The Mundanes were somewhere near the back, and this time, Suzuki didn't feel comfortable trying to make his way to the front.

He was thinking about what Fred had said. He knew that there was still a lot to learn about Stew and Sandy, but he had not been expecting their reasons for coming to Middang3ard. It made him wonder about his own reasons for being in this new realm. Was there any truth to what Fred had said or was he just playing the imp? Suzuki wondered what purpose Fred would have for unnerving him.

By the time that Suzuki got to the head of the line, he felt as if he was going to pass out. It was hard to tell how long he'd been standing, absorbed in his own thoughts. There were no clocks anywhere, and his cellphone had stopped working a long time ago. His legs were sore, and his feet were numb. He assumed that Stew and Sandy were in the same boat. Neither of them was talking. Sandy's eyes were closed, and she was leaning haphazardly on Stew's shoulder. Suzuki stepped up to the desk, where four dwarves sat at a long table like a panel of judges.

"Name, please?" the robed dwarf asked.

"Robert 'Suzuki' Fletcher," Suzuki answered.

"Ah...Suzuki." The dwarf said, looking at the panel. "You are a warrior-mage, correct?"

"Yeah, I used to play as a warrior-mage."

"I did not ask what you used to play as. I asked what you are."

"A warrior-mage."

"Good. Take your HUD. Your armor will deploy from your HUD. Next!"

Suzuki took the HUD that the dwarf held in his hand and moved out of the way. He went over to the wall, away from the line.

The further that Suzuki got in all of this nonsense, the more hardcore everyone seemed to be. He was getting a little annoyed at the constant reiterations that this was not a game. Anyone who hadn't realized that by now wasn't going to make it out alive—even if he was constantly being supplied with devices that blurred the distinction between game, reality, and fantasy.

Suzuki held the HUD in his hand. It was rough and scratched. It was used, and Suzuki tried to put out of his mind any thoughts as to what had happened to its original user.

A single earpiece that fit snugly over his ear, with a visor that stretched across the eyes. The earpiece had a touchpad on it for navigating menus. Suzuki brought the HUD online and pressed the touchpad. As soon as he did, he felt the weight of armor materializing over his body.

When he looked into the reflection of the log cabin's window, he saw himself in standard chainmail that was a tighter fit than anything he'd worn before. It felt as if it had been crafted just for him.

That's probably why there are so many dwarves here. Then a thought occurred to him that made him chuckle. *That's probably why we had so much paperwork. The dwarves were probably buying themselves time to make the damn armor.*

Examining the HUD display, he noted that it was different than any he had seen so far. There was only one corner display in the right-hand corner: the success percentage meter, with several lines below it for modifiers, health, and mana.

This was a step back from anything the military had. Suzuki found it hard to believe that the rumors and propaganda of the spoils of war that Beth and Manny had spoken about were true after seeing his MERC gear.

The MERCs HUDs looked as if they were from the first iteration of Middang3ard, maybe something out of the beta. It didn't appear that the MERCs had any money. If there was loot, it wasn't going into funding the organization.

Suzuki noticed that there was one other icon on the

HUD. At the bottom left of the corner, there was a flashing icon of an imp. Suzuki clicked the icon.

Familiar: Frekreteritdickentrot

Race: Eldritch Imp

Bond: Fragile

Origins: Unknown

Alignment: Unknown

There was another flashing icon beneath the previous information. Suzuki clicked the icon and a message popped on his HUD.

"There is something in Frekreteridickentrot's past that he does not wish you to know," the message read. "Gain his trust and learn about his past. That is the only way to truly bond with your familiar. Until you bond with your familiar, you will be limited in your ability to advance in Middang3ard."

Sandy and Stew were coming over to Suzuki. They were both putting on their own HUDs.

Sandy hit her HUD and little flower buds sprouted and bloomed, sending petals everywhere as robes flew from them, covering her.

When Stew activated his HUD, his shirt vanished and a plate mail kilt rolled out over his waist. A longsword hung from his side.

Stew pulled out his sword and checked its weight and balance. "At least we get started off with some decent gear."

Suzuki agreed, but he wasn't really paying attention. He was thinking about the message that he had just read. *Gain his trust and learn about his past.*

Great, Suzuki thought. *Just great.* Figure out an ancient imp's past and get him to trust you? Taking out the Dark One sounded like a much simpler task.

14

The little bit of sun had disappeared, a swollen full moon hung in the sky, and stars twinkled as the newly- armored recruits trickled out of the log house and back into the marshlands.

Guided by the few lights on in the buildings that made up the village sitting near the swamp, they made their way into town, the dank murkiness of the swamp filling their nostrils as the chirps and screeches of small animals and insects filled their ears.

"We're not in Kansas anymore," Suzuki muttered as the Mundanes separated from the rest of the recruits who were cautiously poking around the various buildings.

"I don't know about that," Sandy said. "Eerie noises, no lights, perfect setting for some wild storm to swoop us away...we very well could be in Kansas."

As they headed for the only source of light, from a structure the size of a motel, Suzuki tried to message Beth. Touching his HUD, he called up her contacts and tried to DM her. "Hi."

A little spindle turned and turned before a red X appeared. Apparently, the message couldn't go through.

"OK," Suzuki murmured, trying to send her an email. He got a short message that said they were in Middang3ard, but as soon as he heard that cyber swoosh of an email being sent, he got a ping with a message that said his email had bounced back.

"What the fuck?" Suzuki growled. Then he remembered how difficult it was to speak to RealDeal, one of the first people he knew to enter Middang3ard. Messaging wasn't as straightforward as on Earth. Probably because they were in the military, but then again, who knows? It wasn't as if there were cables under the ground pumping terabytes of data around. Maybe the Internet hadn't made it here, yet.

"If only Al Gore was a MERC." Suzuki chuckled to himself, resolving to find a way to message Beth. But later.

Now...now he needed to learn more about his new home.

As they approached the structure, Suzuki heard loud shouting and music coming from the building. It sounded like a party.

Suzuki went up to the building and eased open the door.

A bustling bar opened up before the Mundanes. Much like the processing area that Suzuki had just lost six hours of his life in, the bar seemed to stretch back farther than was reasonable for how small the building looked from the outside.

Still, the bar felt cozy.

The wooden walls caught the candlelight cast from chandeliers, and the floor was covered in a variety of different animal skin rugs. The walls were decorated with stuffed big-game heads. Some were recognizable, such as deer and bears, but there were also creatures that Suzuki had never seen before. One looked like a boar, only it had no fur. Instead of fur, the boar had tiny quills like those of a porcupine. Its snout was covered with a dozen eyes of different colors.

Magical creatures from all of the existing realms were sitting together or cloistered off at tables with members of their own race. The majority of the bar patrons were humans and dwarves, and their tables held the most mead. There were no similarities between their armor, other than a red streak, which started at their neckline and stretched down to their waist.

Suzuki scanned the bar and noted that everyone except the recruits had at least one red streak somewhere on their armor or clothing.

"It's a symbol of the MERCs," he muttered to himself. "It's got to be."

As the Mundanes made their way into the bar, a dwarf walked in front of them, cutting them off. The dwarf stumbled and sloshed his mead onto his beard, whirling around and nearly toppling over.

When he caught his balance, he jabbed his finger at the Mundanes. "You watch them gams, human," the dwarf growled. "I'll have 'em strung up someplace, and we all know what to do with them afterward." The dwarf hiccupped, and his face took on the color of a beet.

Sandy knelt down to look the dwarf in the eye. "And what exactly are you going to do with them?"

The dwarf stared long and hard at Sandy. When she didn't budge, he leaned forward and pointed at Stew. "That one's got a nice face," he murmured. "You all got real nice faces!"

Someone at a nearby table shouted, "Leave the newbs alone! Next round is on you."

"Yeah, yeah," the dwarf grumbled as he tottered over, stabilizing himself with chairs and tables as he went. And all the while, he smiled brightly, his cheeks still shining red beneath his scraggly beard.

The Mundanes, not knowing what else to do or where to go, made their way up to the human barkeep, who was bustling about, passing meads and ales out faster than Suzuki ever thought was possible. She looked sixty, but Suzuki suspected that she was probably in her forties and that living here gave her the "older than I am" aura. That and the fact that her arms were covered in scars and burns and her mousy brown eyes looked like stone...it was obvious she'd seen things.

Experienced things.

Suzuki wondered how long the MERCs had been recruiting people.

"Newbs, huh? Well, welcome to the Red Lion. My name's Wendy, and I own this here establishment. Which means, I serve the drinks and you pay me. So what can I grab for you kids?" Wendy sang as she slammed down two huge ales.

"What's the legal drinking age here again?" Stew asked.

"Probably whenever you're old enough to know not to ask that at a bar." She laughed.

Suzuki leaned over the counter and held up three fingers. "Could I get three...uh...meads?"

Sandy held up her finger. Her eyes darted around, and she nervously giggled. "Could I actually get a gin and tonic?"

"A gin and tonic," the bartender repeated. "Looks like we got ourselves a real high-class MERC here, don't we?"

A couple of MERCs sitting at the bar chuckled. One of them burst into uproarious laughter and slapped his hand on the bar. Sandy blushed brightly and looked down at the bar's wood counter as she pushed the hair out of her face.

Stew leaned over and nudged Sandy's elbow. "Sandy," Stew whispered, "you are embarrassing us."

"I don't know what's embarrassing about a gin and tonic."

"Liquor is practically water compared to my mead. Made it myself," Wendy explained as she poured three spittoons of mead and slammed them on the bar.

Sandy picked up one of the spittoons. She sipped the foamy head. "Jesus Christ on a fucking stick," she exclaimed. "That shit is *strong*."

"That'll be fifteen coppers."

"You mean we have to pay you?" Stew groaned.

"Yeah," the bartender said as she took back the drinks. "I give you drinks. You give me money. That's the way that it works. Just like every other bar in any realm."

Suzuki tapped his armor. There wasn't any space for a wallet. He wasn't even sure if there would have been anything in it even if he had one. The Mundanes stood there awkwardly like a trio of children who got caught playing pretend in their parent's clothes.

"They're newbs," a soft voice said.

Suzuki turned around, and another dwarf was standing behind him. This one wore glimmering armor with a golden fox crest on the chest piece; his shoulder blades were sharpened to a razor point. The dwarf's beard was spindly and short, and it stopped at his chest.

He leaned on an ornate sword cane.

Wendy poured mead for the paying customers. "Everyone starts as a newb."

The dwarf motioned to Wendy, who reached over and lowered a small, silver collection tin. Change jangled in the tin as the dwarf tossed in a few pieces of copper. "Come on, newbs," the dwarf said as he gestured for them to follow him.

"Names Milos Winterfell." The dwarf grunted as he took a seat at an empty table. He jerked his head at the empty seats. "Tonight's your first night, aye?"

"Yeah," Suzuki answered as he settled into his seat. The rest of the Mundanes sat down at the table and, one by one, took a sip of their meads.

Milos eyed the Mundanes as he drank his own, stroking his beard; his eyes glimmered like the pieces of copper he had tossed into the tray. "They ship you out and pay two days' worth of board. You gotta get out there and start hustling as soon as you get here. Not the most inviting of situations, I gather."

"It's a little overwhelming," Suzuki answered. "We're not even sure how all of this is supposed to work. Is there a captain or general we can speak to? Someone who's in charge or something."

"In charge? Boy, I've been with the MERCs for years, and I still don't know who's in charge. You got your party, don't you?"

"Yeah, we're a party," Sandy butted in.

"Then y'all know who's in charge. 'Sides, you can figure all that out tomorrow. You should at least celebrate for your first night."

Stew took a huge gulp from his drink. His face flushed, and he belched loudly. "How are we supposed to party when we're broke?"

Milos ran his fingers through his beard in a thoughtful motion. "That would be a problem, now wouldn't it be? Well, I happen to have a solution if you're interested. You see, my party and I split for a quest a few days ago, and they haven't gotten back yet. But here I am with a night of drinking to accomplish. So how's this for a deal? I need drinking buddies. You need drinks. We play a little game of cards and make a little wager. You win, I buy all of your drinks. You lose, I buy all your drinks, and you do me a favor."

"Sounds good to—" Stew started saying.

"What kind of favor?" Sandy interrupted.

"Nothing weird. I don't go into having humans get drunk for me to cover them in butter or anything like that. Just a solid favor between mates. MERCs don't screw other MERCs."

Suzuki shrugged and finished his pint. His face felt very warm and seemed to be made of a sticky substance. As Suzuki acknowledged to himself that this mead truly was strong shit, he felt Fred twisting in his mind.

"Hey, Fred," Suzuki ventured. "Do you think this is a good idea?"

"There is nothing in existence which is good or bad," Fred hissed. "That is a simple lesson that I have learned through my life. There is only experience—which you are all lacking. Now if you excuse me, I'd like to be left to my thoughts."

There was a part of Suzuki that felt this was an obviously bad idea. But as Stew had said, they didn't have any money for a celebration. They hadn't even had money for a drink. And this seemed like the best way to come across some information. Manny had just dropped them off in the forest without a tent or even any supplies. This level of ignorance scared Suzuki. Talking to Milos would at least give them all a moment to get their bearings on what was going on.

"I'll tell you what. I'll sit this one out and watch, but those two are free to do whatever they want," Suzuki said as Stew and Sandy shot him bewildered looks.

Stew threw up his hands. "This one's really into watching. Me, I like doing and doing and then doing some more." He winked at Sandy, who just groaned as she rolled her eyes.

"Aye." Milos smiled. "Just a game with an innocent bet between mates."

"You know, your saying it again and again makes it sound suspicious. It's not comforting at all. But yeah."

"Aye, nothing quite as enjoyable as a friendly competition with a friendly little wager."

"Yes, yes, yes. We got it. We agree."

"Perfect." Milos laughed as he whipped out a pack of cards. He shuffled the deck and dealt the cards.

Stew picked up one of the cards. "What are we playing?"

"Seven Dead Men and a Siren."

"Uh, you in too, Suzuki?"

"Nah," Suzuki muttered. "You guys have fun."

Suzuki leaned back in his chair, feeling relaxed now that the mead had taken effect. He felt he could finally take in the whole scene.

When he had first stepped into the bar, it had all been too much for him, and he had mostly only noticed dwarves and humans.

Now he could really see what was going on in the bar. Besides dwarves and humans, the bar was packed with at least three other magical races.

A group of halflings was sitting closest to Suzuki's table.

They were drinking quietly until one of the halflings knocked over his mead. The halfling closed his eyes solemnly, took his hat off, and pressed it to his chest. Then he stood and climbed onto the table, his hairy feet knocking over a bowl of pretzels. The other halflings pulled out small stringed instruments.

The halfling on the table cleared his throat, and an angelic falsetto rang out over the noise of the bar. The occupants of the tables nearby looked up from their drinks as the halfling began to sing loudly:

It is in bars and battles we find ourselves,
We drink to friends and fear and health,
The night has come, the Dark One gone,
To leave us to our somber song.

The halfling cast his eyes down sorrowfully, and when he looked back up, there were tears in his eyes. Across the bar, more halflings had climbed onto their table as well, covering their hearts with their hats as they joined in on the song.

Our beer, our beer, it has spilled this day,
Of all the days, it spilled today.

The song had lost its classical nature and had shifted to something more like a soccer chant as its pace quickened and they played their instruments more wildly. Within seconds the rest of the halflings started to dance, linking arms with each other, their eyes dancing as they kicked in unison.

All throughout the bar, the halflings climbed onto their tables, threw their arms in the air, and jigged away as the singers chanted. The rest of the bar had returned to their business.

Only the halflings danced, although many of the dwarves and humans swung their mugs back and forth to the tune.

Only the elves didn't join in, their demeanor controlled and completely without mirth.

Milos motioned to one of the barmaids for more mead, and she came by and dropped the meads off at the table. Stew had buried his head in his hands and was pulling his hair, while Sandy peered down at her cards, her tongue sticking out of the corner of her mouth.

Suzuki reached for his mead as a pack of fairies lazily floated in front of his face, obviously drunk. They were about the size of his hands, and he could have reached out and caught them.

One of the fairies bumped into another, their bright, multicolored wings flashing brightly when they touched, and the collision caused their translucent bodies to shine in a way that allowed you to see their bones. The fairy who had been bumped into shone brighter than the rest as a jolt of pink lightning pulsed across its body.

The fairy screwed up its face as if in pain and then there was a loud pop and the fairy burst into the air, rainbow-colored gas shooting out of its ass. Shrill fairy laughter pierced the halfling's chant as the tone of the song gradually descended back into a mournful lament for lost alcohol.

Suzuki couldn't help but laugh as the rest of the fairies started farting and flying around like demented honeybees. The air took on the noticeable scent of cinnamon rolls.

His HUD pinged in his ear, and a notification flashed. He opened it. A message from Beth!

Suzuki turned away from the card game and opened the message to see Beth's face staring back at him. Only her eyes didn't focus on him, so he knew it was another recorded message.

Beth looked exhausted. No, that wasn't right. She looked

older than the last message she had sent. He wasn't sure if it was in his head, but her eyes looked sunken. She rubbed her eyes sleepily as she yawned.

"Hey, Suzuki. I've been trying to send this off to you for a while. Sorry for the last message, but Manny told me I had to get really harsh on you. I told him it probably didn't matter, but he was pretty adamant. Hopefully you've finished all the bullshit and are actually getting out in the field. I heard the MERCs don't waste any time getting their people out there. I'm also assuming you all made it into the MERCs. I wasn't even worried about you guys. You're gonna have to tell me all about all the shit you guys get into. On my end, things have slowed down a lot. I guess we're kind of stationed in the area at the moment to keep the troll situation from getting out of hand, but we haven't seen any in a minute. Some of the guys are getting pretty antsy here. I've been making friends and shit. It's funny, you'd think everyone would be a little more mature, but it's like being back in high school. There's this one really cute guy in my regiment—"

Suzuki's heart jumped up into his throat, which clenched tightly and threatened to give him a heart attack.

"And, I mean, yeah, he's cute and junk, but who isn't a little cute? I showed some of the girls a picture of you, and they said you are a little cute yourself. Anyways, this guy asked me out, and I told him I wasn't interested. No big deal. This kindergarten muthafucker then told everyone in my regiment that he saw me rolling in troll shit. Like, can you believe that bullshit? I had to royally kick his ass. Anyways… uh…what else…um, the commander is a real piece of work. And by piece of work, I mean a sadistic, disgusting bastard. I made sure not to get on his bad side. Last officer he had a problem with ended up losing a limb. So I'm playing it safe.

There are rumors that the Dark One's forces are gathering in Aleria. Which is weird, you know. It's like Ellis Island, but there's a creepy-ass castle there. Same exact place as Ellis Island. It's been making traveling easier, the whole mirror realm thing going on. That's what one of the mages told me it was called. Oh, shit, and you won't believe what my fucking familiar did. Ros'ten literally jumped out of my body in the middle of a fucking firefight just because she thought she smelled honey. Turns out the mountain trolls we were hunting smell like honey when they start to decompose."

"I like her familiar," Fred growled. "Abandoning a human for a snack. Shows a proper order of priorities."

"Shut up," Suzuki snapped.

Beth took a deep breath and smiled before looking over her shoulder. She shouted something that Suzuki couldn't make out. She turned back to the camera.

"All right, I gotta go. Tell those douche nozzles that I asked what's up. Also, I know that it's tough for you guys to message me with how tight-ass the military is. Hell, I need to get permission every time to send something out, too. But apparently, there are these workarounds. Not sure yet, but I'm hoping that pretty soon we'll be able to talk more regularly. That would be good. Real good. I miss you. I..."

Beth's voice trailed off as she muttered something. She looked troubled. When she looked back up at the camera, her bottom lip was slightly trembling.

"I miss you. A lot..."

The video cut out. Suzuki played the last bit of the video again. Beth had started saying something with an "L" before she caught herself. And she had been showing pictures of him to people in her regiment. Suzuki hadn't even known Beth had a picture of him. He felt his throat unclench. His heart was pounding, but in a much different way than before. It made him want to get up and sing with the halflings, to grab a fiddle and start jigging as hard as he could. He felt as if he could run to Beth, wherever she was, right then, as if there were no space between them at all.

He was on Middang3ard. One step closer to bringing the party back together.

"Goddamn it," Stew shouted. "Again?"

Suzuki was grounded back to reality. Across the table, Stew was throwing his cards onto the table, and Sandy had sunk down into her chair. Milos was smiling a wide, shit-eating grin as he shuffled his cards. A barmaid brought another round of drinks and put them down in front of the Mundanes and the dwarf.

"How'd you lose?" Suzuki asked.

Stew grabbed his mead and jugged half of it. "Don't know," Stew replied. "Don't care."

Sandy brushed her hair out of her face and grabbed the cards that Milos dealt her. "It's just for a favor," she reminded Suzuki before turning to glare at Milos.

Milos tossed Stew a couple of cards. "Wouldn't even call it a favor," he said. "It won't be any skin off your teeth. Or back. Whatever you humans say."

Suzuki laughed as he opened up a new text message from Beth.

"And don't forget, Suzuki," the message read, "you're gonna have to jerry-rig it together. Find a chipmaster. They should be able to take care of it. It's not gonna be cheap, but it'll be worth it. Seriously, dude. Make sure to take care of it."

Suzuki closed the message. He had no idea what Beth was talking about, but he figured he could just message her about it later. The card game on the table was starting to look a lot more interesting. Stew was cursing loudly, and Sandy had the drunk giggles. Someone had finally managed to get her a gin and tonic, which she was sipping along with her mead.

Across the bar, the halflings were getting another song started. More drinks were served. Suzuki and Stew were standing on the table, and he had no idea how he had gotten there.

Or at least Suzuki thought that he was on the table. There were halflings everywhere. Cards and pixies flew through the air as Suzuki, Stew, and Sandy slammed their tankards together, trying to muddle their way through the halfling drinking songs.

The whole bar was one loud, drunken singing mess. "This is fucking Middang3ard," a group of dwarves and humans sang. "This is fucking Middang3ard, and the MERCs will take it for what it's worth!"

The chant was sung throughout the night until the last drink was served, and the MERCs stumbled their way to their rooms.

15
_____

S uzuki woke in an unfamiliar bed.
      The sheets were rough and hardly covered his
body. He sat up, his eyes searching the room, trying to make
sense of where he was.

Stew was laying in the other bed in the room, and Sandy
leaned against the foot of the same bed, passed out and
snoring loudly.

Suzuki grabbed his head. He had a headache, and he
groaned as he tried to gather his bearings.

This was Middang3ard, he reminded himself. Suzuki
checked the window. He was still in a muddy marshland. It
as most definitely still Middang3ard.

Suzuki turned around and froze.

There was a shadowy figure standing in the threshold of
the doorway. Suzuki scanned the room for a weapon. Then
he remembered where he was. He hit his HUD, and his
armor rolled over his body. His sword and shield materialized in his hands.

The shadowy figure walked forward to the sound of

clucking chickens. Once he entered the light, Suzuki could see that it was Milos, and he was holding two chickens.

The dwarf held out the chickens and smiled, "What's with the sword?"

"What's with the chickens?" Suzuki countered as he sheathed his sword.

Milos walked farther into the room and stopped to chuckle as he looked at Stew and Sandy. "Looks like they had a great night. I don't usually see humans drink nearly as much as you three did. Looks like you can handle your booze well enough."

"On Earth, gin and tonics aren't anything to mess around with."

"I'll have to visit sometime. After the damned war is over. Which chicken do you like more?"

Milos held up the chickens to Suzuki. They both looked like fairly regular chickens, although much larger than any chickens he'd seen before. One was a speckled brown color, and the other was a glossy, pure white.

Suzuki pointed to the white one. "I guess that's more of a classical looking chicken," Suzuki said. "Kind of like the ideal of a chicken."

"Whatever you say." Milos released the brown chicken. Then he took out a long knife and placed the white chicken on one of the desks in the room. He held the chicken down and chopped through its neck. He tossed the chicken head and the chicken on the ground.

Suzuki jumped back as his eyes zeroed in on the splatter of chicken blood on the wall. "What the hell are you doing?"

The dead chicken was running around the room. It tripped over its own head and skidded across the floor, still kicking its legs in the air.

Milos stepped over the chicken and went to the fireplace in the room. He shifted through the pantry next to the fireplace and pulled out a pot.

"I thought humans like breakfast in bed," the dwarf mumbled as he looked for other cooking tools. "I heard it was considered romantic to most of 'em. Not that I'm trying to romance you. You ain't my type. But hospitality is hospitality as far as I'm concerned."

Stew cracked his eyes open as he rolled over and pulled the covers up to his face. The headless chicken ran past his bed and into the wall. Stew screamed and snapped bolt upright. "What the fuck is going on?"

"By the realms," Milos groaned, "are you all so love-starved that you've never gotten breakfast in bed before?"

The chicken turned and ran over Sandy's leg, tripped, and fell in her lap. Sandy yawned, wiped the sleep from her eyes, and grabbed the chicken. When she fully opened her eyes, the color drained from her face.

"Where is the chicken's head?" Sandy was still clutching the chicken. Her voice was surprisingly calm.

Suzuki pointed at the door where the chicken's head lay, its eyes staring at the fire Milos was building in the fireplace. Milos motioned for Sandy to bring the chicken to her.

Sandy did as she was told, using one hand to hold the chicken by its feet and her other hand over her mouth to hold in the mounting vomit.

"Thank you, lass. Now we gotta get this little one cleaned, and we'll have a nice lil' meal for you whelps. You wanna give me a hand?"

"Sure," Sandy squeaked, swallowing hard.

"Dump him in here."

Sandy dumped the fowl into the pot of boiling water.

Milos looked into the pot and nodded his approval. He went over to Stew's bed and sat on it. "How's everyone adjusting to the whole thing?"

"Well enough," Suzuki answered. "I guess. How exactly are we supposed to be adjusting?"

"Some people leave and go home. One night of being broke in a different realm is more than they signed up for. Others get a little frisky, if you know what I mean. Sharing beds and all that sort of thing. And others decide to flex a little, see what they're made of. Brawls and shit of that nature. Never a good idea, though. Whelps fighting with whelps is a waste of time, and whelps picking fights with veterans usually ends up with someone losing a body part."

"Wait, we can leave?"

"Get the chicken out of the pot, will you, lass?" Milos pointed to the bag he had brought with him. "There are tongs on the side."

Sandy pulled out the tongs and, using them, fished the chicken out of the pot.

Milos looked at the dripping, headless bird. "She'll be a tasty one." Then pointing at Suzuki, he added, "And yes, you can leave. Anytime you like. No one is forcing you to be here. It's not like we're abducting you or something. All you have to do is ask your familiar to release you from Middang3ard and you'll separate. Once your ties to magic are severed, you'll be whisked back home. We'll take care of the paperwork. Though, I will tell you, not all of your spoils will make it back to you. The processing office tends to have an interesting idea of ownership when it comes to dropouts."

Sandy brought the chicken over with the tongs. It was still steaming.

Milos lifted the chicken carcass over the pot. "Thank

you, Sandy. If I may ask a wee bit more from you, please, dump the water and bring the pot over here. Have you ever done this before?"

"No. I'm not sure what it is that I'm doing," Sandy answered.

"You've never made breakfast?"

Stew chuckled as he shook his head in disbelief. "We've all made breakfast before, but our food tends to come in boxes and doesn't bleed all over our walls."

"Well, you all better pay attention then. If you're gonna be out there, you're gonna have to figure out how to eat. So here's a crash course."

When Sandy returned with the pot, Milos took it from her and dropped the dead chicken in her lap. "Start defeathering," he commanded.

Sandy didn't ask any questions. She started plucking the feathers off the chicken and dropping them into the pot. She held the bald chicken carcass up when she was finished.

"Now you're gonna want to make a few cuts along its arsehole." Milos pointed at the bird's bottom.

"So gross," Stew muttered.

"Have you never seen anyone butcher meat before? Where do you think those little hunks of flesh come from?"

Stew shrugged and picked at his skin for lack of anything to say.

"Cut up its arse," Milos repeated.

Sandy made a few cuts around the chicken's sphincter.

"Now you're gonna slide your hand up its bum and pull out its guts."

"That's disgusting," Sandy grumbled as her lips curled up into a devilish smile. The color had come back into her face, and she flipped the chicken over and slid her hand up its rear. "Oooooooh, that's so gross. It's like fisting a corpse."

Sandy whipped the dead chicken around to look at her and moaned in a high-pitched voice. "Oh...your hand feels so good, touching all my organs, lover." She winked at Stew and Suzuki, who both watched, horrified.

Milos laughed and slapped his knee.

"Looks like she's the only one of you with a stomach *and* a sense of humor. You can dump the guts out there, lass."

Sandy ripped out the chicken's guts and gizzards and tossed them into the pot. Milos handed her a handkerchief to wipe her bloody hands with. Then he gave her the knife and instructed her on how to properly butcher the chicken.

Suzuki was paying close attention. Even if he was initially grossed out and deeply troubled by Sandy's love of tearing out entrails, he knew this was something that he was going to have to be doing at some point.

These were the parts of quests that were left out in the books and the games. Consequently, he knew nothing about surviving. He had just assumed that there would be a lot of magic involved.

He guessed there were some things even magic didn't take care of. Though he found it hard to imagine elves ever butchering their own food.

Once Sandy had finished degutting the chicken, Milos pulled out a small pouch. He spread a variety of herbs and seasonings on a makeshift cutting board. He seasoned the meat as he explained what each herb was and where it could be found in different parts of Middang3ard.

Suzuki took notes in a leather-bound notebook that had come with his HUD. Sandy appeared to be losing interest. Stew still watched on with a morbid sort of fascination.

"Who wants to take care of the cooking?" Milos asked.

Suzuki raised his hand. He and Milos returned to the blazing fire, and Milos took a pan from the cupboard. He procured some lard from a compartment in his pouch and slathered the pan with it.

The room was soon filled with the savory smell of frying chicken, basil, and ginseng. Suzuki didn't think that he'd ever smelled anything so heavenly before. The room could have been confused with a restaurant in Paris from the smell alone.

"You cook it all the way through," Milos lectured as he flipped the chicken over. "Make sure you don't get sick. There we go. It should be perfect."

Milos took the chicken from the fire and pulled out a few plates from the cupboard. He served each of the Mundanes and the dwarf and took a bit for himself.

They ate in silence.

Suzuki wouldn't have talked even if there had been interesting conversation. The chicken was amazing. Each of the seasonings popped and brought out a flavor that he didn't know chicken was capable of possessing. It was a good introduction to Middang3ard cuisine.

Once they all finished eating, Milos cleaned up the plates, dumped them into the largest pot, hit a button on his HUD, and the dishes vanished.

Milos patted his fat belly. "Now that that's done, I'll have Wendy set you all up with some cookware and supplies before you head out."

Stew picked some chicken out of his teeth and flicked it on the ground. "What do you mean 'head out'?" Stew asked as Sandy turned her nose up at the piece of chicken that landed next to her. "Sorry, babe."

"That favor that you owe me. I got a contract a few days ago to clear out some black flies from the swamp. Not too many. Hardly even a swarm from what I've been told. Still, the number of black flies is more than these parts are used to, so I got contracted to check it out. It pays a bit, but I don't really feel like schlepping around for a few hours when there's plenty of food and drink to be had here. So I had the contract transferred to you. Perfect kind of work for newbs."

"Are you serious?" Stew protested. "If you don't want to go mucking around in the swamp all day, what makes you think that we want to?"

"Well, you see, I wasn't really concerned with what you wanted to do. That's the whole point of a favor. Besides, it's just the right kind of work for lil' whelps such as yourself."

Sandy turned to Milos. Her eyes had darkened. A storm was brewing across her brow, and she seemed to have grown a couple of inches. She leaned close to Milos so that their noses were almost touching.

Milos tried to escape, but Sandy just leaned closer, her eyes locking in on Milos'. "I'm not a whelp," Sandy growled.

"No," Milos stammered. "Of course not. How 'bout this? A couple of copper pieces advance to ensure good faith. How's that sound?"

"Good."

Sandy's demeanor returned to normal. She took the copper pieces that Milos offered and pocketed them.

Suzuki laughed to himself. He had always thought that the tough guy routine Sandy put on while they were playing was hilarious. Seeing it in real life was even better—especially seeing it alongside Stew.

Sandy was tossing bits of chicken guts at Stew, who was cowering under his covers and yelping for Sandy to stop.

The good mood was not meant to last, though. Suzuki felt Fred uncoiling in his mind, and his joy almost completely dissipated. "My previous host used to sleep in silk beds and waged wars with the Twelve Mute Mages of Unherial. And now, here I am...sleeping in rags and playing the role of a glorified exterminator with children who don't even know how to defeather a chicken."

Suzuki had had enough. Every time Fred opened his mouth, it was to complain about something or make a snide comment. Suzuki had hoped that the prickly conversations he'd shared with Fred would lighten up. It was obvious by now that Fred had no intention of being personable or even agreeable.

"If your old host was so great, why don't you just go back to him," Suzuki snapped.

Fred was silent. Suzuki felt him withdrawing deeper into his being. Within a few seconds, it seemed that Fred had vanished.

Suzuki was glad to have that space of his mind back. He knew, however, that Fred had only retreated into some recess of their shared body. If Fred had left his body, there would have been a much more violent reaction. This situation was tolerable, though. At least Suzuki felt he could speak to his friends in peace.

Milos stood up abruptly and headed toward the door. "Come on," he called to the Mundanes. "Let's get you situated. Don't want you heading out on your first quest unprepared."

The Mundanes finally all got out of bed. Sandy and Stew hit their HUDs and armored up. They all looked uncertainly at each other.

"Black flies." Stew groaned.

"Black flies," Suzuki repeated. "We gotta start somewhere."

The Mundanes followed Milos and marched out of the room. Suzuki shut the door softly behind them as they went downstairs to pick up whatever Milos thought they would need. Wendy, the barkeep, supplied them with basic cooking tools, a map, and vague directions. Then they unceremoniously left the Red Lion and went out into the swamplands.

16

The Mundanes had left the Red Lion far behind, trekking into the depths of the swamps. The smell of mold and moss was everywhere, and they slogged through knee-high mud. It was slow going.

The map they'd been given had only a rough estimate of the area, and it was difficult to gauge the landmarks that had been scribbled in with fading ink.

Sandy's familiar, Niv, had suggested that they upload the map to their HUDs to make it easier to track their progress. The upload hadn't taken long, but the map was still difficult to decipher.

They got turned around more than a couple of times, but it didn't really bother anyone. They were all in fairly good spirits.

Stew and Sandy were talking quietly with each other. Suzuki appreciated hearing the conversation, even if he wasn't involved. This was the way their party had been since Beth had left.

Suzuki found that he enjoyed the silence. It gave him time to think, time to anticipate. When they had been playing the VR version of *Middang3ard*, all of the quiet time had allowed him to make plans and contingencies. Most of them had been jotted down in a notebook that he had brought along with him.

He wasn't sure what battle would be like in real life, but he thought this would give him a good framework to work from. Now that he thought of it, he didn't even know what kind of magic spells he had or could perform. There wasn't a slot for any on his HUD. Just a readout of his health and mana.

The sun tried to beam down on the Mundanes through the thick canopy of leaves, but very little sunlight made it down. Still, it was very hot. The air was thick and humid. Suzuki felt as if he were wearing a second layer of skin.

Suzuki cleared his throat to get the other Mundanes' attention. "You guys hot at all?"

Sandy and Stew both shook their heads. But it made sense for them. Stew was only wearing an armored kilt and Sandy was wearing robes which looked like they breathed a hell of a lot better than chainmail.

"Well, hold on." Suzuki thumbed through his HUD. "I'm going to see if I can pare down what I'm wearing."

Suzuki went through his HUD and found a quick description of how to remove some of his armor squirreled away in "inventory notes." He double-tapped his helmet, breastplate, and arms. His armor glowed bright green, and when it dimmed, he was wearing thinner leather armor. "That's better." Suzuki whipped his arms around like windmills. "So much better."

"Are you tired at all?" Stew asked.

"No, why?"

"You've been walking around for a couple of hours in

full armor. I don't remember you being a gym rat back home. Just thought you'd be tired."

"Actually," Sandy cut in, "I thought we would all be tired. This isn't exactly a cakewalk."

"You ever see anyone walk to get cake?" Stew asked.

"What?"

"I mean, everyone says cakewalk. But I've never seen anyone walk with a cake. Walk to the store to get a cake, sure. But walk with a cake? Never."

Suzuki groaned as he continued to examine the map. "How do you get the cake home after you've bought it? That's walking with cake, isn't it?"

Stew shrugged. "I'm just saying. Ain't ever seen anyone walking with a cake before."

"Whatever," Suzuki said, before calling out silently in his head, "Hey Fred, is there a reason that we aren't getting tired?"

Suzuki could feel the imp coming to the foreground of his thoughts before hearing the demonic creature sigh. "The composition of Middang3ard is not the same as your realm. Your realm is heavier than the rest of the realms. As a result, you're generally stronger and faster. Not any more intelligent, unfortunately."

"Like a superhero or something?" Suzuki mused.

"I would not go so far as to describe any of you as "super." Just not excessively fragile."

Suzuki walked over to a tree stump decaying in the rancid mud. He reached for it and lifted part of it out of the mud with hardly any strain or effort. "I don't know man. I kind of feel like I'm Captain America."

"And given how fast our wounds heal here, I'd say Captain American spliced with Wolverine."

"What are you doing with that tree?" Sandy asked.

Suzuki dropped the stump back into the mud. "I was just messing around with the tree, trying to figure out exactly how strong we are now. That's something we haven't really done since we've gotten here."

"What do you mean?"

"We hardly know how anything works. Sandy, how do you cast a spell? Stew, how are you going to go Berserk?"

Stew and Sandy stared blankly at each other.

Suzuki drew his sword. He brought it crashing down on the tree trunk. The trunk split in two, sending chunks of wood flying everywhere. "The only thing I've figured out is that I'm strong as hell. It never even clicked before that this sword is probably the heaviest thing I've ever lifted."

"Yeah, yeah," Stew interrupted. "You're a weak nerd's wet dream. Now you have the strength to do basic activities."

"I'm just saying."

"Trust me, dude. It can't be too hard. We'll figure it out."

Sandy smiled reassuringly at Suzuki. "Yeah, it shouldn't be too hard. I burned down those plants without a problem. Plus we have our familiars."

"We should still have a plan."

Stew let out an exaggerated yawn. "What kind of plan are we going to need for some flies? Unless you wanna conjure a giant flyswatter. Otherwise, let's just have Sandy torch them."

Sandy mimed shooting a gun. She blew imaginary smoke from the barrel. "Toast."

"Fine, fine," Suzuki agreed. "Guess we'll only know when we get there." He pointed to the sky. "The sun's almost down. Guess we're camping tonight."

"Out here?" Stew objected.

"Seriously, dude. Where did you think we were going to camp?"

The barbarian threw up his arms in frustration. "I don't know. I didn't think we were going to be walking all day."

Suzuki shrugged. "Well, unless you want to be walking all night too, we're gonna have to set up camp. Come on, let's look for some dry land. Or at least something stable enough to pitch a tent."

The Mundanes continued on through the mud. The air was full of buzzing mosquitos. There were strange bird calls. These were accompanied with sounds that Suzuki had never heard before, sounds that served as a reminder that the swampland was teeming with life.

Sandy and Stew had stopped talking. Stew was practically pouting. He looked like a giant hulking child poured into some armor. It was hard to take him seriously, especially since none of them were getting tired at all. Suzuki figured Stew was just complaining out of boredom.

If Suzuki were honest with himself, this wasn't how he thought his first adventure into Middang3ard was going to be.

That being said, he was glad that they hadn't taken on anything too advanced. They were still new to this whole MERC thing...best to take things slowly until they knew more.

The Mundanes came to a patch of solid ground, and Suzuki surveyed the area until he was comfortable with the spot. Spreading his arms wide, he theatrically spun around as he spoke. "This will make a fine base camp."

"You're not impressing anyone," Stew grumbled.

"Jesus, Stew," Sandy jabbed. "Haven't you ever gone camping before?"

"No. I haven't. If I had known camping required being eaten alive by mosquitos, I might have objected."

The sun had already begun to set, so Suzuki got to

picking up sticks for a fire. When Sandy saw Suzuki working, she did the same. Stew reluctantly joined in after a
couple of minutes, and once they had gathered a substantial
amount of wood, they stopped to admire the stockpile.

Then Suzuki picked up a few sticks and piled them
neatly before digging a small moat about them. "Could you
do us the honors, Sandy?" Suzuki asked.

Sandy walked up to the bundle of sticks, snapped her
fingers, and the wood burst into a modest fire.

"Good to know that you got fire down."

"Yeah," Sandy answered. "I was chatting with Niv while
we were hiking. I figured he probably knew about how
magic works seeing as how he's the only way I can use
magic."

Suzuki selected his camping gear from his HUD's inventory and it materialized in front of him. He got started
setting up his tent. Sandy chose her camping gear as well.
She stared at it blankly when it materialized at her feet.

When Suzuki saw the obvious confusion on Stew's and
Sandy's faces, he finished up his tent and came over to them.
"You guys don't know how to pitch a tent, huh?"

Sandy smiled sheepishly as she played with her robes.
"My family and I grew up in a city. We didn't really have
anywhere to camp."

"What about you, Stew?"

Stew turned bright red and stammered. "It's not important! I just don't know how to make up a tent. Not everyone
is Bear Wilderness. And how'd you figure out how to do this
shit anyway? You're kind of a pasty nerd."

"I am not pasty!"

Sandy laughed as she manipulated the flames of the fire
with her hand. "I think we'll all benefit from being out in
nature. And Stew and I are going to share my tent."

Stew's eyes got wide. They quickly narrowed as he rubbed his hands together.

"All right," Suzuki said. "But please, for the love of God, don't—"

"Don't worry, Suzuki." Sandy chuckled. "It'll be like a silent film."

Suzuki nodded, lifting a finger up in the way he always did when he was about to say something interesting. Well, interesting to him at least. "You know the first silent films were actually nickelodeons. They weren't kid-friendly, though. Most of them were porn and...oh...I get it," he added when he saw Sandy's massive grin.

Stew trotted over to Sandy's side and smacked her butt as he passed. "All right. I could get into this camping shit."

"Good." Suzuki sighed. "Then let me show you how to get this tent up."

"It's not going to be the only thing getting up tonight," Sandy muttered under her breath.

"Okay, okay," Suzuki exclaimed. "I get it. You two are fucking tonight. Now give me a hand."

Suzuki walked them through how to get their tent up and going. He explained each step of setting down the spikes and how to get up the canvas of the tent. The work was satisfying to him.

The MERCs hadn't supplied them with anything fancy. Instead, they had been given traditional tents that required a bit of know-how to get pitched.

Suzuki wondered how many of the new MERCs were floundering about trying to figure out the basics of getting a comfortable night's rest.

Stew hammered in one of the spikes with the hilt of his sword. "How'd you learn all this shit anyway? All jokes aside, I never pegged you as someone who spent much time outdoors."

Suzuki stretched the canvas over the frame of the tent and motioned for Stew and Sandy to pull the canvas up and over the various rods and spikes. "I really liked *Lord of the Rings* when I was growing up. I used to make my parents take me camping out in the forests so I could pretend that I was one of the Hobbits."

"Niv says they're halflings," Sandy chimed in.

"No, hobbits," Suzuki corrected. "Hobbits and halflings are different."

"Yes, but Niv tells me we're not allowed to use the word 'hobbit' because Tolkien's people copyrighted it."

Suzuki looked around. "We're in the middle of nowhere. Who's going to sue us out here?"

Sandy lifted a silencing finger to her lips. "Shush—you never know who's listening."

Suzuki threw his hands up in surrender. "Whatever...the point is that when I got older, I started LARPing with a couple of friends. We used to go out and camp in the forest a couple weekends out of the month."

"God, you even have nerdy reasons for being outdoors. I guess you've been training for this whole fantasy life for a long time."

"Yeah, I guess you could say that. But haven't we all?"

The Mundanes finished setting up their tents and stepped back to admire their work. Even Stew looked impressed with what they had accomplished. Suzuki made his way to the fire and sat down. Sandy and Stew joined him.

"So what do we do now?" Stew asked. Irritation and impatience were creeping into his voice.

"Well," Suzuki mused. "My parents used to bring instruments along so we could sing, but I guess we don't have any. And my friends used to bring beer, but that's out of the question too."

"Not quite," Sandy chimed in. She tapped her HUD a couple of times, and three beers and a lute appeared next to the fire. "Niv told me I should grab a couple of drinks for the road. I put them on Milos' tab and figured he wouldn't mind. When I saw the bar had a lute, I asked to borrow it. I used to take lessons when I was a kid."

Stew let out a roaring laugh. "The semifinals for the world's biggest nerd continues. The competition is fierce."

Niv popped out from behind Sandy's back. He hopped over to the fire, sat up on his hind legs, and warmed his front paws. "You don't mind if I join you? It's a beautiful night, and you have a very toasty fire."

"No, no." Suzuki gestured at the fire. "Please do."

Sandy plucked a few strings on the lute and began tuning as Suzuki pulled a bag of salted meats from his inventory. He passed the jerky to Stew, along with a beer.

Sandy started strumming the lute as Niv sang softly under his breath.

Suzuki couldn't tell what the almiraj was singing, but it sounded like another language. The words flowed together like water, and Niv had a soft, sweet voice. After a couple of minutes, Suzuki saw that GB had walked out from behind Stew. He was listening quietly, his donkey face looking more than a little sleepy. Suzuki wondered if Fred was interested in joining them.

"Hey, Fred," Suzuki broached. "You wanna hang out with us?"

There was a long pause before Fred spoke. "I suppose."

Suzuki felt a slight jerk and Fred exited his body, floating above him for a moment before perching on a tree branch.

When she was finished playing, Sandy stretched out and rested her head on Stew's lap. "So how's your first camping trip, babe?"

Stew took a sip from his drink and nodded his head. "Not half-bad," he replied.

Even though he was happy for his friends, Suzuki couldn't help but feel jealous: watching Sandy and Stew just reminded him that Beth wasn't with them. Even if she had been, he doubted that he'd have had the guts to put his arm around her or even flirt. Nothing with him and Beth seemed as easy as with Sandy and Stew. Ever since they'd started playing together, Sandy and Stew had been inseparable. He wasn't surprised when he heard that they were dating. Sometimes he was surprised that they were still dating, but that was another story.

But him and Beth?

Nothing about them ever seemed easy.

Stew cocked his thumb upward. "You know, I've never seen these many stars before. I've never been anywhere that I could hear bugs."

From overhead, there was a plume of smoke, and Fred descended to sit with the rest of the Mundanes. "The stars each have a story. The old ones, such as me, have names and stories for all of them."

"You mean like constellations?"

"No. Each star has a name and a story. Unlike humans, we do not need to make up tales. We have seen each star come into life, and we shall watch as they all fade."

"Could you tell us one?" Sandy asked.

Fred pointed to a flickering red star. "That is Glagorethroashin. One of the first Elder Ones was born from its fire. He drowned the first created realm in his madness and was banished by the other Elder Ones. It is said that he will return when the realms have achieved peace and will spread his madness to all of the realms once more."

"Damn, dude," Stew grumbled. "You really know how to be a buzzkill."

"What buzz have I killed? It will be a beautiful thing to see all of reality thrown into confusion and chaos."

Sandy laughed and pointed to a group of stars directly above her. "Okay, my turn. My mom told me a story about that constellation over there. The one with the bright white star at its apex." Sandy waved a hand and the constellation illuminated. "According to Chinese mythology, that's Vega. In the story, she's in love with this human farm boy, Niulang, something forbidden by the gods. Still they continued to defy their fate, and when the gods eventually saw their love was true, they allowed the two lovers to meet, but only once a year—on the 7th night of the 7th moon, when a bridge of magpies forms across the Celestial River. Now China celebrates that time as the Qixi Festival. Kind of romantic, right?"

"Yeah," Suzuki agreed. "I wish Beth were here to hear that one."

Sandy nodded and took back up her lute. "You should show them to her the next time you see her, Suzuki. She'd probably get a kick out of it. She'd love it."

Fred flapped his wings, returning to the tree branch. "I do not understand your story. As is typical of your human stories, it lacks substance."

"Maybe." Suzuki stared up at the shining stars. "I thought it was a pretty good story, though."

The Mundanes sat and drank as the night passed on around them. The stars did not grow dim, nor did their laughter or conversation. They shared stories and fears with each other as the night wore on. Stew fell asleep first, and he didn't wake until Sandy nudged him hard in the side and they both retired to their tent. Suzuki stayed outside a bit longer, watching the stars.

Then he went into his tent, closed the flap, lay down and drifted to sleep, hoping to dream of Beth, if only for a moment.

17

S uzuki rose with the gray dawn and slipped out of his tent as quietly as he could. The marsh was smoky in the early morning before the sun had fully climbed into its proper place in the sky, painting the sky in hues of red and yellow.

This was the perfect time of day for him. He'd never enjoyed mornings before, but that was back when he was on Earth. There was nothing remotely pleasant about waking up before the sun so that you could go to work or cram for the last test of the semester.

Even if there were a reason to get out of bed, there wasn't anything worth seeing.

The only thing that Suzuki had ever appreciated about waking up early was the silence. The suburbs had a special sort of silence which he'd never heard anywhere else, vastly different from what he was listening to now.

Even though *he* had just woken up, it sounded as if the swamp had never gone to sleep. The frogs were still croaking loudly, and birds were singing overhead.

Suzuki walked a little way from Sandy and Stew's tent. He wanted to give them a bit more privacy.

He took some of the wood with him, and when he was far enough away, he knelt and cleared a spot for a fire. There was a piece of flint and stone in his inventory. He selected it and the flint materialized in his hand. It took a few attempts at striking the flint before a spark caught, but the kindling was soon on fire, burning healthily.

The fire invited Suzuki to think, to let his mind wander. Not that he needed much imagination in a place like this. The last few days had been like a dream. Getting drunk and singing with halflings? Exploring a poisonous marsh? This was way better than any campaign he'd ever played before, even given the hours of paperwork. That, however, had grounded him back in reality: no dream could have gotten that level of bureaucracy right.

Suzuki wondered if the blackfly quest was going to be as easy as Milos had made it sound. If the paperwork was any indication of Middang3ard, Suzuki was certain that nothing was ever going to be as easy as it looked.

Even getting out of the small village and into the thick of the marsh had taken more real-life skills than Suzuki had anticipated.

Were things any easier for the military?

How was Beth faring?

He tried to message her again but was met with the same restrictions. Whatever she used to get around them was tech or magic that he didn't have access to. Yet.

Suzuki tried to imagine what Beth was doing right at this moment. Probably waking up. He remembered her saying that she had a hard time getting out of bed in the morning. She was probably still trying to get her eyes to stay open.

Pulling up the screenshot that he'd taken of the last video Beth had sent him, he tried to think of what she looked like in the morning. Her hair was probably a mess, and she'd probably hate talking. He wouldn't have been surprised if she'd hit him over the head if he tried to speak to her.

But he wouldn't mind because he'd be sleeping next to her, seeing her first thing in the morning, running his fingers across hers, staring into her eyes, feeling himself getting lost as he leaned forward, both of their lips parting slightly.

An ember from the fire cracked loudly and Suzuki jumped to his feet, unsheathing his sword. He whirled around, looking for the source of the noise. When he realized it was the fire, he sat down again.

Man, I need to get more comfortable with the sounds of nature...and fire, he thought.

He pulled up some of the salted meat from his inventory and chomped into it. The meat was indeed salty. His whole mouth puckered, but he thanked whoever was listening that they had gotten enough food to negate needing to hunt. Cooking a chicken would have been a godsend compared to hunting down frogs in the mud. He wasn't even sure what you would make from frogs.

Whatever it would be, it didn't sound appetizing at the moment.

After he had finished eating, Suzuki stood and stretched.

At the camp, Sandy was stepping out of her tent. She apparently had just woken up and was fiddling with her robes. She tripped over the pile of wood near their dead fire from the night before. Her hair was a mess, sticking up on one side, and she tried to pat it down to no effect.

Stew came out of the tent a little after Sandy. He dropped to the ground almost instantly and started doing pushups. He powered through more than a dozen, and when he was done, he flipped over and resumed with sit-ups.

Sandy took a seat on a dead tree trunk near Stew, pulled out a book, and read.

Suzuki gave them a little time with their morning routine and then approached. "Morning," Suzuki called.

Sandy waved at Suzuki as he walked up. Stew continued with his work out. Squats now. He nodded at Suzuki but, other than that, didn't acknowledge him.

"How'd you guys sleep?"

"Good...once we got to it," Sandy bragged. "How about you?"

"Ground was surprisingly comfortable."

"So what now, O Fearless Leader?" Stew asked.

"Well, I was looking at the map last night before I went to sleep and drew a pretty clear path to where we're going. Should take a couple of more hours and we'll be there. You guys ready for a walk?"

Sandy shook her head and looked in the direction of Suzuki's abandoned fire. "Not yet," she answered. "I could do with a little bit more campfire before I get going. It's freezing. And I want to finish this chapter."

"What are you reading?"

"Niv suggested that I grab the book that was in our room. It's a book on spellcraft. It's kind of confusing, but I like it. It's like building your own spells or something."

"All right, you guys should eat anyway. But we gotta get going soon."

Sandy and Suzuki went over to the fire, while Stew finished up his morning workout. They both sat, and Suzuki tossed Sandy some salted meat, which she ate while she kept reading.

Suzuki read through a couple of his HUD's tutorials to kill time. They were mostly basic instructions -- nothing that he couldn't have figured out on his own. He wished he had brought something to read like Sandy, but he hadn't assumed there would be any downtime.

It made sense, though. Half of the *Lord of the Rings* movies were shots of halflings and elves walking for miles. After a half an hour or so, Stew came over and sat at the fire. He grabbed some meat and ate in silence.

After he finished eating, Stew smiled and looked up at Suzuki. "Morning, dude."

"Morning," Suzuki replied. "I was beginning to think you'd become a mute."

"Nope. Just gotta start the day right. Sandy, you still reading that thing?"

"Until I'm done," she answered. "That's usually the way that a book works. You start it and read it until you're done."

"I know how books work. I just meant that we have other things to do. Like killing stuff things to do."

"I'm aware that we're going to be killing things today. Just trying to make sure I don't disappoint myself with a lack of style."

"Any tips?" Suzuki asked.

"Not for you. It looks like magic is pretty specific here. Like everything in the book is geared toward a specific type of magic. It's all offensive shit. Mostly elemental. I haven't come across anything healing based. Makes me wonder if they have any necromantic tomes out there. That would be wild. I never got into necromancy before, but I figure now is as good a time as any."

"Sandy, are you saying that you actually want to raise the dead?"

"No, I'm saying that I want to raise an army of the dead."

Sandy walked Suzuki and Stew through some of the things she had picked up from her reading. The way she was understanding magic was that it wasn't based on incantations, not for humans at least.

Elves still relied on incantations for their casting, but that was because elves were more formal in all aspects of life.

Humans, on the other hand, could "free-flow," as the book put it. That meant that they only needed to have a general idea of what it was that they were casting. The spell work was more about intention and less about rules.

As a result, humans could get more creative with their spell work. Sandy showed them how there were instructions for how to cast a flaming icicle. The book was full of examples like that.

Stew took out his sword and started sharpening it. "What does that mean for someone like me?"

"Well, you know the barbarian spells better than I. I guess you'd have to figure out what you were casting, commit to it, and then use your familiar to cast it. You should probably be talking to GB about that. I've been talking to Niv all day."

Suzuki wondered what it was like to have a familiar that actually wanted to talk. There were scores of questions Suzuki had, and he knew that Fred probably had the answers. He hadn't wanted to ask any of them, though.

Every time Fred opened his mouth, his words were coated with such a heavy layer of condescension that Suzuki didn't even want to bother talking to him. But he knew the imp probably was aware of secrets in Middang3ard that they couldn't even dream of. What was the point of being an eldritch creature if you didn't have eldritch knowledge?

Suzuki made a mental note to work on his relationship with Fred. *I wonder if there's familiar/ human counseling on Middang3ard?*

"Come on, guys." Suzuki stepped on the fire. "We should get going."

The Mundanes tore down their camp and headed farther into the marshlands. They were making better time than they had yesterday. There was a level of confidence that had been lacking.

Maybe it was just having spent their first real night out on a quest, but the Mundanes were trekking through the forest as if they'd been doing it their entire life.

Even Stew was starting to get into it. He would sometimes stop and point to interesting plants as they passed by, wondering if they could use them for potions or alchemy.

Suzuki didn't have the heart to tell Stew that whatever potion-making looked like in Middang3ard, it was probably much more labor-intensive than clicking a few buttons. It would be better to let Stew have his enthusiasm while it lasted.

"Hey, Fred," Suzuki asked tentatively. "How do I use magic?"

Suzuki could feel Fred rolling his eyes. "Simple, human. You think of what you'd like to accomplish and I facilitate it for you. Your HUD is already set up for the spells of a warrior-mage. When you imagine what you would like, I will do a rough estimate of the spell, and help you cast something that will have the desired effect."

There might have been a tone of condescension in his voice, but at least Fred had answered him in a direct, simple way.

Maybe that is the key. Direct questions get direct answers, Suzuki thought as he brushed a low hanging branch out of his way.

"Thanks," Suzuki offered. Fred didn't reply.

The Mundanes continued on their way through the marsh until they came to a large clearing where the marsh's water dried up and the ground was more solid, albeit muddy.

The air was full of buzzing. Thousands of wings were beating, and it sounded like a swarm of bees.

Suzuki couldn't locate the source of the noise, but he knew that the black flies were close by.

As the Mundanes walked farther into the clearing, Sandy pointed ahead.

There was a small swarm of black flies moving in between the trees. It looked like a black cloud of moving bodies. The flies were going somewhere in a hurry.

"Maybe there's a hive," Stew suggested.

"Flies don't have hives," Sandy countered. "Bees have hives. Flies are attracted to things."

"Let's find what these flies think are attractive then."

Suzuki sighed. "Not that kind of attractive, Stew."

They followed the swarm as the flies meandered through the swamp. The flies didn't seem to notice. Despite his worries that everything in Middang3ard might want to kill him, the black flies seemed to be more of an obvious irritation than a threat. Maybe he was a little bit too gung-ho about the whole quest. Milos probably wouldn't have sent them to take care of something that was way out of their league.

The worst thing that the MERCs had done so far was drop them off at an office without explaining how much paperwork they were going to have to finish.

The flies flew behind some trees and Suzuki raised his hand for the Mundanes to stop. Up ahead, where the flies were congregating, there were dozens of animal carcasses laid out on the ground. Their entrails had been ripped out and piled high. That was what the flies were swarming to.

Maggots covered the entrails, and there was the rank smell of putrefaction. It was hard to tell what the animals were at this advanced stage of decomposition.

As the Mundanes watched, a pair of goblins stumbled from the woods, holding some four-legged game between the pair of them. The goblins were short and squat, which was unsurprising. But they were oddly muscular, and they chatted with each other in hoarse, loud voices. Swords hung from their waists.

The goblins threw the fresh game down and set upon it with their knives. Bits of the animal were cut off and placed to the side as the entrails and other unmentionables were tossed into the large pile of viscera.

Once the goblins were finished, they picked up the parts of meat they wished to keep and went back into the darker part of the forests.

Suzuki spoke. Or at least he tried to, but every time he opened his mouth, he gagged, and he had to use every ounce of willpower to not throw up. Finally, on his third attempt, he managed to whisper, "I guess that's where the flies are coming from."

Stew covered his nose. "We could just go in there and take out the goblins. Then torch the flies."

"We don't know how many there are," Sandy countered. "I doubt they need that much meat just for a couple of goblins."

"True," Suzuki agreed. "There's probably a handful of them."

"So we're goblin hunting?" Stew asked.

"Yeah, but slowly. We gotta take this slowly and not get in over our heads."

Stew looked at the goblins like a lion watching grazing gazelles. "The only ones who are gonna be over their heads are these goblins. If they still have heads when I'm done with them."

Sandy rested her hand on Stew's shoulder and smiled sweetly at him. "Babe, you really gotta work on your pre-fight trash talking."

Suzuki stood. "Whatever we do, we need to find their camp first and see exactly how many we're up against."

The Mundanes followed the goblins, who carried their butchered meat back to camp. There they saw at least twenty of the gray imp-like creatures gathered around a fire.

They were roasting strips of recently-butchered flesh, talking and grunting quietly among themselves. They wore warpaint which varied in color from goblin to goblin. Some of them were covered from head to toe in a dark, inky black color, others with delicate, intricate patterns of blues and blood red. Their sloped foreheads shined with sweat from the heat of the fire.

Two of them were snapping at each other over what looked to be a goat's leg, before a third larger goblin stabbed the two fighting goblins with his cutlass, taking the meat for himself. This seemed a completely acceptable thing to do, as evidenced by the fact that the rest of the goblins ignored the screams of the two smaller goblins, who eventually scampered off to tend their wounds.

Suzuki considered just charging in, *Leeroy Jenkinsing* the situation. He ran the plan, or rather total lack of one, through his HUD. The percentage of success read at only twelve percent.

Stew poked his head over the bushes he was crouched behind. "These guys do not look friendly. If they're ready to kill each other, what do you think they're gonna do to us? Maybe we should just take care of the flies."

Suzuki scrolled through his HUD. There was nothing there to help him. Just the glaring twelve percent chance of success. "No." Suzuki sighed. "We got contracted to take care of the black fly problem. It looks like the goblins are causing that. So we have to take care of the goblin problem."

"Any ideas on how to get started?"

Suzuki wracked his brain. Nothing was coming to him. He was freezing up.

"I know exactly what to do," Stew broke in, ruining Suzuki's concentration. "We Leeroy this shit." Stew was already standing, unsheathing his sword, and preparing to launch a full-scale attack.

Suzuki shook his head. "Already ran that scenario through the HUD. Twelve percent, dude. Way too low to risk it."

"No Leeroying here, Stew," Sandy scolded. "We fuck this up and we're dead. And not the kind of dead where you order a pizza and jerk off to make yourself feel better. We're dead, dead here. Don't forget that."

Stew lowered his eyes. "I was kidding. Sorta."

"All right," Suzuki said finally. "We can do this. We just gotta take it slow. First thing...first thing....uh..." But Suzuki couldn't think of what to do next. He just stammered, his hand shaking.

What the fuck is wrong with me? he thought.

You're scared, Fred's voice chimed in his head.

Private thoughts here, Suzuki silently shot back.

Pish posh. I'm literally in your head. Any hope of privacy was lost when you agreed to that infernal contract and let me in. Or did you not read the fine print?

No one reads the User's Terms and Services, Suzuki lamented.

A failing of your species. But as I was saying, you're frightened. As well you should be. The wrong decision will be the death of you and your friends. But there is one decision that you are making right now that will most certainly lead to your doom.

What? Suzuki thought, imagining himself throwing up his arms in frustration. *I haven't decided anything.*

Exactly, Fred said. Not *making a decision is making a very big and dangerous decision. This is Middang3ard. You must act to survive. A moment spent not acting is a moment in which your enemy can impale you on a sword. Or a horn. Or whatever sharp object's available.*

So, what should I do?

I cannot decide for you. But let me put this in human terms. Pull up your big boy pants and do something.

Thanks for the pep talk, Suzuki thought, in the most menacing voice he could imagine.

Anytime. Fred disappeared into the recesses of his mind.

Sandy took Suzuki's hand and held it tight. "Hey, where are you, bud? We need you. Here. Now. You got this."

Stew nodded his agreement and put his hand on top of Sandy's. "Yeah. Give us the plan, Oh Fearless Leader."

Suzuki clenched his fists. They needed a decision. They needed action. Fine. He'd give them both.

"We gotta scatter them. If they're all together, they're gonna overwhelm us. If we split them up, get 'em running around and off-balance, we can take 'em. They aren't that big. And if they're anything like the goblins we've come across before, they shouldn't be too strong. Although everything seems to be stronger in Middang3ard. Or maybe that's just us."

"So how are we going to scatter them?"

"Uh...Sandy...can you blow their fire up?"

"You mean make it explode?"

"I don't know. Shit, this is harder in real-time...yeah...do something with the fire. Stick to crowd control. Keep everyone from getting too close. I want you up above, raining death down, all right?"

"Can do."

"Stew, you and me are gonna tank and knock 'em down while they're scurrying."

Stew shook his head. "Dude, Beth is the Tank. You're support."

"Beth isn't here. And that's why I'm gonna need you to watch my back. Just make sure I don't get swarmed. You guys ready?"

"As ready as we'll be."

"For honor."

"For glory."

"For XP," they all whispered.

"Again, there's no XP," Stew lamented.

"Shut up," Sandy said as she closed her eyes tightly, her brow furrowing with concentration. Her feet slowly lifted off the ground. She opened her eyes and almost burst into giddy laughter. "I'm doing it," she softly exclaimed. "Oh my God, I'm flying. I'm actually flying."

"Floating," Stew corrected.

"Really? You're gonna be the semantics police right now?"

"Sorry."

"Stop fucking around," Suzuki broke in. "Let's get going."

Sandy nodded, floating higher and higher, until she was

a good ten feet above them. A blue aura covered her body as her robes flared out, sparks of electricity jumping off her body.

Suzuki held his breath. "On my call."

This was it. It was now or never.

Raising his voice for all to hear, Suzuki cried out, "Today we find out if we deserve to be in Middang3ard. Go!"

Sandy exploded forward, swooping into the goblin camp. She raised her hand. There was a spark in her palm, large and dense, and she tossed it onto the goblin fire.

A few goblins instantly were ablaze. They screeched and ran around the camp, fanning themselves, trying to put out the fire. Sandy twisted her hand, and the flame started to take shape. Tendrils stretched out and snapped at the goblins.

Sandy laughed maniacally as Stew and Suzuki jumped over the bushes and ran into the fray.

Suzuki ran as fast as he could while sliding forward through the mud, unsheathing his sword before he swung up his shield, taking out the legs of the goblin in front of him. The goblin went down and Suzuki brought his sword down on its skull, cracking it instantly and sending blood everywhere, splashing up in Suzuki's face. He wiped it away, whirling around with horror.

The blood was so warm, so wet.

Suzuki hit his HUD, and his helmet phased over his face. He spun around to see Stew squaring off with two goblins as the rest of the goblins rushed to try and put out the fire Sandy had started.

A goblin jumped forward at Suzuki, and his HUD flashed twenty percent. Suzuki raised his shield and the goblin hit him, sending both of them falling to the ground. The goblin scrambled faster than Suzuki could have imagined and was instantly on his feet. He brought his scimitar down hard on Suzuki, who was barely able to raise his shield in time.

The shock of the attack pushed Suzuki back to the ground as another goblin flanked him. He felt the force of the blow and his armor vibrated so hard that Suzuki thought he was having a heart attack.

"Stew," Suzuki shouted as he tried to beat back the goblin in front of him with his shield.

There was another explosion of fire. Sandy was floating a little way off, tossing fireballs, laughing as if she had gone mad.

A dagger flew through the air and impaled the goblin in front of Suzuki. Stew ran over and tackled the goblin hacking on Suzuki's back. Blood was running down Stew's chest, and his eyes were wide with panic. He helped Suzuki to his feet as the goblins banded together.

"They're too fast." Suzuki gasped. "Too fast."

"It's your armor," Stew growled, turning to face the advancing goblins. "It's too heavy. You're too heavy."

Suzuki scrolled through his HUD as Stew stepped forward and slashed a goblin across the face. He switched to leather armor and felt his body instantly lighten.

And then he felt the sharp, hot pain of steel cutting into his skin. He turned around as fast as he could. There was a goblin behind him, preparing to attack again. Suzuki looked at the blood pouring down his arm.

He felt cold all over.

He needed to run.

He needed to get out of this place as soon as possible.

The goblin lunged forward. Suzuki raised his shield out of instinct. The goblin's attack rolled off Suzuki, who felt his body moving on its own. He sidestepped and brought his sword down on the goblin's neck, sending the goblin's head flying.

"That's one," Suzuki shouted, adrenaline coursing through him, imbuing him with courage. "I can do this," he told himself. "I can do this."

Stew turned and looked at Suzuki. "What the fuck are you talking about?"

Suzuki let out a war cry before leaping higher and farther than he ever could have on Earth. He landed in the middle of the mob, spun around, his shield knocking two of them over, his sword ending another one. "I am friggin' Captain America," he shouted with glee.

Impaling one with his sword, he slashed at another goblin with his kite. But he wasn't quick enough. The goblin managed to slash at Suzuki's leg.

Not that Suzuki noticed. He was in it now, and the adrenaline coursing through him covered the pain.

"Four," Suzuki shouted. "Where are you at, Stew?"

Stew blinked in shock. "Four," he said as four goblins advanced on him. "Four?"

"Yeah! I got four. Where are you at?"

Stew pulled two daggers from his side. He pressed them to his chest and drew blood as he screamed in pain. The panic had fled his eyes. There was something else now. Suzuki could see it from afar. It was just what they needed.

"Where are you at, Stew?" Suzuki shouted again.

Stew ran forward, his daggers flashing. Two of the goblins swung at him, cutting him, but it didn't stop his onslaught. Stew barreled into the goblins, sending them flying. He grabbed one of the goblins from the air and throw it into the ground. He brought a dagger down, cracking the goblin's chest, and he flung the other dagger at the adjacent goblin, finally pulling his short sword out and burying it in the last goblin.

"Five," Stew shouted.

Sandy landed, sending fire flying everywhere. Suzuki could feel the flame's heat, and he grabbed the closest goblin and tossed it into the fire Sandy was generating.

"How about you, Sandy?" Suzuki called.

"Lost track," Sandy said, smiling. Then an arrow hit her in the arm, breaking her concentration, causing her to fall to the ground.

"Sandy," Stew shouted. He pulled his short sword out of a goblin and leapt, soaring over the remaining goblins. He landed with a heavy thud that sent the goblins near him flying through the air. Stew helped Sandy to her feet. "Are you okay?"

Sandy touched her shoulder. The arrow was still in her. She screamed, horrified, as she tried to pull the arrow out. "It's fucking in me," she shouted. "There's a fucking arrow in me!"

Stew grabbed the arrow and broke it off, leaving the head in her skin.

"Yeah, there's an arrow in you." Stew pointed at the remaining goblins. "And it was one of those bastards who did it. So the question is, are you gonna cry about it, or are you gonna go all DeeStruck on their asses?"

Sandy nodded as her brow furrowed and dark energy enveloped her.

She floated back into the air and raised her hands to the sky. She touched her shoulder again for a moment before calling a lightning bolt down in the middle of the clearing. Electricity shot through the ground as Suzuki and Stew leapt in the air. The goblins jerked as they were electrocuted.

A few fell.

Most of them remained standing, screeching.

"Let's end this," Suzuki growled as he sprang forward. He blocked a goblin, spun around and slashed the goblin in half.

Stew bellowed with berserker rage to get the attention of the rest of the goblins. He swung his short sword and floored two more as Sandy dashed forward, disappearing for a second and reappearing in front of a goblin, her hands glowing brightly. She grabbed the goblin by the throat and it burst into flames.

Within a few seconds, the Mundanes had cleared out the last of the goblins. They stood in the clearing, surrounded by dead goblin bodies, panting, trying to catch their breath.

Stew found a tree and collapsed next to it. "Holy fucking shit," Stew breathed. "Holy fucking shit."

Suzuki took a seat next to Stew, as did Sandy.

"Now that was a fucking fight," Sandy panted.

"Yeah. It was," Suzuki agreed.

"I can't believe we just did that. I can't fucking believe we just did that."

Stew felt his chest. He was covered in open wounds. "You know, casting Berserker Rage in the VR game didn't use to hurt this much," he complained. "I think I'm going to have to pick another class that doesn't need to hurt themselves to use magic."

"I'm gonna have to watch the mana use too," Sandy mused as she touched her HUD, assessing her inventory. "I was practically running on empty back there. If Niv hadn't told me about channeling a little magic into my hands, I would have been shooting blanks."

"Looks like we all learned something useful," Suzuki agreed.

"Yeah, like you learned you can fight like a badass," Stew exclaimed. "I never saw you move like that in-game. And that Rally spell really fucking worked."

"What are you talking about?"

"You cast Rally, didn't you? Back when I was freaking out. That's when I got that...I don't know...like a surge of confidence."

"Huh..." Suzuki thought back to the fight. He had noticed that his chance for survival had jumped up when he was shouting at Stew. He had been thinking about casting Rally but hadn't actually called the spell.

Was casting magic that easy?

I took the necessary steps of casting your spell, Fred interjected into Suzuki's mind. *For future reference, actually communicating what you would like to do would be extremely helpful. I do not have a running list of spells to save your life.*

Thanks, Suzuki said. *I'll keep that in mind.*

"So that's a fight in Middang3ard." Sandy was looking herself, over noting the tears her robes had sustained. "I don't think we held up too badly."

"I still feel a little beat up," Stew complained.

Suzuki stood up and raised his shield. "Let's see if we can fix—"

There was a massive crash from the trees a little distance away.

The Mundanes looked up at the sound of cracking wood. Something big was moving through the swamps, pushing the trees out of the way as if they were sticks. Suzuki could see the trees falling in the distance.

The cracking of the trees intensified. In the faint shadows, Suzuki saw the face of a giant, a giant who was at least twelve feet. Its face looked human but stretched out, as if it had been pulled taut by a great weight. Its arms nearly touched the ground, and it roared furiously as it broke into the clearing.

"Oh fuck, oh fuck," Suzuki shouted as he and the Mundanes jumped to their feet and took off running into the swamp.

Branches whipped across Suzuki's face as he ran, trying to form a plan while concentrating on *not* falling.

That was impossible, however, so Suzuki decided to focus on running for the moment.

Sandy was already ahead of the rest of the group. She motioned in front and to the right. There was a group of bushes that had low hanging branches partially obscuring them.

The Mundanes pushed into the bushes and pulled the branches lower.

"Sandy," Suzuki stammered as he wildly looked around, trying to keep his cool. "Can you cast invisibility or something on us?"

"I don't know how," Sandy said.

"I thought you were the mage?"

"Only offensively. I mostly know attacks and small bluffs. Nothing like that."

Stew was scanning the ground behind them. "For fuck sake, try!"

"All right, all right!" Sandy closed her eyes. "Invisible. Invisible. I cast Invisibility."

Stew raised his hand and stared at it as if he were trying to solve the world's oldest puzzle. "Are we invisible?"

Suzuki shook his head. "I can still see you."

"Maybe it's 'cause you're invisible too. Is that how it works?"

More trees crashed in the distance. The giant roared loudly, and it took everything in Suzuki's power not to piss his greaves right then and there. He was trying to get his nerves under control.

A giant couldn't be that much worse than a whole tribe of goblins. They had just been caught off guard, that was all. This was something they could handle. There was a way. Now he just had to figure out how.

"God damn it." Sandy sighed. "We're not invisible. Niv says I can't cast it because I don't know how light refraction works."

"What the hell does that have to do with being invisible?"

"If I knew that, we'd be pulling a Frodo right now!"

The giant screamed again, and Stew peeked over the leaves to see where it was. "I can't see it."

Suzuki touched his HUD. "I'm more worried that we can't hear it."

"Maybe it left and—"

The silence was shattered by the branches covering the Mundanes being ripped away, along with the trees they hung on.

The giant loomed over the Mundanes, drool dripping from its slack-jawed mouth. He pointed at Suzuki with a huge, stubby finger.

"Englishman," the giant bellowed as the Mundanes scurried away.

The word was like a slap in his face. They couldn't run or hide from this thing, not as long as Suzuki was there. His blood—well, his grandfathers' blood—was like a homing beacon to this thing.

"Come on," Suzuki shouted. "We gotta make a stand!"

The Mundanes squared up against the giant,

unsheathing their weapons, Sandy floating slightly above the ground, her hands glowing. The giant looked at them. His face was devoid of any understanding, with barely a glimmer of awareness in his eyes. Then he pointed again and screamed, "Englishman die now!"

"Sandy," Suzuki commanded, "Try to slow it down with Paralyze. His skin is going to be—"

Suzuki was cut off by the giant's club smashing into his chest, sending him flying through the air, crashing into a tree. He coughed blood, turned off his helmet, and spit it out. Ahead, Sandy barely dodged the giant's club as Stew slashed at the giant's leg.

The giant hardly noticed. Suzuki looked down at his sword and his HUD read ten percent.

"This isn't going to cut it." Suzuki groaned to himself.

He wiped the rest of the blood off his lips and jumped through the air, landing a few feet in front of the giant. He swung his sword over his head and slashed at the giant's leg, alongside Stew. The giant swatted Stew and sent him flying. Stew hit the ground hard and didn't move.

Suzuki leapt to Stew and shook the barbarian awake. "Come on, get up."

"Christ, that thing hits like a truck. And I don't think I'm tanking this thing."

"It's okay, I got a plan. Sandy! I need some water. Drench it and the ground. Stew, follow my lead."

Suzuki raised his sword and pressed his forehead to its blade. He hoped that Fred was listening. He wasn't sure what he was going to say though. He'd never cast a spell in real life before. Did he just shout it out like an anime character calling out an attack? What was the spell that he was thinking about anyway?

Fuck it, Suzuki thought. *Gotta start somewhere.*

"Let our holy strength vanquish our enemies," Suzuki shouted. His sword glowed a pale gold and from that glow emanated bright, burning fireflies which flew from his sword to Stew's. Both of their weapons took on the same hue of gold. "Come on, we need to get its attention."

Stew and Suzuki charged the giant. Suzuki slid through the mud, in between the giant's legs, and slashed at its ankles. The giant screamed and lumbered forward as Stew stabbed at the giant's kneecap. Water was pouring from the sky, and the ground was slick and muddy.

The giant took a step forward, swinging its club, its feet sinking farther into the mud.

"Snap-freeze it, Sandy!"

Sandy flew in front of the giant and clasped her hands together. "Taste the chill of death, beast," Sandy screamed as frost formed over her hand.

The giant was knee-deep in mud. Ice crystals formed over the mud and up the giant's body. It screamed in rage as it thrashed about, but it could not break the ice trapping its legs.

"All right," Suzuki shouted, "Death by decapitation!"

Suzuki knelt down and clasped his hands together for Stew, who ran toward him, stepping into Suzuki's foothold.

Stew soared through the air, two short swords in hand, and collided with the giant's chest, driving his swords into the giant's pale, discolored flesh. The giant fumbled about, trying to break free. Suzuki's HUD flashed one hundred percent as he flanked the creature, slashed at the back of its partially exposed kneecaps as Sandy hit the giant's chest, sending fire and ice flying everywhere.

And with that, the giant fell, shaking the ground as it crashed.

Stew pulled his broad sword from his back and

approached the giant. It fell with a heavy thud. The giant lay before them, beheaded.

The Mundanes looked down at the bloody mess they had made.

Stew's face crinkled into a grimace. "That is so gross."

"Better him than us, babe."

"True too. Too true," Suzuki agreed. He raised his shield, and it began glowing. "Healing."

The scars on Stew's chest scabbed over. After a few seconds, the scabs burst and there was pink flesh underneath.

Stew prodded the giant with his sword. "Usually a chest or something shows up after these things are finished, right? And dude, you're going to have to work on your spell casting. You sound lame as shit."

"Sandy didn't sound any better," Suzuki objected.

"True," Sandy agreed. "We both could use some work. Not bad for a first time, though."

"I guess we could check the camp. There might be some cool loot there. Hm...this feels a lot more like looting. Like actually looting."

"We did just murder a bunch of goblins. I think it'd be disrespectful if we didn't loot their corpses."

Stew nodded in agreement. The Mundanes left the giant and made their way back to the goblin camp. Suzuki lowered his helmet and smacked his head. "Sandy?" he asked. "Could you go back and torch that giant? And then the goblins?"

"What for?"

"The whole reason we're here is to deal with that black fly problem. If we're just leaving more dead creatures in the swamp, we're just gonna get more flies. Stew and I will stack the bodies."

"What," Stew objected. "Why do we have to touch those—"

"We do the dirty work. I guess Manny wasn't joking about that."

Stew sighed laboriously as Sandy floated off, her hands flaming brightly. Suzuki walked up to a goblin. The smell of decay was already setting in. Suzuki leaned over, held his breath, and hoisted the goblin's limp body over his shoulder. He walked it over to another one of the goblins and tossed it on top of its fallen comrade.

Stew sighed loudly again, and Suzuki snapped at him, "Come on, Stew. This is what we're getting paid for."

Both Stew and Suzuki collected the rest of the goblin bodies and piled them onto each other in a large pile. By the time Sandy came back, they had erected a monument to their victory. Sandy didn't look twice at the gruesome display before she set it on fire.

"I took care of the deer carcass too. Now let's go find some loot."

The Mundanes went to the goblins' tents. They went through everything that they could find. The process made Suzuki feel sleazy. This felt less like getting a reward and more like spitting on the graves of the goblins they just killed. Suzuki could still see the goblin's flashing teeth and sneering smiles as he had sunk his sword into them.

None of these were comforting thoughts.

"Hey, guys," Stew shouted. "I found something!"

Suzuki and Sandy went over to Stew, who was standing in one of the large tents. There were a few chests and a rack of weapons. Stew broke the locks on the chests and then kicked them open.

As Sandy and Suzuki dug through the chests, Stew wandered off to look at the weapons rack.

One of the chests was filled with a bag of copper pieces and trinkets. A silver cup. A couple of pieces of dining ware.

Suzuki picked up the cup. "Seriously? This is the first haul?"

"Maybe for you." Stew sauntered over to the other Mundanes. He was holding a large battle-ax. The ax had a gold hilt, and there was an inscription in elvish that wrapped up the handle, starting at the hilt, and then splitting to cover both blades. "My HUD says that it's magical. It'll boost my elemental damage."

Sandy flicked her fingers at Stew, sending a handful of sparks his way. The sparks practically bounced off of him. Only one connected. The tiny spark set a few strands of Stew's chest hair on fire.

Stew fanned the small fire and slapped it until it went out. "Cut it out," Stew shouted. "Not funny."

Suzuki couldn't keep himself from laughing as he turned back to the chests. He found a small, wooden box in the chest furthest from him. A small SD card was in the box. Suzuki's HUD displayed some notes on the card while he looked it over.

"SD crystal used for upgrades," the HUD read. "Grants Stone Skin perk indefinitely."

"What's that?" Stew asked.

"An upgrade slot. Says it grants Stone Skin."

"Dude, that should totally go to me. I am *in fact* the tank. We don't want me bleeding out during a battle."

"God, Stew you can't get all of the cool shit. Besides, Sandy could use this. Her armor is a little...light."

Sandy looked down at her robes. Most of them were singed from the fire spells she had been casting. She waved her robes as if she were a ghost. "Stew," she moaned. "If I die, I'll haunt you for all of eternity. And not in a sexy way."

"Fine, fine. She can have it. I don't ever want to be haunted by her."

Sandy snatched up the card. "Thanks, babe."

"Guess it's time to head back."

"More camping?" Stew asked.

"More camping."

Milos sat in the Red Lion, drinking ale at the bar. Wendy was leaning against the bar, counting copper pieces as she sipped a drink.

The rest of the Red Lion was empty, which went a long way to diminishing the dramatic entrance the Mundanes were going for when they stepped in.

Covered in mud and filth, wearing looks of exhaustion, they stumbled over to a table. Without a word, Sandy folded her arms on the table and rested her head, snoring almost instantly.

Stew leaned back, not saying a word.

Suzuki raised his hand in Wendy's direction. "Three of your strongest, largest alcohols, please," Suzuki called.

"You got any money?" Wendy called back, seemingly oblivious to their desperate state.

"I got enough for a month's stay and to get shitfaced every night, so please, three of your strongest, largest alcohols!"

Wendy poured three ales and put them in front of Milos. "Tell them these are on the house. Give them my congratulations. They're MERCs now."

Milos scooped the drinks up and brought them to the Mundanes' table with the care and efficiency of a seasoned barmaid. He put the drinks down and took a seat next to Sandy.

Suzuki took the mead and glared at Milos. "You guys really talked up the whole loot thing," Suzuki started. "We hardly got anything."

Milos looked at Sandy and poked her. When she didn't move, he took her mead and started drinking. "You think that you're going to lift something amazing off of killing black flies, you're crazy."

"There were goblins."

"And a giant," Stew added.

Milos looked at them, his eyes narrowing in thought before his usual jovial smile returned. "All this loot from rancid goblins? I'd say you did well for yourselves. With goblins, you're lucky if you find anything that isn't stained with shit. So I'm assuming from your ballsy ordering, that you finished up the task."

"Swamp is fly free."

"Why'd it take you so long to get back?"

Stew leaned forward and grabbed the dwarf by the beard. "Because we've been chasing down every fucking fly in that swamp," he growled. "So if you want to talk shit, you should go somewhere else."

Milos snatched his beard out of Stew's grasp and chuckled. "If you didn't know, grabbing a dwarf's beard means you're either instigating a duel or trying to fuck." Milos laughed. "Which one is it for you, sweetie?"

"Not now, Milos," Suzuki said. "We're kind of exhausted."

Milos tossed a pouch of coins on the table.

"Full pay for full work. Also a little bonus. Some settlers out there told us you cleaned up those goblins. Figures that deserves a little extra."

Suzuki took the pouch and opened it. Piles of silver stared back at him.

"Thanks." Suzuki scooped up the coins. "Glad to see you guys take notice of good work."

"Wouldn't have anyone on board if we didn't. Now, I'm going to get in touch with Wendy about throwing you guys a right decent party tonight."

"No, no. I'm so—"

"MERC tradition. You can only leave the bar if you're going to go freshen up. Which, no offense, you all very badly need to do."

Milos got up and practically skipped to the bar. Stew groaned loudly as he leaned back in his chair and sipped his ale. "Guess we gotta bring the fire tonight too."

Suzuki laughed as he got started on his ale. "I could get used to this," he cheered.

As Suzuki drank, he looked at Wendy and Milos. There were two icons hanging over both of their heads. Suzuki hit his HUD to click on the icon hanging over Milos. The icon read, "Relationship changed from use them carelessly to use them wisely." Suzuki then clicked on Wendy's. Hers read, "Increased from Disdain to Friendly." There was also a small notification at the bottom of the HUD which read, "Local knowledge increase from 0 to 5."

"Huh," Suzuki wondered aloud. "Info about relationships, but I haven't seen one stat for any of our armor or experience."

Suzuki felt Fred uncurling around his mind. By now, he'd figured out that meant the imp had something to say. Suzuki prepared himself for whatever snide remark was going to slither out of Fred's fanged mouth.

Your HUD is only doing a little bit of work, Fred hissed, his voice low and almost enticing. *It's picking up on their body language, and that is all. It's a tool to help you navigate the different communication style of different races. That way you don't look like more of a jackass than necessary.*

How come there's nothing about my stats?

Because this is real life and not a game. You cannot quantify your skill or aptitude at a certain task. As Sandy realized earlier, if you lack knowledge, you don't need a computer screen to tell you. Any talent you may have will be based on your actual talent. You don't need a status effect notification if you wake up hungover and aren't able to lift your sword without vomiting. Which, may I add, I think you should try to avoid this evening. The Red Lion is unsurprisingly poorly stocked on Weetabix.

Weetabix? How do you know about that? Doesn't look like there's a Costco anywhere around here.

Fred didn't answer. A heavy silence hung over the table as Stew silently sipped at his ale and Fred refrained from speaking. This was a different quiet than Fred usually doled out.

This time it seemed like something might be wrong.

Your previous host? Suzuki ventured.

Fred sighed. It sounded like a balloon being forced to vacate all of its helium. *That is none of your business. But you are right to assume that I am troubled. The goblins had a giant within their employment.*

Yeah, what's the big deal?

Goblins and giants hate each other. Giants are notorious for not looking where they are stepping, and goblins are notorious for being squashed under their feet like cockroaches.

Why do you think they're working together?

You must excuse me, but I am feeling a little tired. All of that combat...I believe that it's worn me down. Goodnight.

Suzuki felt Fred shut himself away. That was the end of the conversation. That last bit of information was more than

Suzuki had been ready for. He hadn't really thought much about the racial politics between those who were serving the Dark One.

Now that Fred had mentioned it, giants and goblins working together was a very odd thing. It seemed like a sign, but Suzuki did not know of what. He wondered if maybe there was something that either Sandy or Stew's familiar could tell him about goblin and giant relations.

Milos slammed another round of meads on the table and broke Suzuki's concentration.

"The celebration starts now," Milos growled as he climbed onto his chair to tower over Suzuki. "The rest of the MERCs are coming, and they're coming to party. Try to keep up."

Suzuki shrugged. He wasn't in the mood for a huge party, but it didn't seem it mattered. He'd worry about the giant and goblin problem later. Now was the time to celebrate. Even if he would rather have slept for a week straight.

18

The festivities began after nightfall.

Dwarven MERCs were the first to enter the Red Lion. Many of their ales were ready for them before they opened the door. They looked as if they had all just returned from their own quests. Most of them were covered in blood of some color. Their armor was dented and dirty. They took their drinks and retired to the far end of the bar, their small dark eyes watching the Mundanes from afar.

Next to arrive were the halflings. There were fewer of them than the dwarves, but they held themselves proudly. They took their meads and went to their seats. A few mixed in with the dwarves. Most of the halflings sat closer to the Mundanes.

Third to arrive were the elves. Their force was nearly the same as the company of dwarves. The elves took their time ordering their drinks. As the halflings had, some of them mixed with the other races and the rest of them secured seats by themselves.

Last were the humans. They arrived at the bar with a

herald of noise and cheers coming from themselves. In a flurry of song and yells, they were milling about the bar yet still keeping mostly to themselves.

As the crowd grew, slowly the human, dwarf, elf, and halfling parties intermixed. The bar was two-deep, and the tables were filled. The barmaids were already starting to make their rounds. Many of the MERCs were still watching the Mundanes.

Suzuki cleared his throat as he shifted in his seat. He didn't know whose eyes to meet, and looking down at the table seemed like the obvious wrong thing to do. Instead, he cleared his throat and put his sword on the table. He wasn't sure what that meant, but he figured it must mean something.

Across from him, Stew was also fidgeting in his seat.

"What are they all looking at?" Stew asked. "And why is your sword on the table?"

"I don't know," Suzuki answered. He started to remove the sword and then stopped. "Milos, what are they staring at?"

"You two lads," Milos said. "Word's gotten out about your little quest."

"Why would word have gotten out? You just said it was a little quest."

Milos shrugged his shoulders and leaned back in his chair. "I might have neglected to mention some important details of safety and concern, but you all figured things out well enough, so I don't see the point of getting—"

"Did you know there was a giant?"

"What do people really know, you know?"

"God damn it, Milos!"

Milos raised his tankard and smiled widely as if he could power through the uncomfortable situation by sheer goodwill. "I didn't *know* the giant would be there, lads," Milos stammered. "There were rumors, but rumors are usually just that: rumors. And to be frank, I wouldn't have thought that any newbs would be able to take down a giant. I never would have sent you if I had known. But here you are, alive. There, the giant is dead. So it all worked out in the end."

"You could have gotten us killed," Sandy mumbled as she sat up. She appeared halfway in and out of a dream. Her eyes were distant and glassy.

"No," Milos disagreed. He drained the last of his mead and slammed it on the table, causing everyone to jump. "You would have gotten yourselves killed. Every job that a MERC takes involves risk of death. It's no one's fault but your own if you get yourself killed. Keep that in mind. We'll mourn you all the same. A stupid MERC is still a MERC as far as we're concerned. And only stupid MERCs die stupid deaths. Got it?"

The silence of the Mundanes was close enough to an agreement. Milos surveyed the table. There was a noticeable change in tone. The Mundanes didn't seem to care that they were being honored.

Suzuki would have rather been sleeping than drinking his second mead. Their quest had taken a lot out of him. Taking on a small horde of goblins and a giant had not been as draining as he would have assumed but, that being said, he still wanted to sleep for the next ten to twelve hours.

"Ah, come on," Milos shouted. "Let's get a little party in you guys. You deserve it. Hey, Diana, get over here!"

A MERC from a table not far away turned her head at the sound of her name. She wore a turban, and her armor was loose and vaguely Arabic. A scimitar hung from her side, and her face was veiled with black silk.

"What the fuck you want, half-man?" Diana asked.

"We need a little pick me up."

Diana stood and wafted over to the table. She moved as if she were somewhat separate from their reality. Her feet didn't seem to touch the ground, and as she turned the corner to come sit at their table, her body shifted out of focus and she was gone. Within less than a second, she was sitting across from Suzuki.

"Hey, how are you doing that?" Suzuki asked.

Diana raised her hand and ran it over her face. The black veil shimmered and then lengthened with the motion of her hand. "Illusion magic is my specialty. Some people like to swing a sword. I prefer to play to my own sensibilities."

"Can you teach me?" Sandy's eyes suddenly were alive with excitement. Any trace of tiredness had been obliterated by curiosity. "I tried to cast an invisibility spell while we out in the field but couldn't. My familiar said—"

"You weren't well-versed enough in the theory of color or light? Some bullshit like that, aye?"

"Yeah. I mean, aye."

Diana leaned back and kicked her boots up on the table, knocking over one of the drinks. She motioned for the barmaid. "First things first. Pick me ups for the victorious adventurers." Diana reached into a pouch hanging from her side. She pulled out five long, green peppers which ended with a small blossom on their ends. A pepper was tossed to everyone at the table. "All right. We all take a bite. Count of three."

Stew prodded his pepper with his finger, eyeing it suspiciously. "What exactly is this?"

"Don't worry, it's nothing illegal. Just a little something I picked up while I was doing research. It has healing properties, specifically involving sleep and energy. Kind of like a

Blood Rage spell, minus the part where you want to kill everything. Hopefully. One. Two. Three."

They all bit into their peppers. Suzuki's entire face went numb for a second before flushing with intense heat. His mouth felt on fire. Then he saw actual smoke pouring out, and he realized it didn't just feel as if he were on fire. His mouth actually was.

He grabbed his drink and started guzzling. As the mead soothed Suzuki's mouth, he felt his muscles relax—and euphoria hit him like a tidal wave. Then his tongue started tingling. The tingle traveled down the back of his throat and to his stomach.

He burped and expelled a little smoke. Any residual sleepiness was gone.

"That usually helps with late-night stakeouts or watches." As Diana spoke, bits of her pepper inelegantly fell out of her mouth. "Plus, it doubles as a delectable garnish. Now, what were you asking me?" She pointed at Sandy with the stem of a pepper.

"How did you learn to do illusions?" Sandy queried.

"Research. And more research. You're a mage, right?"

"Yeah."

"And you've been having fun throwing fireballs and making little snowstorms."

Sandy's smile faded, and she looked crushed. She had the look of a child who's answered a teacher's question incorrectly. Suzuki didn't think that Sandy had anything to be embarrassed about. Those fireballs had pulled the Mundanes' asses out of the fire on multiple occasions.

"Sandy's been holding up just fine," Suzuki chimed in.

"Yeah." Stew put a hand on Sandy's shoulder. "She's been killing it out there."

"I don't doubt that. Mages have the easiest time their

first few quests. Everyone else has to run around, swinging swords and tiring themselves out. Even with the improved stamina and strength, we're all still only human. Except for the non-humans, obviously. But mages? They just swoop around and start dropping fireballs and earthquakes. They don't last forever, though."

Diana hit her HUD and a book materialized in her hand. She tossed the book in front of Sandy. "It's an introductory primer for magic. It's pretty basic, but you'll find everything you need in it to get started. This, however, is only the beginning. I suggest hitting the books too. Your friends will get better with real-world experience. You, on the other hand, are going to have to do a lot of reading to diversify your spells. You might want to start using the Red Lion's library too while you're here."

Diana popped her pepper stem before standing. She spat a small fireball out on the table and put it out with a snap of her fingers. "Pay attention to the section on Magical Dependency."

Standing, she pulled down the veil to cover her face and the skin on the sides of her neck cracked as a bright blue light emanated out of the cracks as if her body were made entirely of pure energy. She winked at Sandy. "If you're planning on being here for a while, you might as well know what you're getting yourself into," she said as she walked off.

Sandy was awestruck, her mouth wide open before she remembered the book in her hands. Seeing the tome and realizing that this book was the beginning of her journey to be like Diana, Sandy tucked into it, a devilish smile painting her face.

"Milos." Suzuki turned to the dwarf. "Who was that?"

"Diana," Milos answered, his drunken gaze obviously admiring Diana's ass as she walked away.

Suzuki snapped his finger twice. "Focus, dwarf. I know her name. That's not what I'm asking. I'm asking, 'Who is she?' What's her story?"

Milos lifted his hand in defeat. "Her story? Well, Diana, there is a living legend. She was responsible for ending the Siege of Tulmarth single-handedly. She's probably the second-best MERC to have ever lived."

"And who's the first?" Suzuki asked.

"José. He's part of her party and the oldest known MERC. José was one of the first humans to come to Middang3ard, and it is legend that he's so old his HUD only displays in ancient Aramaic."

Stew laughed, downing his drink and reaching for Sandy's. "Aramaic? Who is this guy? Jesus?"

"He just might be," Milos said with an air of deadly seriousness. "We don't really know, but the man is nearly invincible. No one knows much about him except that some elder Chipmaster installed something weird in his HUD the day before he died...for the first time."

"Did you say, 'Died for the first time?' As in he's died more than once?" Suzuki asked. "I thought death here is real death, right?"

Milos nodded. "For most of us. But for José, it's different. The legend is that he went on some quest, where his party gets in heavy with a cave troll. The troll clear rips his face off and slams him against a rock. After his party finally puts the troll down, most of them are half-dead mind you, they walk up to José, you know, getting ready to bury him and everything. They all saw how hard of a hit he took. So they finally get to him, and he's still breathing. Faceless, but still breathing. So they bring him back to the Red Lion. None of the mages can fix him up. They say the damage is too permanent. So he spends the night holed up in his room, probably trying to figure out how he's gonna live a life without a face.

"When his party sees him the next day, first thing in the morning, they all lose their shit. José's staring at them with a brand new face. Like nothing ever happened. And that was just the first time. I've been out with José. He should be dead. But here he is, every night with the rest of us."

"Cool story," Suzuki said skeptically.

Milos leaned in close. "You're right to have your doubts, human, but make no mistake. José and Diana are fucking powerful MERCs and the last muthafuckers you want to piss off."

"Fine, fine." Suzuki took a sip as he gathered his thoughts. "I get it. I get it." Suzuki narrowed his eyes and in his drunken haze remembered another piece of Milos' story. "Say, Milos, what's a 'Chipmaster'?"

Milos burst into laughter. "Boy, they fucking told you lot nothing when they signed you up! A Chipmaster is something that hooks up your SD chips. I wouldn't recommend doing it yourself. Usually the damn thing shorts out and fries your brain. It's better to pay for quality work."

"And where can I find one?"

Milos' eyebrow rose. "Got an SD chip or something?"

"Sandy does, but I got this dongle." Suzuki fished out the little piece of electronics that Beth had sent him. "I'm not sure what it does, though."

"A dongle." Milos looked it over, appreciatively. "Did you find this with the goblins."

Suzuki shook his head. "A friend sent it to me."

"That must be some friend. These things aren't cheap. These things are rare. And very fucking expensive." Milos scanned the bar. "One of the members of José and Diana's party is a Chipmaster. I can introduce you two."

Across the table, Stew yawned loudly as Sandy continued to read her book. "I'm going to go grab some more drinks."

Sandy nodded absentmindedly, completely absorbed in her reading.

Suzuki and Milos were talking and neither heard Stew, who sighed and walked off to the bar, raising his hand to catch Wendy's attention. "Could I get another round?"

"Yeah, yeah," Wendy shouted over the roar of the bar.

One of the barmaids took a seat next to Stew. Her uniform was cut lower than the rest of the servers, allowing her breasts to bulge out of her blouse. Her lips were bright red, and her makeup brought out her strong cheekbones. She smiled at Stew and placed her hand on his.

Stew jerked away and yelped before realizing what was happening. "Uh...hi...," Stew stuttered. "Can I help you?"

"The real question is, 'Can I help *you*?'" the barmaid asked. "You're Stew, right? The Mundane barbarian."

"Yeah, that's me."

The barmaid leaned closer and whispered in Stew's ear. Her voice was low and breathy. "I have a room upstairs. I'm very discreet." She rubbed her index and middle finger against her thumb. "And reasonable."

"Oh," Stew gasped as he grabbed his round of drinks, his voice cracking loudly. "Oh, I'm okay. I'm with my girlfriend. I'm actually grabbing her drink. Thank you, though. I mean, no, thank you. But thank you for the offer. Uh...yeah...I gotta go."

Stew rushed off with his meads and set them on the Mundanes table, before sitting down and burying his face in his mead.

"Everything okay, Stew?" Sandy asked without taking her eyes off her book.

Stew looked up, a Got Beer? mustache on his upper lip. "Yep, babe, everything is super awesome and totally cool."

The barmaid who had spoken to Stew pulled a chair from another table and sat it down next to Sandy. As soon as he saw her, Stew yelped. Loudly.

"Do you mind if I join you guys?" the barmaid asked Sandy. "I don't really like being on my feet during my breaks."

Sandy shrugged as she turned the page. "Not at all."

"I'd prefer to spend it on my back."

Sandy looked up from her book for the first time and at the barmaid. "Uh...you should probably lay down then."

The barmaid leaned over the table and met Sandy's eyes. "We could both take a lay down for a bit."

"That's very flattering, but I'm here with my boyfriend. That one." She pointed at Stew. "You know, the guy who's making that weird face."

"I know. We've met."

Sandy slammed her hand on the table. "God damn it, Stew, what did I tell you about asking for threesomes!"

"I didn't say anything," Stew objected, raising his hands in his own defense.

Milos chugged the last of his drink and stood up. He kicked Suzuki in the shins and motioned for Suzuki to follow him. "Come on. I feel like this is the kind of drunken conversation we can bow out of. Let's go try and get your HUD upgraded."

Suzuki followed Milos, who dropped a couple of copper pieces in Sandy's lap and winked, and they left the barmaid with Stew and Sandy, who were both fumbling over their words as the barmaid laughed good-naturedly.

Milos led Suzuki through the maze of moving, loudly cheering MERCs to a backroom of the Red Lion. It was dark, lit only by a few candles.

The room was mostly empty. The few chairs were filled with MERCs who were smoking, drinking, and laughing.

One of the MERCs blew a huge cloud of smoke that shifted its shape until it looked like a flower. The MERC pursed her lips and whistled, causing the petals of the flower to fall off, one-by-one.

Next to a table was a recliner which looked like a dentist's chair. A man sat in the chair as a woman seated next to him was soldering something in his head.

When she moved, Suzuki could see that the HUD which the MERC was wearing had been dismantled, even though it was still connected to his head.

His eyes were closed, and he appeared to be in some pain. The woman sitting in the chair reached over to a box of tools sitting on the table beside her.

She took out a pair of tweezers. "Almost done." Then she started soldering again, this time sending sparks flying up from the MERC's HUD.

The backroom reminded Suzuki of a seedy tattoo parlor.

Milos took a seat near the reclining chair and Suzuki sat next to him. "That's the Chipmaster."

Under the light, Suzuki could get a better look at the Chipmaster. She wore a thick smithy apron over a short-sleeved blouse that showed off arms covered in tattoos that weren't the sort popular with the MERCs. There was nothing elvish. No arcane symbols. Just images of 1980s TV cartoons—*Tom and Jerry, Donald Duck...the Tasmanian Devil.*

"Whattaya want?" the Chipmaster asked without looking up.

"Kid's got a dongle," Milos answered.

"A dongle?"

"Aye."

"Military?"

"You know of any other."

"Let me finish this one up, boyo, and I'll take a look."

The Chipmaster soldered the MERC's HUD. The MERC groaned in pain a few times, but both he and the Chipmaster laughed it off as they talked, occasionally taking a break for the MERC to wince and sigh dramatically.

After a couple of minutes, Chipmaster put down her tools and closed up the MERC's HUD. She motioned for Suzuki to take a seat once the other MERC had moved. She held out her hand for the dongle, and Suzuki passed it to her.

"Hmm..." Chipmaster mused. "Definitely military. Where'd you catch an admirable piece of this sort?"

"A friend sent it to me," Suzuki answered.

"Aye, military indeed. Impressive. Not the sort of tech we see floating around these sorts of parts. What does it do?"

Suzuki shrugged. "All she said was that it might save my life one day."

The Chipmaster pursed her lips before shaking her head. "That's the trouble with these dongles. We don't know what they do. Could be amazing. Could be horrible, too. Tell you what. Fancy a trade?"

"A trade?"

The Chipmaster pulled open one of the drawers in her toolbox and pulled out an SD card. "This is premium stuff. It will open up a brand new pair of peepers in ye skull. Lifetime guarantee too. Pop 'em in, everything changes. Sure, there's a teensy bit of pain. But what's an evening of migraines for a lifetime of perks? I'll set you up very legit wise too, seeing how it'd be ye first time. A dongle don't feel too pretty, and we're all under this great roof to give you and your pals a little of the ol' show and spectacle, ya know?"

"No, thanks. I want the dongle."

"Even though it's a gamble? For all we know, this is the dongle of Dicklessness, then you lose yer dick...as in forever. Get it?"

"So whatever this does is permanent," Suzuki mused. "But it came from a trusted friend and she told me it would save my life, so, yeah, I get it. Put it in."

The Chipmaster pointed her soldering gun at him. "A gambler. I like you. Let me set ye all up, and we'll take your skull for a spin. Little bit of pain, the process. Slightly little trip. Mighty eye-opening though. Some of the folk can't get enough of that part, but to each their own. Not for me. Some of the dark brain dreams should be reserved for the eves when they can be held accountable, don't ye think?"

"Yeah, sure."

Suzuki sat in the recliner, pushing away his doubt. He wasn't in Middang3ard to play it safe, and Beth had told him that it was important to get this dongle installed. Besides, Suzuki had always wanted a tattoo. This seemed infinitely cooler.

"Let's do it," Suzuki said.

Chipmaster clapped her hands together and pulled up her goggles. "Thank the gods," she exclaimed. "Ain't had something this robust and shiny in a considerable amount of time. José's the only one who ever brings back anything with this amount of sheen to it. Heyo, José, come and check in on this dongle I got betwixt me nimble fingers."

Chipmaster strapped Suzuki's head to the chair and started whistling as she fired up the soldering iron.

"You're gonna feel a bit of a pinch," Chipmaster

explained. "And then your brain is going to go all sizzly and you might see God or something, but you'll live through the whole thing, on me father's sordid life, I promise ye. Gotcha?"

"Gotcha."

Chipmaster flipped Suzuki's HUD open. He couldn't see what she was doing, but he could feel the heat from the soldering iron. Other MERCs were crowding the chair now, some of them clanking tankards together.

Suzuki tried not to wince in any noticeable way. That thought faded from his mind the moment that his brain went "sizzly." Everything in the room got fuzzy and muddled together as if he were looking through an unfocused telescope. The eyes of the surrounding MERCs began to glow. Then they ejected themselves from the MERCs sockets and floated up into the air.

He followed them with his eyes, which he now could see were floating out of his head as well. The eyes went up, out of the ceiling, and into the sky, past the ozone layer, out to the stars. They floated and grew larger, and stars and planets zoomed around them.

Suzuki could see that one of the planets was Earth. His eyes bobbed closer to Earth, smashed straight through it, and came out the other side. The moon was revolving around Earth and Earth was revolving around a similarly-shaped planet. The planet was followed by another planet of the same shape and size. There were at least seven earths floating around one large, pale planet. When Suzuki strained his eyes, he could see billions of eyeballs walking around on the pale planet. One of them looked straight up and stared at Suzuki in his detached eyeballs.

Then, as suddenly as it had begun, Suzuki was back in

his chair. Chipmaster blew on her soldering iron and closed up Suzuki's HUD.

"What the fuck was that?"

"Oh, the visions. You see, your electric boogaloo dance-with-the-stars moment was brought to you by the HUD that's been pretty close to stapled into your skull. HUDs perceive reality. I just splintered yours a little for a fraction of a bit. Let you see all the reality out there that our little brains don't want to deal with. See it enough, and it'll drive ya beyond mad. But for a tickle of a minute while I torch ye ol' HUD won't do no damage. Now let's see what we got here. Up and at 'em, young squire."

Suzuki assumed that Chipmaster wanted him out of the seat. His legs were wobbly and it was difficult to stand, but he made it up. He used the chair for support until one of the MERCs reached out and gave him a hand. The MERC was tall and extremely lanky. He had greasy hair that hung over his face and a beard that made one question if he indeed did have a face.

"Get 'im up and straight, José," Chipmaster chirped.

"Thanks," Suzuki murmured as he got his bearings.

"Now what you got?"

"What?"

Chipmaster tapped her HUD. Suzuki nodded in understanding and clicked his own HUD. As soon as he touched it, a bright green message flashed.

"Scent Modification," the message read.

Suzuki clicked the message. A variety of racial scents appeared on his HUD. Suzuki chose French.

"Scent Modification," Suzuki said. "Could have used that today."

"Aye, sounds dull as an elvish orgy," the Chipmaster said as she put her equipment away.

José tapped Suzuki's HUD with enough force to nearly knock Suzuki over. *All that from just one finger*, Suzuki thought. *How strong is this guy?*

"That's because you lack imagination." José voice was calm, even, —reassuring. "Most everything hunts using their noses. You just upgraded this kid to a warrior with an exceptional edge over most assassins. Don't waste it, kid."

Suzuki choked back his words. He didn't know why, but he was overcome with a sense of awe. He felt he was meeting a childhood hero. Something about José just exuded greatness. Suzuki held back the urge to ask for an autograph as José walked off to party with the other MERCs.

"Ahem," Chipmaster said. "Now that'll be the flavor of my choosing."

"Flavor?"

"Tall, dark, and holy is all I need, ya know." She chuckled as she absently twirled her hair around a finger. Then she seemed to come to her senses because she looked up at Suzuki and pointed at his HUD. "Make good use of that there dongle. Now get out of here and go enjoy yourself."

Suzuki and Milos left the back room to the sound of MERCs chanting a drinking song and shattering glass. Their table was empty. As Suzuki took a seat, he turned to the dwarf. "Milos, can I ask you a question?"

"You just did."

"You know what I mean."

"Human, just speak. This preamble serves no purpose -- you're a MERC now. That makes you family. And we MERCs ask, say, command, fight, fuck...like any good family."

Suzuki nodded. "OK, do MERCs ever join the army?"

At that, Milos spit out his drink. "Why would you? All the drills, the early morning, the utter lack of loot?"

Suzuki shrugged. "Higher purpose?"

Milos leaned in close, scanning Suzuki's eyes. "There are only two reasons why someone would choose army over MERC life: because he's delusional or in love, and those two things are basically one and the same if you ask me. So which one are you?"

Suzuki didn't answer.

"So, love it is. Who is she?"

"No one."

"Bah, humbug." Milos took another sip of his mead. "We all know she's not "no one." And let me guess, she joined the army and you, a reject, wound up here, right? Now you want to join up and fight the good fight by her side."

Suzuki pursed his lips. He thought about trying to wiggle his way out of this conversation. Some lie or excuse. Instead, he opted for honesty. "Something like that," he said.

Milos slammed his hand on the table. "That's my boy! Want to join the army? Then finish some big mission that's a thorn in their ass and impress 'em. That will get you a one-way ticket into that hell."

"So it's possible?" There was a ding in his HUD. He just received a message.

"It is possible," Milos said with a nod.

Another ding. He checked his HUD. It was a message. From Beth.

"Hey, Milos, I gotta take this. Thanks for everything. Really. I'll catch you around."

Milos winked as he took a long draught from his tankard. "Ah, let me guess, your delusion beckons." He chuckled as Suzuki rushed off.

Suzuki wasn't even halfway up the stairs before he had opened the message from Beth. The message was short, almost terse. It read, "Hey Suzuki. Just wanted to let you know I'm still alive. Troll duty has gotten out of hand. We're also seeing a lot of red orcs. They've been attacking nearby villages. It's getting pretty rough. Anyways, just wanted to remind you about the present I sent you. Tell those douche nozzles that I asked what's up. Miss you lots. Love, Beth."

Love, Beth.

Suzuki read the sentence over three times before he finally closed the message. He stumbled to his room in a daze, hardly taking notice of anything. Love, Beth. He mouthed the words to himself, fully aware of how ridiculous he looked as he fumbled the door handle to get into the Mundanes' room.

Opening the door, he read the message one last time.

Love, Beth.

Still wasn't getting old.

Suzuki clicked 'Reply,' but again the option was denied. Suzuki was trying to figure out a workaround or hack when he heard a discrete cough.

Looking up from his HUD for the first time since entering the room, he saw Stew laying on the bed, Sandy straddling him.

"Jesus fucking Christ," Suzuki shouted as he covered his eyes. "You guys can lock the door, you know."

"Come here." Sandy gestured for Suzuki to come closer. "Look, he's sleeping."

"Okay, I'm just gonna say, right now, I am so not down being a part of your weird, kinky sex games."

"No, dude, seriously. Come here."

Suzuki cautiously approached the bed. Stew was snoring loudly. Sandy handed Suzuki an inkwell. She was holding a quill pen in her hand. She already had covered Stew's forehead with drawings of a variety of penises.

"How old are you?" Suzuki asked.

"Always a child at heart. Now gimme a hand."

Sandy and Suzuki worked on what Sandy referred to as her magnum opus.

There was a knock on the door. "Come in," Suzuki shouted.

Milos swung the door open and barged into the room. He came to a complete freeze when he saw Sandy on top of Stew and Suzuki kneeling over Stew's face.

Milos hiked up his pants and sauntered farther into the room. "Oh, I see this is where the real party is." Milos grinned.

Sandy shrugged and leaned over so that Milos could see Stew's recently-decorated face. "Wanna lend a hand?"

"Not my cup of tea." Milos was noticeably disappointed. "You all have a good time. I just came by to tell you we're leaving early tomorrow."

"Early? For what?" Suzuki asked.

"How long did you think you were going to rest between contracts? This time I'm coming with you. I'll help show you how it's done. Stew's got the right idea. You might want to get some sleep."

Milos slammed the door as he left. The sound woke Stew, who sat bolt upright, nearly knocking Sandy over. They peered into each other's eyes.

"Babe," Stew mumbled. "Babe, what's going on."

Stew sleepily looked at Suzuki, who managed to pull off an encouraging smile without laughing.

"Suzuki," Stew said. "What are you doing at breakfast?"

Suzuki gently pushed Stew's head back onto the pillow. "Just getting the sausages, buddy. That's all."

Stew rolled over and buried his head in his pillow. "All right. Just make sure I get extra. I'm really hungry, mom."

Stew was snoring in a couple of seconds.

Suzuki got up. "We should let him sleep."

"But he said he wanted extras."

"You know what? He did say he wanted extras."

19

"At least it wasn't breakfast in bed."

Stew had managed to scrub most of the dick drawings off, but a few stubborn penises still stained his skin.

Once Stew had resolved himself that he'd spend the day with dicks on his face, he, Sandy, and Suzuki went down to the bar.

There were three plates of eggs and sausage alongside fresh coffee. The plates were drizzled with grease, and there was a bowl of congealed fat from some blubbery creature.

Milos waltzed up to the Mundanes, whistling. He sat at the bowl of fat, picked it up, and started slurping. He wiped the fat off of his beard. "Compliments to the chef." He belched. "Ready to head out?"

Suzuki crammed a handful of sausages into his mouth and washed them down with coffee. "What exactly are we doing?" he asked, careful not to let any food slip out of his mouth.

Wendy set another cup of fat down in front of Milos, who hungrily swallowed it down. "Basic kidnapping," he explained. "Nothing too exciting. Not by MERC standards at least. But it'll be fun enough for me to come along for. Plus, it pays well."

Sandy ate while reading. She turned a page with her fork. Without looking up, she asked, "Any specific details we should know about? You were more than a little vague last time."

"Specifics? Sure. A krampus kidnapped a group of elvish children. We got to get 'em back before they get eaten."

"*A* krampus? I thought there was only one Krampus," Suzuki interjected.

"It's a story most cultures have. But like most of the stories that humans have, it's meant to point you toward the truth. Krampuses are truly demons. They're kind of like a pest throughout the realms. I think Earth is the only one lucky enough to have them centralized in one location. The realms are lousy with them."

"So it's just a run-of-the-mill demon? What about all of the Christmas stuff?"

"Oh, still applies. I don't know where they picked it up, but they love Christmas. You'll probably get a kick out of the damn thing's den. Usually good for a laugh or two."

Milos pulled out a pocket watch, checked the time, and slipped it back into his pocket. "All right, kids. Time to go. Wendy, will you do us the honor?"

Wendy nodded and came out from behind the bar. She went to the side door. A large lever and a bulletin board covered with various scribbles and charts were beside the door. Wendy knocked on the door twice. There was no answer.

"The krampus kidnapping, right?" Wendy asked as she reviewed the bulletin board.

"Yes, ma'am," Milos answered.

"Got it. Just ring me if you find another junction, all right?"

"Will do."

Wendy flung the lever and the door swung open. Suzuki approached the door after Milos. There wasn't another room beyond the door. Instead, Suzuki could see into a dimly-lit cave. He could hear screams coming from the cave. "A portal?" he asked.

"Wendy takes care of all the organization for this MERC base," Milos said. "She scouts and maps out our mission areas for us, provides coordinates, and gets us there. Not quite as streamlined as having Manny run you out for missions, but that little ball of eyes is a busy Beholder. All right, come on. One at a time."

Milos waved the Mundanes over to the door. Stew scrambled to shovel the last of his eggs into his mouth while Sandy finished her coffee, never taking her eyes off her book.

"Seems a lot more organized than our first mission," Sandy muttered.

And more complicated, Fred chimed in Suzuki's head.

Suzuki stepped up to the door and poked his head through. He instantly felt the draft from the cave. *What do you mean?*

There's more than a single krampus in there. And what's more, I can feel other...creatures.

What are they?

Wouldn't that knowledge kill the fun?

Suzuki sighed internally. It was too early to deal with Fred. The imp was consistently getting on his nerves. Between the condescending remarks and the vague threats of impending doom, Suzuki had realized that his familiar was a constant source of irritation. Suzuki was jealous of

Sandy and Stew. Both of them seemed to be getting along with their familiars way better than he was.

Niv was helping Sandy get a better grasp of magic.

As for GB, Stew never complained. And Stew was a complainer, so if GB was getting on his nerves, they'd all know about it.

Meanwhile, Suzuki had to practically drag out the information about his mage spells (as limited as they were) and the damn imp was a constant source of irritation.

Tell me, human. Fred sneered. *Do you think that you'll be trembling in your boots?*

Maybe. After all, whatever's inside is probably much scarier than you, Suzuki snapped. *You're practically a talking bat with stick arms.*

Duly noted, Fred coolly said. *A talking bat. Quite creative.*

Suzuki tried to pretend that Fred had vanished from his body. There were more important things to worry about than arguing with his familiar, and he didn't want a repeat of their last mission.

Granted, it was the first time that they had been in the field, but the whole thing had been chaotic. Suzuki knew there were areas that he wanted to improve, and even though this was nothing like the VR game, he had mastered that...so he figured that in time he'd get the hang of this, too.

He hated feeling like a newb.

Still, fighting in the real Middang3ard had been easier than he'd thought it would be.

It was the planning in the midst of a battle while his body was flooded with adrenaline and fear that was the hard part.

Milos crossed through the door and into the cave. He grabbed Suzuki and pulled him over the threshold.

Stew and Sandy followed close behind.

The Red Lion was behind them. They had been seamlessly transported into the cave. Suzuki greatly preferred this over the other teleportation methods he'd experienced. At least this method didn't turn his stomach inside out.

The cave was small and cramped with only enough room for them to walk single file. As the Mundanes and the dwarf made their way through its corridors, Suzuki felt like the walls were squeezing in around them.

Milos took the lead because, as a dwarf, he didn't have to bother ducking under hanging stalactites. Unfortunately, the rest of the Mundanes had to occasionally duck or even crawl on their knees to avoid the sharp pieces of rock jutting out of the ceiling.

Finally, the walls of the cave opened up a bit and they could breathe a little easier.

But the sense of relief was short-lived when they discovered they were standing at the edge of a ledge.

Milos walked to the edge and looked over, pressing his finger to his lips as he waved the Mundanes over to him. "Take a look," he whispered.

Beneath the ledge, about twenty feet down, was the krampus den. Christmas lights were strung up from the ceiling, and there was a burning wooden effigy of St. Nick in the corner.

There were also dozens of Christmas trees everywhere that were all decorated with shards of broken glass and the skeletons of small animals.

The bizarreness of the scene was accentuated by the scent of pine and eggnog.

In the middle of the den was a large nativity scene. The animals were all skeletons, as were the wise men, Mary, and Joseph. Scraps of clothes draped the bones, and the manger was filled with rotten fruit.

Across from the manger were a large blackboard and a row of school desks. The elf children were all tied up, each one sitting at a desk, being forced to listen to an old record player that played a crackling version of "Jingle Bells."

The haunting notes partially covered the crying of the elvish children.

"José would get a kick out of this," Milos mumbled.

"José," Suzuki muttered to himself, remembering his brief encounter with the MERC. "That guy was...was unique."

"Jesus, Suzuki." Stew groaned. "You need to stop your fanboying. It's embarrassing."

"Yeah. Right. Sure. Ahh, OK, we need to come up with a plan."

There was a loud, screeching roar coming from the passageway they had just exited.

But because they were on the ledge, Suzuki couldn't see what was making the noise. Still, he drew his sword, ready to fight.

That's when he felt something hit him hard in the stomach, knocking him against the wall's edge.

As his vision went blurry, he felt something large and heavy sit on his stomach. It pried his mouth open and poured in a hot liquid.

Suzuki tried to fight the thing, but it was too heavy...and the hot liquid too delicious.

Immediately Suzuki felt overwhelming exhaustion as his eyes closed under their own weight and he drifted off into the blackness of sleep.

20

W *ake up, human.*
     Suzuki's eyes snapped open, and as soon as he realized where he was, he tried to stand but couldn't.

Whatever had captured them had also bound them.

As his eyes were adjusting to the dark, he tried to make out what shapes were surrounding him.

He was still in the cave. Sandy was leaning against the cave wall, and Milos was slumped over on his side. Both of them were snoring loudly.

But Stew was nowhere to be seen.

I said, wake up, the voice sleepily repeated.

What? Who? Fred? Is that you? Suzuki asked.

There was no answer, but Suzuki could feel the imp curling up in his mind as if he were going to sleep.

Seriously, Fred. Now's not the time to sleep, damn it.

Fred's voice came back weak and distant. *Can't...help it. So very, very tired.*

Whatever, Suzuki thought, angrier than ever at his familiar. When they got out of here...if they got out of here,

Suzuki planned on looking into trading Fred for anything else.

Fred might be of no use, but Sandy wasn't. Suzuki rocked himself back and forth, edging closer until he fell on top of her. She yelped softly. "Be quiet," he whispered.

"Christ, I was having such weird dreams." Sandy teased some pebbles out of her hair. "Sugarplums and shit. Where's Milos?"

"Here," Milos groggily muttered. There was white liquid in his beard.

"What the fuck is in your beard?" Suzuki asked.

"Well, I can't exactly see it now, can I?"

Sandy face contorted. "It looks like cum."

"Cum?" Milos frantically picked at his beard. "Why would there be cum in my beard?" Then, pointing a trembling finger at the mage, added, "And how would you know?"

"Dude, I know what cum looks like. White, thick, sticky. Just like that stuff in your beard."

Milos looked at Suzuki for help, but all the warrior-mage could do was shrug and say, "Whatever is in your beard is all of those things."

"In all the domains what the fuck is—?" but before Milos could finish what Suzuki was sure would be a colorful string of curses, a rumbling was heard ahead in the cave, followed by slow, plodding steps of something large.

Another inhuman roar echoed as one of the krampuses walked into the cave, bending low so it didn't scrape its horns.

The creature was at least ten feet tall. Its body was covered in thick, black fur, all except its face, which looked like a parody of an old human woman, all wrinkled and furrowed, with a long, hooked nose below deep-set, piercing black eyes, and with a slack-jawed mouth filled with jagged, yellow teeth.

The krampus wore a tattered red robe and, cradled in its spindly arms held close to her bosom was Stew, who suckled at the krampus' teat as if he were a babe.

"Guess we know what's on your beard," Sandy offered.

Milos leaned over and started spitting. "Sucking a krampus' tits," he moaned. "If a word of this gets out to anyone, I'll have you all gutted."

The krampus lumbered farther into the cave and gingerly placed Stew on the ground next to the rest of the Mundanes. It grabbed tinsel and Christmas wreaths from a pile of yuletide junk piled in the corner and then tied Stew's hands and feet. The krampus then thoroughly observed each of the party. It was only a few inches from Suzuki's face, breathing heavily, the scent of fresh gingerbread wafting from its mouth.

Suzuki wanted to pull away in disgust, but the smell was oddly satisfying. He breathed deeply, and his head started to swim.

The krampus pulled back its robe and exposed its hairy breast to Suzuki. It pressed its teat to Suzuki's lips, forcing him to suckle.

He tried to resist but couldn't.

Suzuki was starting to get sleepy again and slumped onto his side. Sugarplums danced in his head. Satisfied that Suzuki had had his fill, the krampus moaned loudly, a sound like a train screeching to a stop, before shuffling off, leaving the Mundanes in the dark.

"Dude," Sandy called, rousing Suzuki. "I think you just gave her the big O."

"Shut up," Suzuki murmured, trying to drive the sleepy visions from his mind.

"Just couldn't wait to get seconds," Milos chided.

"Have you seen yourself? You look like a 'Got Milk' commercial."

"Come on," Sandy said. "We need to focus. How are we getting out of here?"

"How many krampuses are there in this cave?" Suzuki asked.

"There's the big one, for sure. And the one with the maternal instinct, but outside that ...." Sandy shook her head.

Suzuki nodded, trying to think, but he felt very sleepy and very thirsty. So very, very thirsty. "Is anyone else in desperate need of water?" Suzuki hesitated before adding, "Or more milk?"

No one answered.

"Seriously. I'm really thirsty."

More silence. Finally, Sandy cleared her throat. "It was pretty tasty," she admitted.

"Fucking spook missions," Milos mumbled under his breath.

"What'd you say?" Suzuki asked.

"Military. This was a military-grade mission. They handed it over to MERCs 'cause, who knows? Someone just didn't want to do it."

"Huh. Guess Manny wasn't joking about us taking out the military's garbage."

"They think they have more important things to do. Not everyone cares about rescuing kids."

"And you do?"

"Someone has to."

This level of sincerity was not what Suzuki was expecting. Milos had been all booze and laughter since Suzuki had met him. He didn't seem like someone who would be risking his life for children because he "cared."

None of the MERCs had seemed like that.

That being said, Suzuki didn't know many MERCs. The most he'd interacted with any of them had been at the Red Lion while they were celebrating the Mundanes' first mission. That in itself should have told Suzuki something about the nature of the MERCs.

At the time, Suzuki had just assumed that they all just liked to get drunk. Any reason to party was a good reason to party. Reflecting on Milos' reaction to the kidnapping made Suzuki question his initial assumption.

Maybe the MERCs were the kind of people who honestly did want to celebrate for the newbs and their first mission. He'd read online that MERCs considered themselves to be something of a family.

They all chose to come to Middang3ard on their own terms.

Suzuki felt childish for assuming that MERCs were just money hungry sons of bitches out to make a little extra coin. If the Mundanes had their own reasons for coming to Middang3ard, any other MERC must have just as valid a reason.

"So since we're all being vulnerable before our deaths, what's with the whole Suzuki thing?" Milos queried. "Is that an actual name?"

Suzuki rolled over and pushed himself up against the wall. "It's not important. And we aren't dying here. We're just tied up...with tinsel. I'm sure we can work our way out of this." Suzuki strained as he tried to pull his arms apart.

"I'm pretty strong, lad. You see me breaking my bonds?"

"Fine, but what about our familiars? They can get us

out?" Suzuki searched for Fred, but he wasn't anywhere in the recesses of his mind.

Sandy shook her head. "Niv is still out. Whatever was in the milk affected her more than us. Might be a size thing."

"Or a magic thing," Suzuki added.

"Whatever it is, they're of no use right now."

"Fine." Suzuki fiddled with his hands. "It's just tinsel. Christmas tinsel. Highly flammable tinsel. Sandy, can you burn through yours?"

"Can't see my hands," Sandy replied. "Can't cast what I can't see."

Suzuki bunny-hopped over to where he heard Sandy's voice. He crashed into her, and they both fell onto the ground. "If you can hold mine, can you get it burning?"

"Yeah, I think so."

"All right. Feel around."

Suzuki felt Sandy's pointed fingers prodding him. He tried to adjust so that she could get to the tinsel around his hand without bumping into other body parts. Sandy jabbed Suzuki in the stomach, and he yelped, "Higher."

After a few more uncomfortable moments in which Suzuki horrifyingly imagined Sandy accidentally crushing his testicles, Sandy finally got her hands around the tinsel binding Suzuki's hands.

"Got it."

Suzuki saw a spark and the cave brightened for a second before fading. Then he felt the heat around his wrists. It was getting hotter. "Shit," Suzuki whined. "I did not think this one through enough."

The tinsel caught flame fast and kept on burning. Suzuki's hands were ringed with fire, and it wasn't showing any sign of going out.

Suzuki could feel the skin of his wrists boiling and

burning away. He clenched his jaw tight to keep from screaming in pain. Soon the pain faded and his hands went numb. He assumed that was because the fire had finally made it to his nerves. When Suzuki looked down, the tinsel had burned itself away.

His hands were free.

He quickly untied his feet, pulled out his sword, and cast a healing spell. In the dark, he could faintly see his skin stretching over the burned area. He thanked God that he hadn't seen how bad the damage had been. After he got himself untied, he released Sandy and went over to Milos to unbind him.

"Didn't think you'd be the first one to give up," Suzuki teased.

Milos straightened up, rubbing his wrists. "Hardly," he countered. "Just wanted to see if you whelps were the sort that cracked under pressure. I been twiddling my thumbs waiting for you to get your shit together."

"Why didn't you just cut us free then? And what was up with the whole sob story?"

"I'm not gonna hold your hand through a mission. Just wanted to see what your resolve was like. And as for the sob story, well, we all gotta find ways to entertain ourselves."

"So you don't care about the kids? Is it just for the money?"

"I can care about both the kids and the money. Now come on. We got monsters to kill. They took my weapons and pretty much everything else on me." Milos was patting himself down. "But they left your HUDs. They probably don't know what they are and thought they were part of you or some crap like that. How about you go through your inventory and get me a weapon?"

Suzuki groaned, thinking of some witty retort to get back

at him for all the "We're going to die" crap, but in the end, he did as Milos suggested, pulling at an ax for chopping wood as a weapon.

"This will do." Milos chuckled. "Time to cut me down some Christmas trees."

"Lame." Sandy groaned as she knelt down next to Stew and shook him awake. "Come on," she whispered. "Nap-time's over."

Stew was dazed. He looked around frantically as if he were trying to piece together where he was. "But Mom," he murmured. "I haven't even eaten yet. And—"

"I'm not your mom, Stew. Not unless mom gives you the occasional hand job. Now get the fuck up. I'm thinking this might be time for a Leeroy Jenkins."

Sandy grabbed Stew by his arms and helped him to his feet. Once Stew was more stable on his legs, Sandy cast a small spark, and the Mundanes crept through the cave until they found an exit. A pair of horns could be seen in the shadows cast by Sandy's spark.

Suzuki pointed ahead.

A krampus was sitting at the foot of the cave, its head tilted downward. It was breathing slowly. *Sleeping*, Suzuki thought.

Suzuki pressed his finger to his lips. "We gotta be quiet," he whispered.

Milos gripped the small ax. "Fuck that," he growled as he turned and threw the ax. It sailed silently and struck the krampus in the skull. The krampus opened its eyes as blood dripped down its forehead, and then it slumped to the side.

Milos shrugged. "We've already been here long enough. We gotta get a move on. I don't wanna miss Wendy's lunch. She's cooking yak haggis."

As the Mundanes made their way past the dead krampus, Milos scooped up his ax and wiped the blood from its edge.

They were close to where they had been before, the ledge overlooking the bizarre classroom that the krampuses had set up.

There were four krampuses roughly the same size as the hulking one they had seen earlier. Two grey orcs were slouched in the corner of the subterranean classroom. Stoking the fire were three red orcs, their bodies swollen with muscles, making their gray cousins look nearly as small as a dwarf.

Hm, Fred said. *This is not good.*

What? Where the fuck were you? And what do you mean? Suzuki growled in his head.

First off, little human, I was asleep. Whatever krampus milk does to a non-magical homo sapiens, it affects us higher, more magical beings even more. And secondly, the orcs. That's what is not good. Red orcs hate grey orcs. And all orcs hate seasonal demons such as krampuses. None of these creatures should be together. This is not a good sign.

Stew came up beside Suzuki. "Please tell me Sandy was right about Leeroy Jenkinsing this shit. Please." Stew wore a look of a child asking for a second dessert.

"I might have over-promised that, babe. I just wanted to motivate you to get up," Sandy admitted. "Besides, since when do you ask permission to go all Leeroy on us? Shouldn't you just be charging ahead as we scream your name in panic?"

"Yeah, whatever. That was the old me. This me is gonna play things a bit more cautious from now on. And since fearless Suzuki here is good at figuring shit out, I thought I'd ask him first."

Suzuki surveyed the area. There was a fire. Almost ten

enemies. Children who couldn't defend themselves and very limited space to move around. Some of his usual tactics that involved Sandy were completely out of the question. Any area of effect attack could hurt the kids, probably kill them.

A close-quarters fight was also impossible. There wasn't enough room to move around. The hulking creatures below would rip the Mundanes apart.

Probably not Milos, though. The dwarf was small and could probably slip into spots that the rest of them couldn't.

No options were coming to Suzuki. He looked out over the ledge with his HUD, and it read eleven percent. Not nearly good enough.

"Anyone got any new tricks?" Suzuki asked. "Sandy? You figure out how to become invisible or something?"

"I already told you, I need to study more," Sandy said defensively. "It's been, like, a day. I can't just learn all this shit in a day."

Suzuki nodded. "Ok, so that's out. All right, everyone, let's put all our cards on the table. What can we do now that we couldn't do yesterday?"

"Uh," Stew stammered as he picked at his face. "I got this new ax. It's got this...uh...this perk that lets you transfer elements to it or something."

"And I got that Stoneskin SD card installed last night," Sandy added.

Milos stepped into the center of the group and puffed out his chest. "I'm ferocious," he stated. "And compact. Oh, also handsome."

"Yeah...you are handsome," Suzuki noted. "And very small."

"Not that small, whelp."

"Small enough. And I can change my smell...which seems extremely useless. Except that orcs are mostly blind.

Milos, what are those krampuses planning on doing to those kids?"

"Eat them."

"So they're predators. Hanging out with orcs who are also predators. In an extremely dark cave. They probably don't need to see."

Suzuki snapped his fingers and his eyes lit up.

"Think he's got something." Sandy chuckled.

"Sandy, I'm going to need you to come with me. We're getting the kids out. Milos and Stew, I'm gonna need you to wait for my signal. That's when you're gonna roll."

"What's the signal?"

"You'll know it when you see it."

Suzuki grabbed Sandy's hand and led her down to the bottom of the cave.

The closer they got to the krampuses and orcs, the harder it was to ignore the stench. The bottom of the cave smelled like wet hair and mold. *The smell coming off of them was probably body odor*, Suzuki thought. But that smell wouldn't be strong enough to counter what Suzuki was thinking.

The orcs were mostly hairless, their faces devoid of any kind of intelligence, whereas the krampuses looked as if there was something nefarious and festive going on in their shallow eyes.

The fire in the middle of the room cast heavy shadows on the cave's walls, and Suzuki could barely make out the tables where the children were sitting. There were only vague outlines. The only definite shapes were those of the monsters...and that was only because of their size.

"All right, Sandy, kill the fire."

"Okay...wait, what?"

"Kill the fire. Get the kids out of the room and toward where we entered. Then come back in to help us clean everything up. There's going to be a lot going on, so you should use that SD card to keep you from getting crushed. Come back and wait for me to get everything started."

"What are you going to do?"

"Something stupid. It'll make a great story, though. If, that is, I don't die," Suzuki added.

Suzuki crept toward one of the piles of Christmas junk that lay on the ground. He pulled out a large red cloak and tapped his HUD, closing his eyes and trying to concentrate. The scent display popped up, and he changed his smell from "Frenchman" to "krampus youth."

With that done, Suzuki wrapped himself up in the red cloak. "Start moving those kids," Suzuki whispered.

Sandy stared at the fire in the center of the cave. She puckered her lips and blew. The fire went out.

Suzuki crawled on all fours past the elvish children as they murmured to themselves. Near the walls, the orcs were grumbling, but they weren't moving much.

The newfound darkness was obviously not really bothering them, but a couple grunted, and the smallest orc stood to start making the fire again.

Suzuki made it past the rows of tables. His heart was pounding so loudly he thought the creatures would be able to hear it.

But he knew that was just fear. Orcs were practically deaf and blind. Even if they weren't, it didn't matter as it would take a special kind of ears to hear him over the elves' crying and the demonic "Jingle Bells."

So Suzuki made his way to the small group of krampuses, fairly confident that he could do so undetected.

One of the krampuses stood upright and sniffed the air, its nostrils flaring widely. Then it took a step toward Suzuki.

Suzuki was ready. He pulled out his sword and held it close to his chest. "Let the holy waters wash over me. I cast Holy Blessings."

A golden aura washed over Suzuki and his weapons, and he clutched them closer to his chest as the krampus leaned over and scooped him into its arms.

Ribbons of flesh hung from the krampus' jaws only a few inches away from Suzuki's face, and Suzuki almost passed out from the smell alone. Hopefully, it was from a meal before the children had been captured.

Best not to think about that now.

The krampus was humming softly under its breath. Suzuki couldn't place the tune, but it sounded like a nursery rhyme. In another context, it could have been comforting. The krampus returned to where it was sitting next to the others and grunted something under its breath in low, deep guttural sounds .

The other krampuses responded, and the one holding Suzuki pulled back its robe and exposed its breast. It popped its nipple into Suzuki's mouth, forcing him to suckle.

But this time he was ready and, through considerable effort, forced himself not to swallow, letting the flow dribble out of the side of his mouth.

After a few moments, the krampus withdrew its teat and leaned against the wall. The grunting from the other creatures had died down.

Suzuki let the milk trickle from his mouth as slowly and quietly as he could. He looked over in the direction of the children's tables. There was a brief spark of light, and Suzuki caught Sandy's face. She had returned from moving the children. *I hope she doesn't see this shit*, Suzuki thought as he looked up at the krampus cradling him. He checked his HUD.

Seventy-five percent.

Suzuki leaned his head back and pushed his sword straight up into the krampus' throat. The krampus screamed, gushing blood everywhere as it tossed Suzuki to the ground. Suzuki rolled as the rest of the krampuses rose and started roaring. He crawled to where the krampus that he'd struck was flailing about, lifted his sword, and cleaved through the rest of her throat.

Across the cave, a spark. "Now comes death," Sandy shouted. There was a flash of light, and the entire cave lit up. Sandy was standing near the blackboard, the grey and red orcs behind her.

She lifted her hand and the spark in the palm of her hand exploded, covering her entire body in fire as she sprinted toward Suzuki and the krampuses. Sandy dove straight into the already tangled mass of hairy legs and snapping claws. She grabbed a leg of one of the krampuses, and its matted hair caught fire.

"Is that the sign?" Stew called from above.

"Yes, it's the fucking sign," Suzuki shouted as a krampus grabbed him and tossed him across the cave.

Stew and Milos leapt down from the ledge, Milos landing on top of one of the krampuses, instantly crushing its skull. Stew pulled out his short swords and cut down the other krampus.

The orcs roared on the other side of the cave.

"Scatter," Suzuki shouted.

The Mundanes and Milos broke formation, each of them putting some distance between themselves. Suzuki scanned the cave for more krampuses. They had just killed four of them. That left one more, the largest.

And the orcs.

"Stew, Milos," Suzuki commanded. "Steamroll the orcs! Sandy, clear a path to the exit. Let's get the fuck out of here now!"

Sandy shot a stream of fire out into the dimness of the cave. It scorched through the tables, the blackboard, and an orc. The orcs' screams bounced off the walls of the cave and mixed with Stew and Milos' bloodthirsty whoops and yells.

Stew and Milos ran into the thick of the orcs. Neither was slowing down. Stew's ax caught the light from the flames that Sandy shot out. The ax's blade caught fire.

"Flaming Ax of Total Badassness," Stew shouted as he cut through an orc.

"Typical human." Milos sighed as he rolled underneath an orc's leg. "Gets his first magic ax and almost busts his ball juice all over the place."

"Come on, Mundanes," Suzuki shouted. "I want us all out pronto! Move it, move it, move it!"

Sandy lifted her hands and made a pulling motion at the flames, which jumped from the ground and in the direction of the orcs.

"Sandy, you're gonna burn us alive," Stew yelped as he dodged the flames.

"Then move your ass and stop trying to stab everything!"

Stew and Milos leapt out of the way of the flames and followed after Sandy.

Suzuki had already caught up to them, and they all ran toward the cave's exit. The children were crowded together outside.

The Mundanes burst out from the cave and into the cool, sunny open air. They were on the ridge of a mountain.

"Now would be a good time to teleport us back, Milos," Stew cried out, his voice cracking with nervous energy.

"Uh," Milos muttered. "It doesn't quite work like that. It's a one-way trip. We gotta hoof it back."

A screeching roar came from the bowels of the cave.

"We didn't kill everything, did we?" Sandy asked.

"Stew, Milos, get the kids out of the way. Just go. Sandy and I will take care of these guys and meet up down the way." Suzuki turned to Sandy, "Come on, DeeStruck, let's make sure that nothing comes after us."

"Gotcha."

Milos and Stew herded the elven children away from the cave's mouth. One by one, they helped the kids start their steady descent down the side of the mountain while Suzuki hacked at the foundation of the cave entrance.

Sandy blasted the top of the mountain, causing bits of it to fall down.

"Not fast enough," Suzuki muttered. *Hey, Fred, is there anything you can do to help us out? Like real fast.*

No, Fred replied.

Wait, what? Why not?

Another screech from within the cave. The krampus was getting closer.

You hurt my feelings earlier, Fred said matter-of-factly.

You have to be fucking kidding me. I hurt an eldritch imp's feelings? Do you even have feelings?

You called me a bat with stick legs.

That was hours ago! You could have said something by now!

Revenge, human, is best served—

Cold, yes, I know! Fred!

The entrance of the cave was shaking from the pounding footsteps coming toward Suzuki and Sandy. Sandy was still tossing fireballs at the cave's entrance.

It wasn't enough.

I was going to say, minutes before death. The pristine moment when life is about to fade but has not started yet. The beautiful anticipation of your death.

Seriously, Fred. That thing in there is huge and it's going to rip me apart when it gets out here. You're gonna lose your host.

As the sage of your realm, Kanye West has said, "There's a thousand yous. There's only one me."

Are you fucking quoting Kanye West lyrics to me? I don't have time for this Fred. I'm sorry. OK? Is that what you wanted to hear? You are not a talking bat.

Most certainly. And my arms?

Your arms?

Tell me about my arms.

Christ. They're huge. Extremely well defined.

Adonis like?

Brad Pitt. Just perfectly Hollywood chiseled.

Was that so hard, human? Tell your friend to stop wasting time with fire. Use an earth-based spell. It is, technically, elemental magic. She should be able to handle it.

The entrance of the cave burst open as the last krampus split the narrow opening.

The top of the cave cracked open and the krampus forced its head outside, nearly goring Sandy as she leapt out of the way, losing her footing. She reached out for Suzuki and he tried to grab her, but she was too far away.

The krampus forced more of itself outside the cave's opening, sending rocks and boulders flying. A large rock shot out and struck Sandy in the head, causing her to stumble and pitch over the side of the mountain.

"No," Suzuki screamed. "Sandy!"

Sandy was gone.

Suzuki stared at the krampus as it forced itself farther

out of the cave. He narrowed his eyes and raised his sword as the krampus clawed at him.

Suzuki raised his sword into the air and screamed, "Fuck you, dude."

Above the krampus' head, a massive golden sword materialized. It hung in the air for a second before crashing down into the krampus' neck, breaking apart the rest of the cavern, sending rocks flying everywhere. The ground around Suzuki shook and crumbled. It gave way, and Suzuki went sliding down the side of the mountain into the sloping evergreens.

Then the world went black.

21

Suzuki snapped awake.

He was laying in the middle of the forest, his forehead bloody from a cut above his brow. When he stood, his entire body ached, and he had to stumble to a tree to keep himself from falling.

He drew his sword and spun around awkwardly, trying to find a threat. It took a while for the adrenaline to drain from his system. He sat down when the energy passed and racked his brain for what had happened.

The last thing he could remember was the krampus attacking.

And Sandy freefalling.

"Sandy," Suzuki shouted as he remembered. He took off into the forest, screaming her name. He couldn't tell how long he was running before he stopped. *Fred?*

Yes, human?" Fred answered, writhing around in Suzuki's mind.

"I need to find Sandy. Help me find Sandy."

She is most likely dead. Besides, you are in no condition to—

"What the hell are you talking about? I'm fine," Suzuki

forced out. In truth, he was anything but fine. "We have to help Sandy."

No, human, you are hurt. You are also wearing a full set of armor. And you did not get hit in the head with a rock. If you're lucky, she's in a nice pile without blood every—

Shut the fuck up, Fred. I'm not in the mood. Are you going to help me find her or not? Suzuki was making his way to the cliff's edge.

Fred sighed loudly. *I know you are panicking. So let me remind you of one word: magic.*

Suzuki raised his sword and shield. He closed his eyes and hoped that this was going to work. "I cast Find My Target," Suzuki whispered, and his shield began to glow as a bright light shot out of it into the forest.

It zigged between trees and Suzuki took off running after it. He wasn't able to catch up with the front of the trail of light, but he was close. Blood was pumping in his ears. He couldn't hear himself think.

All he could see was Sandy, laying somewhere, broken, her limbs jutting out in odd angles, a pool of blood haloing her face, her blank eyes staring ahead.

Suzuki pushed the image out of his mind. This wasn't the time for any of that. He couldn't completely rid himself of the dread that was bubbling up in his stomach like vomit.

"Sandy," Suzuki shouted. "Sandy, can you hear me!?"

The light suddenly dipped and stopped. Suzuki ran up to it until it disappeared in a flash, momentarily blinding him. His vision returned slowly. Laying at the foot of a tree was Sandy. Her forehead was covered in blood, and her eyes were closed. Suzuki ran up to her, cradled her head in his hand, and gently shook her.

"Sandy," he whispered, trying to hold back his tears. "Sandy, can you hear me?"

Sandy groaned quietly as her eyes fluttered open. She looked up at Suzuki, obviously still dazed. "Suzuki?"

"Holy shit, I thought you were dead!"

"Me? The future Queen of the Armies of the Dead? Psh. Not happening." Sandy tried to sit up and winced in pain. She touched her side tenderly. "Guess I got a little beat up. That SD card wasn't a bad idea. Kinda hard to figure out how bad of a beating you can take without armor stats, though."

Suzuki helped Sandy to her feet. "Hold on." He clasped his hands together and closed his eyes. "Divine Healing."

A golden aura encircled Suzuki and Sandy. Suzuki could feel his own bones healing and his torn skin pulling itself together. He could see the deep gash on Sandy's forehead sealing itself up.

When the circle faded, Suzuki stretched. Everything felt back to normal. All of the pain had disappeared.

He looked at Sandy's forehead. There was only the faintest trace of a scar.

Sandy playfully shoved Suzuki. "Glad you finally remembered that warrior-mage with a few spells up his sleeve." She was smiling and looked as if she had enough energy to take off running into the forest.

"Yeah...I guess I've been so worried about everything else going on in fights that I forget about the magic."

"Improvisation, my dude. You could use a couple of classes. Planning ahead is great and everything, but you can't go forgetting things like this. Maybe it's time we start running drills again."

"Drills?"

"Remember when I was having problems with hotkeys? We used to stay up all night going over different combina-tions and shit. It worked. You, me, and Stew should give it a shot one night. Get a little more organized. Now come on, let's go find everyone else."

"Sounds good." Suzuki clasped his hands together as he cast Find My Target again.

Another beam of light shot out of his chest. "At least, we'll be able to find the others now."

"Yeah," Sandy said as they started after the little beam of floating light. "Time to *un*split this party."

As they walked, Suzuki felt he should say something. There was a lot that could be said. This was the closest that he'd ever come to death. He was pretty sure it was the same for Sandy.

They'd almost died.

Almost.

Suzuki wasn't sure how close they'd actually gotten to the end. But whatever it was about Middang3ard that made them stronger, it also made them more resilient.

But not invisible. If shit ever got out of hand...well, more out of hand than it did already, then they'd be done for and—

Sandy shoved Suzuki, almost knocking him over. "Hey, Suzuki," Sandy broke in. "You got that stupid look you get when you're overthinking something. What's up?"

"I'm not overthinking anything," Suzuki said. "Just thinking. Has anyone...you know, close to you ever died unexpectedly?"

"A couple."

Suzuki nodded. "Not me. And I never really thought about anyone I care about dying before, except my mom."

"No one really does. It just sort of happens. One day,

you're with them, and the next day you know you're just going to be thinking about them for the rest of your life."

Suzuki tapped his HUD so that his helmet disappeared. Sandy pointed at Suzuki's head. "First thing I'm going to do when we get back is find something to cover my head." Her eyes were tearing up. She wiped away a tear that fell down her face and sniffed loudly. "That's how my aunt died. Blunt force trauma to her head."

"Holy shit. What happened?"

"Her husband killed her."

"Oh my God, Sandy. I'm sorry."

"There are monsters back home too. At least, here we can do something about it." Sandy stopped walking and took Suzuki's hand in hers. "I know we fuck around and joke a lot, but Stew and I know how serious this is." She smiled. "Fun as hell and very, very crazy. But serious. We talk about it all the time when we're alone. But you don't have someone. Beth's not here. So if you ever need to talk about that, just say something. You don't have to freak out all alone."

"I don't really freak out," Suzuki said, pulling away to follow the spell.

"Cut the shit. We hear you at night."

"What the hell are you talking about?"

"You talk in your sleep. And you always say the same thing."

Suzuki was taken back by this. He had no idea he even snored, let alone actually spoke. "What do I say?"

"Please, Beth. Don't go."

Suzuki felt his cheeks get hot with embarrassment. "I...I..."

"It's okay. You love her."

Suzuki felt his eyes well up. This was all too much. The fight. The krampuses. Sandy almost dying. And now this.

He shook his head. "Ahh, I think...I think we should talk about something else." Suzuki's voice quivered, and he took several deep breaths as he focused on holding his tears in.

"All right." Sandy leaned in and gave him a kiss on his cheek. "But know that Stew and I love you and we're here for you. Always."

Suzuki nodded, taking a couple steps in front of Sandy so she couldn't see the tears he could no longer hold back.

The two Mundanes followed the shining light for another hour. Ahead, Suzuki could see a clearing where a river was flowing, where the beam of light stopped. He could hear children's voices by the river.

Suzuki pointed. "Come on," he exclaimed. "We found them."

Sandy rested her hand on Suzuki's shoulder until it became uncomfortable enough and Suzuki met her eyes. "Hold on, Suzuki. I have one more thing to say."

Suzuki stopped. "Do we have to?"

Sandy stepped in front of Suzuki and held his gaze with hers. "You can be afraid *of* Beth. But you don't have to be afraid *for* Beth. You get what I'm saying?"

"Yeah." Suzuki nodded. "I think so."

"Good. Come on, let's go let those jackasses know we're pissed they aren't out looking for us."

Sandy jogged to the river. Suzuki followed her to where the elvish children were sitting by it.

Milos was sitting with them, talking slowly, telling them a story. Stew was pacing back and forth, alternating between picking his face and scratching his scalp.

"This is what you call a search party?" Sandy shouted once they were in range.

Stew spun around fast enough to almost fall. He ran to Sandy and grabbed her, sweeping her off her feet. Unfortunately, he was still running and tripped. They both went tumbling into the grass.

Sandy pushed Stew off her. "Oh, my God, Stew," Sandy shouted. "Not in public."

Stew grabbed Sandy's face and kissed her. "I thought you were dead."

"Nope, and obviously, you aren't either."

Stew kissed Sandy again and held her close. They both sat there, holding each other for some time. Suzuki thought about what Sandy had said. Then he noticed Milos walking up to him, the children peering from behind his stocky shoulders.

Milos clapped his hand on Suzuki's back. "You three didn't do too bad."

"The krampus," Suzuki started. "It had a...a limb—"

"Not any of the kids', lad. All arms, legs, and heads are accounted for."

"That's good to hear."

"Glad to see that the Mundanes live up to the hype."

"What hype?"

Milos smiled and handed Suzuki back his ax. "The MERCs watch the games. We usually bet on them. You've been winning me money for a long time."

"You guys watched us play *Middang3ard*?"

"Oh, yeah. Streamed it right into the Lion. It's a way for us to keep an eye on the prospectives. And we've been watching you Mundanes for a long time. You're better in the flesh."

"That's good to hear."

Stew and Sandy were finally done hugging. Stew came up to Suzuki.

"Hey, you big lug."

"Hey, back," Stew answered.

Stew grabbed Suzuki and hugged him. Suzuki felt the air being crushed out of his body. He wondered how Sandy could ever survive being hugged like that.

Stew let go, and Suzuki could see the tears in Stew's eyes. "Don't ever do that shit again, dude. Never split the party."

Suzuki nodded. "Never split the party," he repeated.

Milos sighed and waved his hands around like he was trying to ward off a foul gas. "All right, all right, we're all excited we're alive. Now let's get these kids home for Christmas."

When no one laughed, the dwarf hung his head low before saying, "What? Too soon?" Then, shrugging it off, "We've got a long walk and a lot of gold waiting for us, so we best get going."

"Sounds good," Suzuki mused dreamily. "Let's finish this quest. Let's get home."

22

The Mundanes heard the Red Lion from miles away. And when they finally did arrive, they were hoisted into the air in chairs.

Mead and ale were placed before them as they were passed around the bar, and every MERC wanted to shake their hands.

Two missions in a few days? It was practically unheard of for new recruits to be out in the field so much. The rest of the recruits who had come with the Mundanes hadn't even finished a quest yet.

As usual, the bar was filled with elves, halflings, gnomes, dwarves, and humans. There seemed to be more alcohol in the one room than Suzuki had seen in his entire life.

Suzuki wondered if the MERCs at the Red Lion partied like this every night.

They probably did, and he could understand why.

This seemed like a good way to blow off some steam. And after his near-death experience, Suzuki felt more alive than ever. He also understood that life could be taken away at any moment, so he wanted to make sure to enjoy himself as long as he could.

Sandy had been right. This was serious. But it could also be a lot of fun.

"Speaking of Sandy...or rather, *thinking* of her," Suzuki slurred to himself as he looked around the bar. She was nowhere in sight. Neither was Stew.

And, if he was honest with himself, he couldn't quite put a finger on any one moment in the bar since he'd gotten there.

As soon as the Mundanes had opened the door, they had been whisked off in a flurry of congratulations, meads, with everyone wanting to have a minute of their time. At that particular moment, Suzuki was sitting at a table of gnomes, explaining how he had spent the previous night.

"I was nursing," Suzuki said as he finished up his drink. "I wasn't sucking. Sucking has a sexual connotation. There was nothing sexual about what I was doing. It was survival. Pure survival."

A deep voice spoke from behind Suzuki. "Much like a babe." José and the Chipmaster were behind him.

"Wanna join us for a little bit of the ol' sippy-sippy?" Chipmaster asked.

"You're damn right I want to," Suzuki exclaimed. He bid farewell to the gnomes as he jumped out of his seat and followed Chipmaster and José to their table in the quieter corner of the bar.

José put an ale down in front of Suzuki. "Milos told us about that stunt you pulled. That was one ballsy trick."

Chipmaster leaned forward and tapped Suzuki's HUD. "I second that one. Never would have thought a little one like you'd hold onto this one's sage wisdom. Hell, don't know if I would've listened to myself. You Mundanes got a good amount of swagger, don't you?"

"They're good guys," Suzuki replied. "Stew, Sandy, and Beth. They're solid."

"Who's this Beth?"

"She's...ahhh...my friend. Part of the party. Well, she was, until she got drafted."

José playfully shoved Chipmaster. "You know Beth," he reminded her. "The fighter with the buzzcut. Man, she was something else. Your other tank is impressive, but this girl had speed. She was always covering you too. You guys made a great team. Glad to have you with the MERCs. Who knows, maybe you could persuade Beth to drop the whole 'holier than thou' routine and join up with us."

"'Holier than thou?'"

"Not her specifically. I don't know her. But a lot of those military punks think that they're cut from a finer cloth than us."

"Oh."

The table suddenly shook, and Suzuki realized he had been staring at José. He looked to look at the source of the distraction. Stew was slamming his hands on the table.

Stew grabbed Suzuki by the collar. "Dude," Stew stammered. "Meeting, right now. Let's go." Stew turned to José and the Chipmaster. "Sorry...sorry, but...sorry...it's important."

José waved away Stew's concerns. "Don't worry about it. You two probably have a lot of important strategies to discuss. Good job, again. You guys are doing solid work."

"Thanks," Suzuki managed to get out before Stew dragged him upstairs. Stew looked for an open room, shoved Suzuki inside, and slammed the door behind him.

He went to the windows and closed the blinds. "Stew?" Suzuki started. "You're acting *really* weird."

Stew whipped around. His face was pale as if his whole body had been drained of blood. He grabbed Suzuki's hands. His palms were clammy. "It's Sandy," Stew explained. "She's like really...oh my God, man, I can't believe I'm having this conversation right now."

Stew paced back and forth, sat down on the bed, stood back up, and started to pace again.

"One word at a time, Stew."

"Sandy...she...uh...she wants..."

"Breath, Stew. One word. At. A. Time."

"Sandy. Wants. To. Bone."

"Okay, I get it, you guys fuck all the—"

"No, no, dude. We were just messing with you. We've never...uh...I've never..." Stew stammered, unable to get the words out. "Don't get me wrong. We do stuff. Lots of stuff. With our mouths. We just never." The barbarian lifted his pointer finger and made an 'O' with his other hand. Then he tried to get his pointer into the 'O,' but in his drunken haze, missed the mark.

"Oh. Got it." Suzuki grabbed Stew's hands. "I totally get it."

Stew ran his fingers through his hair in exasperation. "What am I going to do?" He hung his head in his hands. "She's so fucking gorgeous. And so cool. What if I fuck it up? Like, get too nervous, and something happens. Or doesn't happen. Oh god, what if I can't get—"

"Again, I get it." Suzuki sat down next to Stew. "You could talk to her about it. Let her know how you're feeling. It might—"

"I could use magic," Stew interrupted.

"Or you could use magic." Suzuki narrowed his eyes, unsure of what Stew had in mind.

"Yeah, I could ask GB." Stew snapped his fingers in rapid succession as he formed some harebrained scheme. "He could help me."

"Stew, you know what Sandy said about magic. You kind of have to know a little about what you're messing with."

"I know enough. I've taken health classes. Hey, GB?" There was a loud pop and a stone donkey's head popped out of Stew's chest. "Woah, cool."

GB brayed lazily. "Yeah?" he asked.

"Is there something you could do to help me? Like some magic spell or something? When we were doing those medical exams, mages were stretching and growing every part of my body. Could you help me with something like that?"

Stew glared at Suzuki and then looked back down at GB. "We should talk privately. Suzuki, out."

Suzuki raised his hands defensively as he got off the bed and slunk away. "Your call. I still think you should talk to her."

"Yeah, yeah. Out."

Suzuki left the room and closed the door quietly behind him. He walked back downstairs. The party was still raging. His fifteen minutes of fame weren't over yet, but he couldn't have been less excited. He snuck around the majority of the crowd, went straight to the bar, and grabbed a drink.

Wendy handed him a tankard. He paid and asked if he could order something to eat and have it brought to his room.

"Hungry? We got chicken liver mousse and hippogriff rump with a glaze of calcified unicorn tears."

"Unicorns can cry?" Suzuki wondered aloud.

"They ain't supposed to. That's why it's a delicacy."

"Sure, I'll take that."

Suzuki paid for his meal, took his mead, talked briefly to the landlord, and went upstairs to the separate room he had taken, given the conversation with Stew. He closed the door, collapsed onto his bed, and rested his mead on his chest. After debating whether he wanted to risk choking to death, Suzuki sat up a little bit and sipped some of the foam off his drink.

Surprisingly, he felt Fred uncurling in his mind.

Human, do you mind if I step out for a moment? Fred ventured.

You don't have to ask me, Suzuki answered. *Pop out whenever you want.*

The room filled with the smell of brimstone, and Suzuki felt his chest opening up. A portal had appeared in his chest and smoke was coming from it. Fred's claws reached out of the portal, and the imp climbed out of Suzuki's chest. The portal shut behind him. Fred stretched his wings and claws. He coughed a little, causing flames to fly from his nose.

"Thanks for the help back there," Suzuki said. "With Sandy. And the krampus."

Fred curled up on the bed and rested his arms between his legs. He looked like a dragon trying to be a cat. "My pleasure," Fred hissed. "You seem to have an affinity for José. You were staring at him for some time. Why is that?"

Suzuki made an odd face, as if he were smelling something he would have preferred never to have never smelled and he laughed awkwardly. "I wasn't staring at him," Suzuki mumbled. "Besides, why are you asking?"

"You did not answer my question. You suggested that Stew talk to Sandy. You also insinuated that I should have discussed my feelings with you earlier. Now you refuse to talk? Are you a hypocrite or just weak-minded?"

"Okay, fine. What do you want to know?"

"Why you are so infatuated with José?"

Suzuki shrugged. "I am not infatuated. Just interested. He is one of the oldest living humans to have been granted access to Middang3ard. He has to know things no one else does."

Fred nodded. "I see. As one who wishes to know before acting, you seek to understand more from that legendary adventurer. I understand and do agree that his aversion to death does make him interesting. Still, I have met many immortals, and as far as immortals are concerned, he is something of a...hmm...how would your soulmate say it? 'Douche nozzle.'"

"Wait, what do you mean soulmate?"

"The human your heart is always drooling over."

Suzuki was getting sick of everyone calling him on his feelings for Beth. "I have the hots for her. Does that make her my soulmate?" He tried to really sell it, but in his heart, he knew he had more than the hots.

"Fine. Then you *wish* her to be your soulmate. Whether this happens or not is largely dependent on your actions. As for José, yes, "douche nozzle." That would be an apt term for him."

"Again, why would you say that about him—?"

But before Suzuki could finish his question, there was a huge crash from upstairs, followed by the sound of wood cracking and furniture being frantically shoved aside.

Then Suzuki heard someone scream, "Get that thing the fuck away from me."

Sandy. She was in trouble.

Fred vanished into Suzuki as he ran upstairs only to see Sandy screaming on the landing of the second floor.

She was pointing into their room, her face twisted in disgust.

There was something in there. An enemy? Maybe another krampus out for revenge.

And if Sandy found something disgusting, it must be truly horrifying Suzuki thought as he took a play out of the Leeroy Jenkins' playbook and charged into the dark room head-first, crashing right into a hulking figure.

They both went tumbling down onto the ground, and when Suzuki finally managed to disentangle himself, his jaw dropped as he got a good look at what was scaring Sandy.

Stew was sitting pants-less on the floor. And in between Stew's legs was his engorged penis, which now stretched to his feet and was nearly the girth of both of Stew's thighs.

The veiny, pulsing mess didn't even look like a human appendage anymore.

"Oh, God...the veins," Suzuki shouted, covering his eyes, desperately wishing he could unsee what he had just seen. "What the fuck did you do to yourself?"

"It was GB's idea. I didn't know—"

Sandy burst into the room, her eyes blazing. "Do you see what this idiot has done to himself?"

Stew turned to face Sandy, but he stumbled over his words. He finally stopped trying and just sat there, with Suzuki and Sandy standing above him, a look of horror on each of their faces.

"Sandy," Stew finally started. "I...I guess...I guess I was worried that you...uh...wouldn't be happy with my... ahh...performance."

"For fuck's sake, Stew." Sandy knelt next to him. "You

could have just talked to me before you decided you wanted to be Ron Jeremy." Sandy kissed Stew on the forehead. "I love you. You don't have to be worried about things like this. Ever."

"I love you too, babe."

Suzuki was inching toward the door. "I feel like this is something you guys should talk about in private," he said as he opened the door, slowly backing out.

If I can just sneak away, he thought, but then there was another crash. This one came from downstairs, and it was louder than what Suzuki had heard before.

The crash was followed by an ominous boom, then another, and finally a third that literally rocked the whole Red Lion.

"What the fuck—" Suzuki started when he heard someone yell, "The Red Lion is under attack!"

23

S uzuki hit his HUD and his armor rolled over his body. "What the fuck? I thought this was our sanctuary. Come on, guys."

"What am I supposed to do?" Stew shouted.

"Can you stand?" Suzuki asked.

"Yeah."

"I don't know. Swing your dick like a windmill or something. But get up. Listen to those screams. They need us."

Stew grumbled and Sandy helped him to his feet, taking care not to touch the flaccid atrocity hanging between Stew's legs.

Stew hit his HUD and his armor shimmered over his body, his kilt stretching down to his ankles to cover his uncomfortable situation.

The Mundanes made their way to the stairs and peered down the staircase.

Running down the stairs, Suzuki saw that the Red Lion was overrun with orcs still pouring in through the front door and two holes they'd made in the side of the inn.

The MERCs were all suited up, and the fight was well

underway. Steel from both sides clashed, and the bar was a cacophony of violence.

"Bar fight," someone shouted.

Lightning crackled from Sandy's hands. "So cliché," she muttered under her breath.

Suzuki raised his shield and tackled an orc, sending it tumbling down the stairs. Another orc charged at Suzuki, swinging at him with its club.

Suzuki managed to deflect the attack, then stepping to the side, he swung his sword downwards, slicing off its arm. The other orc was getting back onto its feet, but before it fully got its balance, Suzuki dove forward, swinging his shield to knock it down and sliding his sword into the first orc's chest in one fluid motion.

Sandy floated downstairs, firing lightning from her hand. The lightning bolts jumped from one orc to another, and when she got to the bottom of the stairs, an orc jumped out at her and knocked her to the ground. Sandy rolled to the side and grabbed the orc's leg, sending thousands of volts of electricity surging through its body.

The air reeked of toasted flesh.

By the time Stew made it down the stairs, Sandy and Suzuki had already cleared a path to the larger fight that was happening in the main room of the inn.

Stew sought to follow them and join the fray, but an orc dove in from the side, pushing him to the ground. Stew scrambled to his feet and the orc squared off with him, watching him closely as he hobbled around trying to balance his third limb in one hand and his ax in the other.

But it was all proving too much, he simply couldn't manage both. "Fuck it," Stew shouted as he grabbed his magically endowed penis with both hands, brandishing it like a club. "You want some? Come get it!"

Sandy had caught up with Suzuki, and they cut and burned their way through the orcs whose backs were turned to them.

Up ahead, Suzuki could see José slashing through orc after orc. Chipmaster was at his side, firing arrows faster than Suzuki could follow.

It was magical watching the two of them working.

Even with an entire bar crawling with orcs, the two of them were working in unison. Back to back.

It was almost like watching a ballet—a ballet which was punctuated by Stew's screams.

Sandy cast a glance back in Stew's direction. He was holding his bloody cock in his hands. The orc lay dead at his feet, its skull bashed in. The sight was so ridiculous that Sandy burst out in laughter.

"It's not funny," Stew objected loudly. "The head is *so* sensitive."

Sandy's hands turned to the consistency of gravel. She waved her hands and cast Stoneskin on Stew. His skin instantly hardened. "There—a magic prophylactic for you."

"Thanks, babe," Stew shouted.

"Don't thank me too much," Sandy called back. "Looks like you have a crush."

Stew turned around to see another orc standing behind him. The orc, a female Stew guessed by its incredible bosom, stared at his crotch for a long, lingering moment before lunging forward with an obscene amount of speed.

Stew took off, hobbling as fast as he could, shouting, "I have a girlfriend!"

Suzuki stepped over the body of an orc and hesitated for a second. "We should go help him?"

Sandy pushed forward, pointing back at the main fray. "More important things right now than Stew's dick."

Steel clashed, and flesh was carved. Suzuki could see the MERCs around him falling alongside orcs. The floor was piling with bodies.

Still, Suzuki and Sandy pushed farther into the growing circle of pain and death.

Then there was a flash of lightning as Sandy came up behind him.

"We gotta clear this out," Suzuki shouted, looking into the room. There were so many bodies fighting against one another in an ebb and flow of movement that it was hard to distinguish between enemy and ally. "There are too many people."

"Yeah, you think," Sandy answered.

Suzuki tried to think of something he could do to help the situation. But nothing came to him. There was simply too much going on.

No time to plan.

So Suzuki did the only thing he'd never thought of doing before. He stopped thinking and let himself go. His body moved on its own. He did not know where it went. It was someplace far away. He was thinking about home.

About the friends he had left behind.

His mother.

Beth.

Everything that he was fighting for...and with those thoughts in mind, his instincts did the rest.

He lost himself to the battle, with only quick flashes of what was happening around him entering his mind.

A club swung on a downward arc, barely missing him.

The whishing sound of a sword grazing his helmet.

The battle cries of all those who fought.

He was caught up in the heat of battle, his rage fueling his instincts.

And in all of it, Suzuki saw one more thing...the orcs were being pushed back out of the bar.

It was a slow retreat but still a retreat.

José had climbed up on top of a table and was leading the rallying cry. The MERCs behind him screamed their battle cries, and the orcs returned their own. Suzuki and Sandy were in the front lines, staring down the orcs.

"We finish this here," José shouted. "MERCs, let's take back our fucking bar! First round is on me!"

Suzuki, Sandy, and the rest of the front line ran forward. The orcs came at them and they smashed into each other in a chorus of screams, steel, and magic.

The final push had been made. The frontline of the MERCs hacked through what was left of the orcs' defenses.

A loud horn sounded in the distance, and what was left of the orcs turned back and fled out into the night.

There was an eerie silence that hung over the bar as everyone assessed the damage. The dead covered the floor, both MERCs and orcs.

The walls were stained with blood. No one spoke. There was only the hush and stillness of the dead.

Suzuki stumbled away from the mess of bodies to the staircase. The rest of the MERCs were also trying to gather themselves together.

In the corner of his eye, Suzuki saw Stew walking out of a room. An orc pushed Stew out of the way and bolted out of the bar, disappearing into the night.

Stew's enlargement spell had worn off.

He walked over next to Suzuki and collapsed on the staircase. Sandy joined them after a bit. They sat there and tried to catch their breath.

But Suzuki couldn't rest. Not yet. Instead, his eyes were fixed on all of the MERCs who lay at his feet. None of them had been prepared for an attack, a fact clearly worn on the dead MERCs' faces.

This was home. And no one expects to be attacked at home.

Across the bar, José was kneeling among the dead, closing their eyes. He looked up at Suzuki but said nothing.

There was nothing to be said.

24

The night chill had set in as the MERCs solemnly went about their work. The bodies of the dead orcs had been dragged out of the Red Lion and piled high in the alley behind the bar.

When all the bodies had been gathered, one of the older MERC mages came up to the pile and snapped, engulfing the dead orc bodies in fires so intense, the bodies turned to instant ash that was caught up in the wind.

It was by the light of that brief fire that the MERCs attended to their own dead.

The casualties were not high, but they were felt throughout the company. Twenty-two MERCs had died in the fight, and each was draped in black silk wrappings, the garments of the fallen.

José and Chipmaster grabbed one of the bodies and took it outside.

Suzuki jabbed Stew. "We should help."

Stew and Sandy nodded but neither said anything, following Suzuki back into the Red Lion in silence.

The three of them took a silk wrapping from the pile

that had been left beside the dead and wrapped up the body as they had seen José and Chipmaster do.

Then the three of them lifted the body.

It was lighter than Suzuki would have expected.

But then again, Suzuki wasn't sure what he expected. After all, how much does death truly weigh?

José looked up at the Mundanes and pointed to a pile of shovels laying on the ground. "Glad to see that MERC pride runs through the new kids. Thanks for the help."

The Mundanes silently grabbed shovels and started digging, tearing up the hard dirt and piling it beside the slowly-growing hole. The two groups worked in silence, the only sound that of their grunting as they dug and the crows cawing in the night.

Once they had finished the first two graves, José and the Mundanes went back into the Red Lion and grabbed two more bodies.

By now, Milos and some other MERCs came over to offer their assistance, and it didn't take long before all of the bodies were underground.

As soon as that was done, the rest of the MERCs gathered around the freshly-dug graves, saying nothing, only offering silent prayers.

José climbed on top of a large, disturbed tree trunk. In a solemn voice, the ancient MERC spoke. "Nights like these are the sort where we must remember first and foremost what we are here for. We are brothers and sisters. We are a family. We are here to fight the Dark One. When one of us bleeds, we all bleed. When one of us falls, we all mourn. The MERCs who sacrificed their lives tonight to defend us are heroes. They are the unsung heroes of this war. I did not know any of them personally. I do not have to have known any of them personally. I know that they were MERCs, just like the rest of you. We are the living, and we honor the dead."

"We are the living, and we honor the dead," the rest of the MERCs echoed back.

José nodded at Diana, who waved her hands, which were glowing bright red. Twenty-two little flames floated from her fingertips and over to the graves...one for each mound of fresh earth.

Once their respects were paid, the MERCs went back to the Red Lion and slowly started to piece the place back together. The work was mostly done by the mages who used magic to repair the chairs and tables and to clean off the walls.

After only half an hour, the Red Lion was restored to its former glory.

Wendy started pouring tankards of booze. "A well-fought battle deserves a stiff drink. It's on the house tonight, boys! Drink to the memory of the fallen."

Sandy, Stew, and Suzuki were sitting at their own table. "I'll go get the first round," Sandy offered as she stood up.

Stew shook his head, still not sure what to make of what just happened. "Attacking us at our own base. That's gutsy."

"No," Suzuki disagreed. "That's stupid. From a tactical point of view, it's insane. I can't even begin to name how many battles have been lost because of that strategy. It would take all night. Historically, that's as bad as Germany trying to invade Russia during winter."

Stew started at Suzuki with a blank look.

"It's just such an obviously bad idea," Suzuki added.

"Sure, whatever. I still don't get your point."

Sandy returned with the drinks, placing them on the table.

Stew sloshed his mead in Suzuki's direction, some of the head tipping out and over the side. "Fearless leader here thinks that it's weird that the orcs attacked here."

"Not weird. Stupid," Suzuki corrected. "Think about it. There's a lot of fucking MERCs here. And most of them are veterans. That was a suicide mission if I've ever seen one. You'd think the Dark One's forces would be better managed given everything I've heard about how terrible he is. But...I don't know...something doesn't add up about tonight."

Sandy shrugged. "Maybe. But then again, maybe the orcs were part of some cell group or something."

Suzuki looked at the mage curiously. "What do you mean?"

"You know, a cell group. Like when a force has a loose hierarchy. You just kind of let them do what they want to do, but they have to do it under your name."

Stew burst out laughing and raised his tankard for a cheer. "Didn't know you were one for military history, babe."

"I'm not. It's just been in the news a lot, and my dad's really into politics. Just picked it up, I guess."

"Maybe they're getting desperate," Suzuki offered. "You know, the war isn't really going their way, so they're starting to make stupid mistakes."

Sandy shrugged and drank. "Who knows? Honestly, who really knows what's going on around here."

"I don't, and I doubt I ever will," Suzuki muttered. "Listen, guys—I think I need to be alone. " And without another word, Suzuki left the Mundanes and went upstairs.

The room was a mess. Stew had made short work of it stumbling around with his "extra limb," and their room was utter chaos.

All this damage from Stew. Imagine what would have happened if an orc did make it up here, he thought as he righted some of the furniture and searched for his pillow and blanket. He considered tidying up the rest of the room. For Stew and Sandy.

But probably more for himself. It was something to do

And something to do was better than nothing, so that's exactly what he did. Something. He tidied the room.

As he did, Suzuki felt Fred moving around in his mind. *What's up, Fred?*

You were right to question the circumstances of the attack, human. But you were wrong to blindly dismiss it as stupidity on their part.

Suzuki sighed. He just wasn't in the mood for the imp. *What do you mean? And speak plainly or go find some corner in my mind to jerk-off in. I'm not interested in another condescending chit-chat.*

Very well, let me speak plainly. The orcs have never attacked the Shire before. This is partly because of what you so rightly pointed out—the Shire is the MERCs home base. But it is also because the Shire is widely regarded as a safe zone. Neutral territory.

Fred projected places into Suzuki's mind that he had not known existed. Once the images were in place, Fred hissed, *There have always been safe zones throughout the realms.*

What good is a safe zone in the middle of a war? Suzuki asked.

Traditions and manners. Even the orcs were not ready to descend into complete savagery. Still, there are two things that trouble me. Firstly that the attack happened at all. The scale was extremely small. I have seen the orc hordes. They stretch for valleys upon valleys. If this realm's orc population wanted to destroy the Red Lion, they would have.

Suzuki took this in before asking, *And what is the second thing?*

That such an attack could not be random. This is not some rogue orc troop as your compatriots suggested. Orcs are stupid, but they are not that stupid. No, they were asked to attack this place. And I can only it assume it was by him. By the Dark One.

Why would the Dark One want to attack here? To what end? We're just a bunch of MERCs.

MERCs who constantly vex him.

So what? He wanted to irritate us back. Seriously what did the Dark One gain by attacking us here and in the way he did.

Fred's silence was his answer. The imp did not know.

Suzuki shook his head. *OK, let's assume that you're right and the Dark One did it for some reason so fucked up that not even you can hazard a guess. What happened then? He went to the closest orc troop and, what? Asked them to sacrifice themselves on some suicide mission, because...what? He asked nicely. I seriously doubt that.*

Yes, I am telling you exactly that. You don't understand, do you, human?

Oh, please, then...enlighten me.

For eons, the children of dust—dwarves, elves, gnomes, and humans—hunted my kind, Fred hissed. *You saw us as evil monsters to be wiped from the face of Middang3ard and all the other realms that surround it.*

Fred conjured images of hunting parties taking down trolls, giants, orcs, goblins...and imps. *We were on the verge of being destroyed until someone came to us. The Dark One. No one questioned where he...or it...had come from. We knew nothing about him. We still know nothing about him. All that is known is that he arrived without ceremony or magic. He simply came into our realms, and he spoke a truth that the beasts of the nine realms could rally around.*

And what was that? Suzuki asked.

Power. Power was something all the races could understand.

That still doesn't explain why a troop of orcs would sacrifice themselves for no good reason. There's more going on here. Mind-control or some spell... Suzuki mused.

Perhaps. But then again, perhaps not. Fred paused as he considered his words. *Do you know what orcs used to be? Do you know the filth and the slavery they were forced into? The elves are not as benevolent as you would assume. They enslaved the orcs. Until, that is, the Dark One gave them the means to escape their bonds. He promised them freedom, and he delivered. Such a service buys one a hell of a lot of loyalty.*

Suzuki was dumbfounded. The whole time that he had been trying to understand why the MERCs and the military were waging war against the Dark One, it had never occurred to him to question what the Dark One was fighting for.

And why would he? Evil was evil, and the only thing any of them had been told about the Dark One was that he was one evil son-of-a-bitch.

If Fred was right and the races deemed monstrous were on the verge of extinction...then it was clear the Dark One wasn't the only evil force in the nine realms.

Fred must have sensed his thoughts...or read them outright, Suzuki still wasn't sure what kind of access Fred had to his mind. Either way the imp sighed before sending, *No, dear human...the Dark One is evil. Just because he sought to help the dark races gain their freedom does not mean he is not using them for his own purposes. Make no mistake, the Dark One is pure evil. Even when he does good, he does so to further his own evil intent. Hence why I fight with the Children of Dust and other lesser creatures. Hence why Myrddin created the game the way he did.*

Suzuki snapped his fingers twice. *And what about the game? If all this shit is happening, why not just pull back the veil and get us here in a more direct way?*

He could feel Fred shaking his head. *Myrddin believed that the humans needed to be convinced to fight. That humans, selfish as they are, would not leave their realm to fight against an evil that lived on another plane of existence,* Fred explained. *Hence why he began to seed your realm with information through different formats. At first, it was legends. They came to your realm and stitched themselves into the tales that your people have been telling for thousands of years. Gilgamesh. Zeus. King Arthur. All of those stories were planted within your culture with an exact purpose: to prepare your kind. An attempt to ready you humans for the trials that were to come.*

Fred conjured up images of all the *Middang3ard* modules and games that had been in circulation. Suzuki knew most of them. Tabletop games, board games, books, movies, video games, and finally the VR version that came out when Suzuki was a kid.

As your people began to change, Fred continued, *to accept these legends, Myrddin sought to deepen your understanding of this realm through fantasy fiction—not that it was fiction at all. The books published under the guise of fiction have more truth in them than any myth. And Myrddin didn't stop there. Eventually, the books became games. And those games grew in complexity until they took on their final, virtual format.*

Images of the VR suits and helmet that Suzuki knew so well popped into his mind. *But the VR suits weren't training like Myrddin explained. No VR game could prepare you for the real thing. They were merely a means to deepen your acceptance of Middang3ard, and to trick eager recruits such as yourself with lies of painless adventure and endless riches.*

Fred sighed. *To be honest, most of us didn't think that he was going to be able to pull any of this off. But look at you: proof that he was on to something. Thousands of humans have come here for the glory of Middang3ard. That in itself is a victory.*

Suzuki sat there, trying to take in everything that Fred had said. It was a lot. All of the games, all of the books that he had spent his childhood with, all of that was nothing more than a recruitment tool.

The best memories of his life were nothing more than someone assuming that he knew enough about what it was that he thought was going to happen to indoctrinate him. It was almost too much to understand, almost too much to cope with.

Yet he knew it was true.

Somehow, he knew that all of the time he had spent reading through myths, trying to understand the technicalities of mythical races, all of what his parents had described as nonsense was hardly a waste of his wits. Here he was in Middang3ard right now. There was no way that any of that was a waste.

There are not many humans from your generation who understand the complexities of these realms," Fred hissed. *"Despite what else I'd like to say about you and your friends, you seem to understand. Since you've arrived in Middang3ard, you seem to have an understanding of this place, of these people, that many others do not.*

What are you trying to say? Suzuki asked.

You understand the customs and rules of Middang3ard far better than you know.

Thank you. I think, Suzuki said as he made his bed. There was something cathartic about pulling the sheets back and placing them on properly. It reminded him of his childhood, a childhood that seemed so very long, long ago.

You know, I'm sure there is a good reason why they attacked, suicide mission or not. It's a good thing there are some very smart MERCs mulling this over right now.

Smart MERCs?

José, Milos, Diana...they know the score. They'll figure this out sooner or later.

Perhaps, but— but before Fred could finish his thought, a notification popped up on Suzuki's HUD.

It said, **Classified. Urgent.**

Suzuki stared at the message. A cold feeling came over his body. Whatever was in that message could not be good.

A chill went down Suzuki's back as he opened the message, and the first thing he saw was the military emblem blazing at the top.

He scrolled down, and what he read made his heart stop cold.

We regret to inform you, the message said, **of the passing of Beth Lovett. She was killed in combat during a raid on her camp. Robert "Suzuki" Fletcher, Sandy Poples, and Stew Harris are listed as her next of kin and, subsequently, you will inherit her personal items. Within two business days, you will receive these items via inter-realm mail. There was a selection of weapons, one which was specifically left for you. The rest can easily be divided up among you three. I am sorry for your loss. Stay strong, we must be ever vigilant against the Dark One.**

Suzuki closed the message.

He did not have any thoughts. He just sat there, staring at the floor of the room.

There must have been some kind of mistake. People make these mistakes all the time.

Only a few months before they left, Suzuki had seen a documentary about a man who had been declared dead in the Vietnam war, only to show up at his family's doorstep thirty years later.

The military constantly made mistakes. He knew that for a fact.

This was just a mistake.

There was no way that Beth was actually dead.

That's not the way that this kind of thing worked. The party was going to get back together. That's what they'd been saying since she left.

The party was going to get back together.

He could hear frantic steps coming up the Red Lion's stairs. The door to Suzuki's room flung open. Stew and Sandy were standing in the doorway.

Suzuki shook his head. "It's not true. It's not true."

Sandy was shaking and crying. She covered her eyes and walked into the room, Stew trailing close behind her, his eyes sunken and his face waxen. They sat on Suzuki's bed.

Suzuki couldn't understand why Sandy was crying. It didn't make any sense.

Beth was okay. She had to be.

Another message pinged on Suzuki's HUD. He opened it and saw Beth's face staring at him.

"Hey, Suzuki, it's me. If you're getting this, then it means I'm nixed. Dead. The game's over for me. Such a weird thing to have to write about, you know? To be honest, I hope you never get this message because, well, I don't want to be dead. Also, I would be surprised if I did die doing the kind of gruntwork they got us doing. I mean, right now they're having us sit around patrolling the fringes of some island in case the village of Red Orcs decides to attack."

Beth sighed as an unescaped tear welled in her eye.

"Still, you never know, so I might as well get to it. Just go right out and say it. I love everything we've ever had. It's weird to say. Cause we only met once. Like really met. But that's whatever. We've had a whole thing outside of just playing games. And it's meant a lot to me. It's funny a game could have brought me to meet one of my favorite people ever. More than just a favorite. I don't know anyone like you, Suzuki. Even if I lived a hundred years, I don't think I ever would. So thanks. I'll miss you. Keep those douche nozzles in check. We'll always be a party. No matter what. Remember what Stew always says—never split the party.

"And when you do, get back together as soon as you can. Cross that bridge, slay that monster—do whatever you can to get the party back together. Seems some monsters can't be slain, some bridges can't be crossed. Sorry to let you guys down like this."

Beth leaned forward. Her eyes were stern as she looked long and hard into the camera.

"But know this: even though I'm gone, we will always be a party. Now and forever." Beth leaned forward, fumbling for the camera button. "Now I just have to figure out a way to come back as a Force Ghost and haunt you guys." She chuckled before turning off the camera.

Sandy was sobbing now. Stew sat beside her, staring at his feet. He was fighting back tears and was barely winning. With one hand, he stroked Sandy's. The other gripped his short sword, which was resting on his knee.

"Didn't think it'd be her," Stew said. "Didn't think it'd be any of us. But definitely not her."

Suzuki threw his hands up and grabbed his hair. He took a deep breath and sat down. "It can't be true," he finally let out. "Beth was the best of us. There's no way..."

Stew flipped his sword over and picked at a couple of its scratches. "Suzuki. She's gone. Face it."

"No! She's not dead! She can't be. Something else is up. We just have to figure it out."

Suzuki knew what the five stages of grief were. He knew what denial was. This wasn't denial. The sinking feeling in his stomach wasn't about Beth dying. It was something bigger. Something more confusing.

Something that he was going to figure out.

Suzuki played her message over and over, looking for something, anything that would prove the feeling he had that she was alive to be right.

And as he did, a second message pinged. He opened it and saw Beth's face staring back at him. "Hey, Suzuki," she said.

"Beth? You're alive?" he checked the timestamp. She had recorded the message about nine hours earlier, right around the time of the attack.

The message continued. "We're under attack, Suzuki. These fuckers are actually attacking our base. There are thousands of Red Orcs. I mean, thousands. I've never seen so many. And they've never attacked our base before." There was the sound of an explosion that caused Beth to look behind her.

"Shit that was close. I've got to go join my platoon. Defend the base. Suzuki, this war is real and...well, I didn't want to go into what could be my last battle without calling you a douche nozzle one last time." She winked at him, forcing a smile. "I love you, Suzuki. I always have. I just wish I'd gotten a chance to tell you in person. Take care of yourself Suzuki, and who knows, if I survive this fight, maybe I will get to tell you in person. God knows I want to."

And with that, the message blinked out.

"What the fuck!" Suzuki yelled.

Suzuki considered the other message from Beth during the attack -- it had been delayed. Suzuki wasn't sure if that meant anything. From what he knew about how the HUDs worked, they needed to be online to send, so maybe, just maybe hers was online.

Then it hit him. Something so small, but obvious. He clicked through the email stamp's metadata, strolling through the code until he found what he was looking for.

The message had been composed nine hours ago. But it was only sent recently.

And not from a military base. No, it was sent from another location altogether.

He was right. Her HUD was online. She was alive.

"Beth isn't dead, guys," Suzuki said, leaping to his feet.

Stew looked up at Suzuki with a mix of rage and frustration, like he was ready to grab Suzuki and kill him. "Cut the shit, Suzuki," Stew shouted. "We all got the message. We—"

"She's not dead."

"What the fuck do you mean, she's not dead? You saw the same thing—"

"I just got another message from her. One she made during the attack." He forwarded the message to Stew and Sandy.

"So?" Stew growled. "The message got stuck in her outbox. Shit like that happens. Doesn't mean she's alive."

"No," he said, projecting the message's metadata on the screen. "Look. That message was sent from...from..." he called up a map, clicking the coordinates and a big red pin appeared on what would have been Ellis Island on Earth. "She's there."

"No, dude," Stew said. "Even if you're right, all it means is some fucking orc accidently sent the message when he was chewing on her skull."

Sandy punched Stew in the gut. Hard. "Shut the fuck up, Stew. Show some fucking respect."

Stew threw his arms up in the air. "I am. Her HUD is there. But she's not. She's dead."

"No, she isn't," Suzuki said. "She was clear that the attack was conducted by red orcs. Not gray orcs. Red."

"Yeah, and?"

"Gray orcs kill. They can't help it. It's all throughout the stories. Tolkien. Lewis. All of the English myths. Gray orcs are killers. But when it comes to RPG campaigns and stories...red orcs take prisoners. Beth mentioned multiple times that her troop was dealing almost exclusively with red orcs. And Beth knows as much as I do, if not more. If she was in a situation where she was being overrun by red orcs, she would have thrown her sword down and let herself be captured."

"How the fuck do you know that?"

"Because that's what I would have done. And when it comes to the history and legends of Middang3ard, Beth knows way more than I."

Sandy wiped the tears from her eyes and looked up at Suzuki. "She's alive?"

"No, no...don't buy Suzuki's bullshit, Sandy. He's a lovesick asshole who is desperate to believe his girlfriend is alive. She's dead."

Suzuki lifted his hands in surrender. "She might be. Yes, I admit it. But she might also be alive. Red orcs don't kill. They enslave. Think about all the times your ass got captured by a band of Red orcs, and we had to come save you."

Stew shook his head. "That was in the game, dude."

"A game designed to train us for this world. For this war. Why would they put in some crazy detail like that if it didn't have some truth to it?"

Stew was silent. It was true, in their gaming time, Stew had been captured not once, but three times by red orcs and it was always the same. Capture, imprisonment, put to work...and then he was eventually saved by Suzuki.

Suzuki stepped up close to Stew and looked him in the eye. "All I'm saying is she might be alive. I mean, I'd still be alive. I don't see how Beth couldn't be."

"I don't know, Suzuki," Stew said, hesitantly.

Suzuki took a step back and pulled up his HUD, clicking on its map again. "Beth sent a message earlier to me where she said that she was close to Ellis Island. Now her HUD is sending messages from there. That's not a coincidence."

"Ellis Island is on Earth, dude." Stew sneered.

"True, but the geography on Middang3ard is the same as ours. She's on whatever Ellis Island is called here. She's on an island, and it's probably still a prison. If Beth is anywhere, it's going to be there."

Suzuki used his HUD to project a 3D map of New York City. Of course in Middang3ard, it was covered with forests and swamps, but from an aerial view, they could make out the unmistakable outlines of Manhattan, Staten Island, and Ellis Island.

The zone flashed red.

Stew growled in frustration. "Shit, dude. Even if you're right, it says we have less than a three percent chance of surviving that zone. It's full of the Dark One's bitches."

Suzuki was about to say something when his inbox

pinged. He checked it and saw another message from Beth. No...that wasn't right.

He saw the same message from Beth. Sent again.

Whatever was happening and wherever she was, she could send the same message more than once.

He hacked into the second message's metadata and saw that it was sent from the same location.

"She's alive guys. And she's there."

"OK, ok." Sandy nodded. "Let's say that you're right. What good does that do us? The HUDs are designed to transport us out of any zone with less than a fifteen percent chance of survival. It's some safety protocol Myrddin installed to stop idiots like us getting in over our heads."

Suzuki threw his hands up in frustration. "This isn't a fucking video game. I don't give a shit what percentage it gives us for survival. We're going to get Beth. Period." And before the other two could say anything, Suzuki unsheathed his sword and pointed it to the heavens. "Never split the party, remember? Come on, guys! For honor," he cried out.

Sandy's hands glowed bright blue, sparks jumping between her fingertips. "Beth might be alive. We owe it to her to find out. And if she's alive, we have to save her. She pressed her fingers on Suzuki's sword. "For glory."

Stew pursed his lips. "Fine," he snarled. "Fine...but I'm not saying, 'For XP'. I'm calling this one for what it is. We're getting the party back together. We're doing this for the Mundanes. We're doing this for Beth."

Suzuki nodded. "That's exactly why we're doing this. For the Mundanes. For Beth."

Always for Beth.

EPILOGUE

When Beth woke up, her head felt as if someone had split it open.

She was lying on the floor, hands and feet bound. Blood caked her forehead. Pain wracked her body as she tried to stretch to test the strength of her binding. Whatever they had tied her up with seemed to grow hotter if she moved too much. She tried to look around wherever she was, but it was too dark. She couldn't make anything out. She could tell that it smelled horrible, though.

"Hello?" Her voice came out hoarse and harsh, like she'd been under for some time.

"Shut up," Allister replied.

"Captain, is that you?"

"Who the hell else would it be?"

Beth was quiet as she tried to put her thoughts together, but all she could remember was being overrun by red orcs. Her platoon had wanted to fight, but Beth knew that would be suicide. Surrender was better because red orcs don't kill.

Not when they don't have too.

She had convinced them all to put down their weapons. And then everything went blank.

"Sir, what happened?" Beth finally managed to ask.

"What's the last thing you remember?"

"Fighting. Then surrendering," Beth said before remembering one last thing. "Falling. I remember surrendering and then falling."

"That would be the magic." The captain sucked in a deep breath. "Best I can tell was that when we laid down our arms, the bastards cast some sleep spell on us. Most of the platoon was knocked out."

Beth looked around and saw about twenty of her fellow soldiers tied up, all sitting in some cave, somewhere on Middang3ard. "I don't...understand. Red orcs don't use magic. How could they have done that?"

The captain shook his head. "Not sure. I don't speak orc, and even if I did, I doubt they'd tell me. Your guess is as good as mine."

"Where the fuck are we? And how many of us are left? And—"

"Soldier," the captain growled. "Get a hold of yourself. Now."

Beth gritted her teeth. "Yes, sir." Then taking a deep breath added, "May I request a quick debrief, sir? That is, if you're not too busy, sir?"

"Now that's more like it," the captain mused. "Keeping your head in shit like this is the greatest weapon. Don't forget that. Now to answer your questions. I woke up while they were bringing me here. We're in some kind of catacomb. I'm not sure how far down. Best I can tell, about half of us are here. Why only half? I have no idea. There should be more of us, so either the other half is dead, or they split us up. Either way, count yourself lucky. Very lucky."

"You have a twisted concept of luck," Beth muttered before adding, "sir."

Allister chuckled, and Beth could hear him struggling in the darkness. After a couple seconds of movement, Allister stopped moving. He let out a heavy sigh. "These aren't your typical red orcs. The sleep spell is one thing, and these braces are obviously magic too."

"Again, sir. Magic? Orcs can't use magic," Beth said as she fiddled with her HUD. It was disabled, and she couldn't get it to display anything. No percentages, inventory. Nothing. "Seems they're pretty good with tech, too. All things that Intelligence said they shouldn't be able to do. So I'm guessing Intelligence ain't so intelligent after all."

Allister laughed again before breaking out into another cough. "You would be the one to keep your sense of humor, soldier."

"I am a comedic juggernaut, Sir," Beth said in a flat tone. She flipped through her disabled inventory. All useless. Except for one thing. Her mailbox was disabled, sending a new message was completely blocked off. But there was one message flashing in her Outbox. A message that she had meant to send to Suzuki.

She held her breath as she clicked the send button.

For a split second, nothing happened. Then she heard the whoosh of an email being sent into cyberspace.

"It's the least I can do to lighten the mood when we are so close to being fucked," Beth said with a devilish grin. The message was sent, hours after the attack. Suzuki would put it together; he'd know that she was alive and kicking.

"Close?" Allister lifted a curious eyebrow. "I'm sorry, but we are royally fucked. Unless you know something I don't."

Beth checked her HUD again and saw that although the message was sent, a copy still sat in her Outbox. Probably a glitch caused by whatever they did to the HUDs to make them inactive.

She clicked Send again and the message whisked away, only to pop back into her Outbox again. She could send and resend the same message again and again. If that didn't get Suzuki off his ass...

"I do, indeed, sir." Beth grinned. "And I'd say we're fucked, but not royally."

"And how is that?"

"Because there was a message stuck in my Outbox. I guess their hack wasn't as complete as they thought it was. I couldn't modify the message, but I was able to send it." She didn't bother mentioning that she could also resend it.

Allister tried to sit up. He ended up groaning in pain instead. "You were able to reach Command?"

Beth tried to move out of reflex. It was a mistake. Her wrists and ankles felt like they had just caught on fire. "Not quite. It was a message to Suzuki. He knows what happened."

"Suzuki again. Always going on about Suzuki. You really think this kid is going to be getting us out of here? We don't even know where here is."

Beth smiled. "Trust me, sir. He'll get us out of here."

"So what's the plan? Sit here and wait for your knight in shining armor?"

"Fuck that, we're not going to wait. We see an opening, we take it. With a little reassurance that we have backup coming."

Allister laughed, and Beth could hear him trying to sit up. "I'm gonna hold you to that."

There was the creak of a door opening. A little sliver of light shone through. Beth was able to make out some of the detail of their surroundings. They were definitely in a cave.

There wasn't much room. It looked like it might have been a cell. Wherever they were, it was far from where they had been fighting. Beth didn't know of any place along the plains where she had been stationed.

A large red orc lumbered into the room. It was carrying several bowls on a large wooden platter. The orc tossed two bowls onto the ground in front of the captain, and then two more.

Two bowls for each prisoner.

Beth wiggled over to the bowls. One was full of water, and the other was full of foul-smelling slop. Even with the intensely disgusting smell, Beth was ravenously hungry. She shoved her face into the bowl and started eating as the orc returned with two more bowls.

Allister chuckled to himself. "Beth, why don't you just make yourself easier to poison?"

Beth's mouth was full of some kind of animal she could never have imagined eating. "They're not going to keep us prisoners and poison us. What would the point of that be?" she managed to get out between slurps. "So while we're figuring a way out of here, I for one am going to keep my strength up."

Beth pushed her face into the bowl, licking up the last of the foul soup.

Suzuki was coming. She had never been so certain of anything in her entire life. Once he got her message and put together the pieces, there wasn't going to be anything to stop him.

He and the Mundanes were coming.

And when they did, the party would be back together.

THE STORY CONTINUES

Book two in the Middang3ard series, LATE TO THE PARTY, is available now at Amazon and through Kindle Unlimited.

Get your copy today.

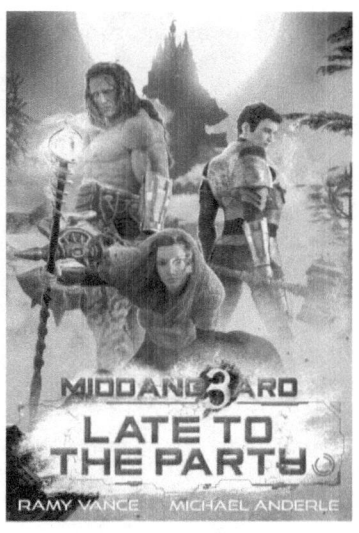

Who knew tabletop RPG's were training manuals to teach humans about our allies?

Robert "Suzuki" Fletcher's on a mission to save to one of his fellow Mundanes who was captured by the Dark One's forces.

His teammate is being held in the heart of enemy territory... *and his HUD gives him a horrible chance of surviving.*

IT'S TIME TO LEVEL UP.

Soliciting the help of other more experienced MERCs, the team needs to gain the skills necessary to rescue Beth. Are they up to the task?

The problem: Gaining experience in Middang3ard is incredibly, horribly painful.

The leader of the Horsemen has a quest that might grant them the experience they need.

But can they survive?

There are no saved games in *Middang3ard*.

Get it now at Amazon.com

AUTHOR NOTES

AUGUST 3, 2019

Joint Author Notes – Ramy Vance (He who shall be called truth-breaker) and Michael Anderle (He who shall be called story-corrector.)

(I'm totally hijacking his author notes because otherwise this poor excuse for the story will become the 'official' story and Ramy will look at me with his eyes full of mischief and just shrug his shoulders. – Michael Anderle)

Author Notes Ramy Vance
and Michael Anderle

Fucking Tolkien.

This was how my elevator pitch went when I met Michael in Vegas last November: "Michael, I got a great idea ... imagine a world where all the stuff we read in Tolkien, Milton, Beowulf was real. Where Dungeons and Dragons wasn't an RPG, but actually training for the some seriously bad shit lurking off-world. Where, when we travel to said off-world location, humans are all super-strong, fast healers, more endurance, etc..."

<Mike: This is so far from the truth (and timeline) that I can't even begin to explain the real timeline and story... But, the short answer is MONTHS apart and we did the idea up together. Next thing you know, Ramy is going to be explaining how he was chilling with J.R.R. himself over the holidays at the University and told him to go with 'some one-eyed creature at the top of a big tower' or other ridiculous assertion. J.R.R. Tolkien deserves all the credit for The Lord of the Rings... Ramy, not so much.>

"So basically, we're all Captain America in said off-world?" Mike asked.

"Yeah! That's exactly it!"

"Cool." His eyes lit up with the possibilities of my proposed universe. "So what's going to happen on that off-world place? Humans--us--we're going to, what? Fight the Dark One?"

"Exactly!" I'll have to come clean here. I hadn't thought of a Dark One or any big bad, really. I had just come up with a cool world.

<Mike: See note above about truth-breaker.>

He took a sip of his Coke. That's Michael for you. Always on brand. "Fight the Dark One before the Dark One brings the fight to Earth?"

<Mike: The real story is Ramy provided me an Amazon Kindle with his stories on it for my review and a document about adoption or something. No, really. I should keep that Kindle in case we ever have an LMBPN museum. It is a black and white Kindle, not even an Oasis. He's kinda cheap that way.>

"It's like you read my mind," I lied. It was more like he was feeding me the story. But who was I to complain?

"A world where the DnD, RPG and video game players are the heroes?"

"Are you psychic?" *<Mike: Yes...yes I am.>*

"I dig it. But what do we call this place?"

And that was when the magic happened. We both ... and I kid you not ... said, "Middle Earth." Or more specifically: Middle3arth.

<Mike: Actually, I can't remember what happened, but I'd be willing to put a few dollars down that Ramy was first out of the mouth with MiddleEarth (note no hyphen).>

We even got a cover commissioned to honor our most awesome title.

Over the next few months, we plotted, planned and wrote until we came up with Suzuki and Beth's story--a three book series to introduce the world and, if successful, kick off the universe.

I couldn't be happier ... I mean, I not only get to collaborate with one of the most successful indie authors ever, but we were actually building a universe.

Talk about Ultimate Cosmic Power (and an itty-bitty laptop). What? Not an Aladdin fan...

<Mike: It's "in an itty-bitty laptop" and I think you forgot the blue guy setup.>

Anyway, I digress. Launch day is fast approaching, we're starting the pre-launch buzz and then it happened. We got hit by an author friend and former lawyer who said, and I quote, "What the fuck are you doing? You can't call your book Middle3arth."

"Why not?" we proclaimed.

"Because it's copyrighted, dingbats." Yes, he really did call us dingbats. People do talk like that. Well, lawyers based out of Alaska do, at least.

<Mike: Technically, "Middle-Earth" is copyrighted or trademarked or something. The actual term Middle Earth existed before Tolkien. However...>

"But ... but ... we like Middle3arth."

"And Tolkien's lawyers like money."

"But ... but ... Middle3arth is a great title."

"And Tolkien's lawyers are great at getting your money."

"But ... but ... we already *have the cover*."

"Fuckity, fuck, fucknessity." Another direct quote. I don't know what Alaskan lawyers are into, but this was getting weird.

"So no way we can call it Middle3arth?"

"No way."

"No way at all?"

"No way at all."

"Fuck. Then what do we call it?"

"I don't know," quoth the lawyer turned author, "it's your fucking story."

So Michael and I scrambled until we finally found

Middang3ard (the '3' is an 'E'). An old word spelling for Middengard (with a better location for the 'E,' too. Looks cooler). And there you have it … the birth of Middang3ard.

Fucking Lawyers.

OTHER BOOKS BY RAMY VANCE

Mortality Bites Series

Keep Evolving Series

BOOKS BY MICHAEL ANDERLE

For a complete list of books by Michael Anderle, please visit:

www.lmbpn.com/ma-books/

All LMBPN Audiobooks are Available at Audible.com and iTunes

To see all LMBPN audiobooks, including those written by Michael Anderle please visit:

www.lmbpn.com/audible

CONNECT WITH THE AUTHORS

Connect with Ramy and sign up for his email list here:

Join Ramy's Newsletter

Join Ramy's FB Group: House of the GoneGod Damned!

Connect with Michael Anderle and sign up for his email list here:

Website: http://lmbpn.com

Email List: http://lmbpn.com/email/

Facebook:
www.facebook.com/TheKurtherianGambitBooks

www.ingramcontent.com/pod-product-compliance
Lightning Source LLC
Chambersburg PA
CBHW031619100726
47898CB00006B/1853